The Blood Bride

Hope just wants to be an ordinary nestling. She went to college and escaped, but now she's back and there's a secret everyone is keeping from her.

Xavier is the new master of the nest, ready to welcome home the daughter of the house who he has never met. He's unprepared for the woman who steals his breath and enchants him.

Now Hope and Xavier must fight for lives and those of the innocents. After all, it is only by overcoming the rogues that they will have a chance of a timeless future together. But will it be in time?

THE BLOOD BRIDE

Blood Secrets Book 1

Imogene Nix

Cover Art (c) Fantasia Frog Designs

Editing by Sassie's Editing

ISBN 978-1-922369-04-8

DEDICATION

I can't believe I'm finally re-releasing The Blood Bride. This was my first paranormal title and although the rights returned in 2018, I purposely waited until I had the entire series before re-releasing it. It's been a labour of love (especially when it comes to the re-working and waiting for the re-release!) I may have even had the covers since 2018! Don't hold that against me!

I've reworked the series, changed a couple of names and added some extra story to "explain" some of the issues concerning Hope and her parents. The answer isn't apparent until the end but highlights the change in the relationship between Hope and her family, as well as Cressida.

I'm sure you'll love the Master - he's been uppermost in my mind for many many years. He's strong but also soft enough to understand Hope is young but has the potential to become a strong woman. He's prepared to accept her as she is, a young woman about to unfurl her wings for the very first time and take flight. A man like that... well, that's sexy.

This book is dedicated to my oldest daughter - Charlotte. Mainly because a lot of the changes were things she told me the story needed... Things I was too close to see for myself. I hope I've done both the book and Miss Charlotte justice!

Thank you as always to my editor, the luscious Sassie, to Tara from Fantasia Frog for the amazing cover art and my family who put up with my foibles with each book.

Oh and who can forget my lovely Makers & Fakers from Facebook!

To my readers, who wait eagerly every release for the next instalment. Thanks for your support!

Imogene
2020

PROLOGUE

As silence descended on the house, the shadows grew—dark grays and blacks that bled into each other. First one figure then another broke away, making a run toward the house. Silent as the grave, they moved swiftly over dew-slicked grass. Then they stopped still. Waiting. Not a movement betrayed them until a signal propelled them back into action and they started crawling upwards. The walls damp coating no barrier to the intruders that ascended in the darkness.

The sound of each window breaking shattered the quiet—the figures were inside. Screams echoed through the night. Yet, in this area of large estates, heavy with noise-absorbing shrubbery, no one could hear those within. The blood-curdling screams went on and on before finally dying away.

Just one sound echoed through the night: The sobbing of a child.

The front door opened and figures trooped out—ghostly specters against an inky night sky, broken by a single outline. A child in white, carried at the center of the pack.

No sound broke the silence as they moved toward the trees surrounded the house.

Flames now licked at the manor: A deathly glow of oily smoke rising.

All that remained was a single person—wrapped in a cape of midnight blue beyond the house—watching them melt away.

Jemima moved toward the burning structure, breaking into a run as she breached the threshold. Vainly she attempted to enter, but the heat drove her back.

Now dashing tears from her face, she raced across the graveled driveway toward the gates, where the guardhouse was located. No sign of life existed within the building and some instinct of survival slowed her pace to a careful creep. Out of breath and heaving from exertion, she nervously checked within.

Small puffs of white vapor colored the glass. She darted from one window to another. Her cloak drawn tightly around her body, hoping it would camouflage her from sight.

Satisfied, Jemima entered through the heavy, wooden front door and moved toward the phone she spied on the floor. Her eyes darting here and there she dialed, listening to the rotary motor as it returned to the proper position. Time was short and if *they* came back, she needed to have shared the message.

The phone rang once. Twice. With a brrping sound it connected.

"Hello?" A male answered and she felt a warm flush of relief at the voice. A voice she knew well.

"The manor has been breached. The girl child taken." The words erupted and her hand trembled.

"On our way." The click of the receiver being replaced echoed loudly in the stillness of the room.

Copper. She smelled copper.

Her stomach soured, knowing it meant more deaths. Jemima looked around for the gun—a gun with deadly, holy water-infused copper bullets—she knew was hidden somewhere in the room. A gun she couldn't find. *No divine intervention exists here*, she thought.

Hopefully *they* didn't remain. Feeding. If they were still here, that's what they would be doing. She found a corner and scrunched down, hiding from sight.

Crouched low, she tried to stay as still as possible, listening for sounds of the vehicles she knew would be coming. She dug her fingers into the flesh of her arms; remaining aware enough to stop before drawing blood. That would surely bring them out. Jemima dragged the cloak around her to capture the warmth, yet there was little to be found.

The sounds of engines roused her from the corner of the room. Jemima inched toward the window, the lead of the old glass distorting her view, hearing raised voices she knew Mistress Cressida had arrived.

Jemima retreated. Remained hidden from the woman because if she knew, all may well be lost. From the shadowed room she listened to the conversation...

"It smells like Estersham." The Mistress' eyes closed. "If it is, we have a problem." She turned once more, her face set and eyes now glacial in intensity. "James?"

The man nodded as if he knew what was to come.

"If I take those steps, I cannot return. Another must stand in my place." Her voice hardened while her eyes glittered in the dim light, piercing in their intensity.

Then the Mistress' voice called out in the near silence. "You and yours have been my loyal servants for so many years. I took an oath to protect you long ago. I renewed it with marriage and births, over and over. Now, my home and yours have been breached and this child taken from us. The girl child, who will be the hope and salvation of our kind, was ripped from the bosom of our nest. I will repay your loyalty and I will get her back." The words of power rippled in the night and licked at Jemima's skin.

This had been foretold. The coming to pass was simply the first step in a long march. Who would win? That was yet to be known.

CHAPTER ONE

9 Years Later

*H*ope nodded, all the while her eyes on her mother's face.

"You will follow these rules Hope. There will be no tolerance of misbehavior. Your father is the *Yeux Secondes* and as such, you will act like a lady at all times. No dalliances with unworthy men. I know you've been eyeing young Sergei off like an ice-cream which is highly inappropriate."

Hope started, wondering how her mother had heard of Sergei, after all, her mother felt the second son of one of the maids was beneath recognition. For a moment, Hope allowed her mind to drift, remembering Cressida and the way the woman had treated her kindly. She wished life were once again so simple. Since the abduction her mother had restricted her contact with others. She'd attended school, been tutored in subjects ensuring she was fluent in four languages. She'd been schooled in music, dance and art appreciation. Everything and anything to make Hope an appropriate wife to a *Yeux Secondes*. The restrictions chafed.

"Mother, I'm attending college. I will study hard, achieve good grades and only mix with socially appropriate individuals." She would appease her mother, if that was the only thing achieved during her time away from the nest.

Her mother's eyes narrowed, and Hope knew it for a sign of her displeasure. "You will remain home when not in the company of the guard or family itself, Hope. You will uphold the honor and status of this family. Anything less, and you will be recalled."

Hope's stomach curdled, just as it did with every conversation, they'd had for the last three or so years.

Why? Why had her mother changed? What was different? It was a refrain Hope couldn't answer, though she'd tried.

"Mother, I will do everything to uphold the honor of the house. I promise."

It didn't matter of course. Right now, she'd agree to anything because on the horizon lay her departure from here. She was going away. Going to taste freedom without the cold fingers of her parents there to correct her. Away from David, who no longer saw her as anything other than a liability to the nest. Their relationship—the closeness of siblings—long faded to little more than a tolerance which was eventually overlaid with what felt like hatred. The home she'd loved was long gone, but hope for a future, happy and bright was the emotion that kept her plodding through her days and nights until she could escape from here.

CHAPTER TWO

4 Years Later

Hope hauled the last heavy box up the stairs of the manor house, occasionally catching glimpses of the way her midnight black hair shone in the sunlight, as she passed the window in the living room of her apartment. "Thank heavens this is the last one," she muttered to herself, sliding the box down to rest on the floor, before straightening and rubbing the nagging ache in her back. She could have had help, all she needed to do was ask. But now that she was an adult, Hope needed and wanted to stand on her own two feet.

Straightening up, she looked around at the mass of boxes waiting for her to delve into. "Well, gone away and back again. Where do I start first?"

The phone trilled and she started for an instant, before extending her hand to the receiver on the shelf beside her. "Hope speaking."

"Miss Hope, do you require any help? Lisi is wondering if you require her assistance." The muffled voice of one of her guardians flowed out of the earpiece. She'd forgotten that living at the manor meant living the fish bowl lifestyle she had tried her best to escape at college. Not that she'd had much opportunity to live a free life. She'd been lodged with a guardian family within the college grounds. Even then, her personal team of five guards had shadowed her every move: to classes, shopping and even the hairdresser's.

They hadn't escaped her notice, the looks some of her classmates had thrown her way. Longing for the lifestyle they'd thought she enjoyed. Little did they know, Hope would have happily swapped. Downtime had existed within a carefully vetted group of companions, each from houses of similar status. The cloying atmosphere she hated, but, nonetheless, she'd submitted to her parents' will. Only a few times had she sought to do activities that they would have deemed inappropriate. Even then, her conscience had kicked in and she'd derived no enjoyment from the guilty feelings that had overcome her.

"No thanks, Jeffrey. I have all the boxes up here and I am going to take my time going through them." How could she explain that she needed a freedom which had been denied? That this small and almost insignificant rebellion was one she embraced? She couldn't. It wasn't fair to Jeffrey to share that.

"Fine, Miss Hope. Oh, and I'm supposed to remind you, the new Master has requested your presence in his library after sundown."

She nodded, knowing it was expected that she would take her oath of fealty. "Oh. Right. I'll be down for sunset." She laid down the receiver. *It's one thing to owe my continued safety to a vampire nest Master, but quite another to be at his beck and call all the time, just as my parents have been.* Her temper spiked momentarily. The emotion coiled through her then she shuddered, pushing away the negativity, while absently reaching for the boxes she needed to stack, store or unpack. The rough exterior of some of them brushed against her hands. For now, she had time.

Lots of time.

Ripping the tape off the first box, she started to root through it, unwrapping reminders of her slightly less constraining college life, formulating arguments to put to her parents, knowing that the dice were stacked against her. Her life had been mapped out since her birth. Perhaps she could find a way around some of the roadblocks. At least she hoped so. With that thought she set to work.

He stretched in the bed, welcoming the sensation of cool sheets, savoring the experience of knowing he could rise when he wanted to. Luxuriating as he came to full awareness of his surroundings. His bed. His home. His nest. Exultation swept through him. One he experienced several times in the last six months since he'd become Master.

Xavier had only recently been transferred to this nest, after Cyrus had been called to ascend to a seat on the Council with his predecessor Cressida, the most senior vampire on the Council.

A new Master had been required for the nest, a situation arising from the ascension of Cressida who had saved the child Hope from the rogues. The death of another of the Council meant that Cyrus had answered a call to accept a seat. It was an almost unheard of event for a nest to have two new Masters in under a hundred years, yet Xavier had accepted his unexpected promotion. Not that he would take it for granted—no, he worked beside his vampires as required, so they knew he would ensure their safety while they protected them.

The household he'd taken over was well run, and he had no fears for the financial status, even though they had lost the manor and many assets during the dark days of clearing the rogues who had attacked the house. Indeed, he'd been with Cyrus the night he'd ascended and had seen the great strides Cyrus had made during his Mastership.

He swiped a hand over his stubbled face, a voice to his left said quietly, "Master, refreshments for you." A crystal goblet appeared in a white hand at the edge of his vision. He accepted it with a grunt, the ruby red liquid inside called to him on a primal level. Blood wine. Sustenance that would ease the clawing hunger he always felt on awakening.

His teeth extended and his mouth opened. The first drop touched his tongue and a frisson moved through him, the ecstasy of drinking flowing into his body. He took his time, savoring the flavors.

Young.

Full bodied.

Tart aftertaste.

The wine, the only human sustenance he could now enjoy. Food was relegated to a memory of things long passed.

He closed his eyes as the last drop flowed and breathed deep. Yes, a Master could very quickly become accustomed to this lifestyle, but not now and not today. He needed to meet this Hope, the one who had turned their entire world upside down. James had told him little about his daughter, save that she would need to remain within the house, protected from the world. That someday she would assume the mantle of leading a house, while her brother oversaw the legal and financial affairs of this nest.

He pushed the bed covers away, unconcerned about nudity as he padded to the bathroom. He still needed to bathe and shave for all he was a vampire—a thought that made him chuckle. Even after all these years, when vampires had made their entry into the human world, humans outside nests thought vampires had no need for those daily rituals.

He moved through his ablutions with speed, aware she'd be waiting for him. He would present himself to her in his most urbane incarnation and she would take her oath of fealty, before he met with his advisers, with James and David leading the human contingent.

No need to rush, he reminded himself. After all, he was the Master now. He stopped and thought. This was not the attitude to take. He might be the Master, however each and every human in the nest had a place and value. He remonstrated with himself, giving a shake of his head, then hurried through his dressing, pulling on a white shirt, suit and tie.

Finally dressed and ready, he left his suite, making his way up the stairs and through the secure door, where he continued to the library. His sanctum, and now office.

In the corridor stood his second, Javed. His origins were Arabic, though, as with most of the vampires Xavier knew, they never discussed the lives they'd led as humans before they became vampires. He waited, looking easy, and no one knew better than Xavier that this belied the soul of a warrior. His friend and most trusted ally would be carrying a range of weaponry. He scanned the room, watching every movement around him, assessing and looking for weaknesses. He also acted as an information conduit where necessary. Tonight, Xavier needed to know the status of the newest to take oath, the daughter of the house whom neither of them had met.

"What is her status?" He looked closely at his second in charge and only confidante.

"She is concerned and upset. Her parents have continued the line that she is to assume the mantel her mother holds. The staff have intimated she is unsettled and angry at the obvious restrictions placed upon her. Apparently after the freer life she experienced whilst away, she is finding the strictures difficult to accept." Javed watched him, waiting for the words of his leader, and Xavier felt the weight of responsibility settle again.

The nod he gave was quick. He would be adding to the strictures that she found so stifling. Something felt wrong about the situation, yet he'd accepted the comments of his *Yeux Secondes* in the matter. Then he dismissed his concerns and considered the day ahead. The sound of steps filled his mind and he moved to the room beyond, knowing that the chandeliers would gleam in the dark and the white tiles beneath his feet would reflect the glow of light as directed by Verity.

The doors opened and he entered the room, only to stop just beyond the threshold as he saw a woman. Her scent, clean and soft, filled his mind. Beautiful, willowy, he noted while she gracefully moved before the bookcases, her long-nailed fingers sliding over the spines of the books she perused. And for a moment pleasure invaded his mind, thoughts of those fingers trailing over his body arousing him. Long black hair, graceful neck and hips that flared slightly. She wasn't angular, just perfectly proportioned.

His mouth dried, even as his gums ached and his body tightened in response. Then she turned around.

The sound of doors opening caught her attention. Hope had been looking through the titles on the bookshelves, running a finger along the spines, and feeling the reassurance of old leather beneath her touch, all the while taking in the scents of wood, lemon-infused beeswax, old paper and remembered cigar smoke. Memories of this room filled her mind. The hours spent poring over the titles she knew were housed here. Titles such as *The Booke of Vampyre* and *The Bloode Promise* resided next to *The Diary of Anne Frank* and *Dune*, and she could tell that the collection had expanded once again.

It seemed almost surreal that many of the titles she'd perused as a child still existed in this room. On some level she knew they weren't the same books, for they had been lost in the old manor when it burned to the ground. It was obvious that time and great care had gone into finding and replacing the titles with the same—a fact that continued to fill her with wonder.

The subtle creak of old hinges pulled her from the reverie, telling her that she was no longer alone. The frisson of power, would have done the same, and she shook slightly, feeling a pull as she turned.

In the doorway stood the most exquisite man she'd ever seen. Piercing green eyes captured her gaze before she looked beyond them to the planes of his face. Lean and olive-skinned, a slight shadow existed even though she could tell he'd recently shaved. She even detected the hint of aftershave.

He was tall. Very tall. She would hazard at least six foot four. Muscular. His well-fitting suit did nothing to hide the rippling muscles the material covered. He had a presence that captured her instantly. Her breath caught. The scent that filled the air called to something deep within her, and her insides quaked.

Dear Gods, if this was the Master, then she had a problem. The thought slammed into her. He moved with a determined stride, displaying his innate grace of both a man and a hunter.

He strode around the room, as if holding his inner predator at bay. His eyes widened and his nostrils flared as he watched her. All these things she saw in bare seconds in which time stood still and she gazed upon him. Her stomach clenched, breath shortened as a primal thrill sang through her veins.

"Master Xavier?" The words slipped out while her heart beat a rapid tattoo at his nearness. The air in her lungs felt as if it had disappeared, and she knew she breathed heavily. Heard it and knew by the narrowing of his eyes, he did too.

"Yes. You would be Miss Hope? Please sit down." He gestured toward a winged chair, and she noted his fingers, long and tapered. "We have important matters to discuss."

Hope stumbled slightly. She reached for the back of the leather chair and gripped the wings hard, fingers shaking. She glanced away briefly, seeking strength as she battled to control her reaction to the man before her. *Vampire not man*, her mind screamed. Once more, she breathed in, expanding her chest and inhaling the deeply masculine scent of him that in turn made her pulse react again. Hope lowered herself, as if her legs were boneless, into the seat. She hadn't felt this ungainly in many years, yet at this time and in front of this man any confidence she had gained melted away.

Hope considered herself quite reserved and contained, yet since this man...this Master...had made himself known to her, she felt like the gawky child she'd once been. Her mind thick and full of nonsense, resembled no more than a jumbled mess. She was unable to clutch and hold on to any thought without it scattering. Twisting her fingers in her lap she sought something to bring her back to reality.

"You have settled into your suite, I take it?" He reclined in the chair opposite her, watching her intently, as she focused on him again.

"Yes, thank you, Master, I... All my items arrived safely. I plan to take the next few days unpacking everything." He sat waiting and she ploughed on, even though she knew he wasn't really interested in the subject. After all, it was small talk, filling the quiet. Wasn't it?

"However, I would like to ask permission to find employment... and to be situated in the city, perhaps in one of the nest apartments?"

She stopped as his face tightened, and she felt a stab of apprehension at the change that overcame him.

The urbane sophisticate was replaced with an icy cold visage, and the deep green pools hardened before her shocked gaze. "No."

Searching his face, she sat forward hoping she could somehow change his mind. Her own churned, looking for a way to explain her wants and needs. Hoping she could salvage the meeting and make him agree.

"I have skills. I have my degree and I need to use it…" Surely, he would see that? His face remained closed as the words died away, and a suffocating feeling filled her chest. The same one she'd experienced several times since returning home.

"No." His words were clear in the sudden silence. "You may find employment within the household. You will not be allowed to move from the manor without the necessary guards."

Inside her chest something shuddered and cracked before rebellion, hot and acidic, rose within her. "Look, all I want is a chance to find *my* future. I can continue to work toward the greater good of the nest." She gripped the plush velvet at the arms of the chair, and she leaned farther forward. Seeking something, some crumb of understanding and, for now, uncaring of the possible danger of arguing with a Master vampire. "I am more than happy to move into the apartments where Lisi and her family reside, if that makes it easier. They're guarded there." The cold of his eyes only seemed to deepen, while her skin tightened and the pressure within her built.

Hope controlled herself with an effort and her words died away. She wanted to scream her frustration at this man who controlled her as effectively as her parents. The yearning in her chest grew, a lump formed in her throat. She struggled to swallow, and with burning eyes she accepted that she would find no ally here.

She wanted freedom. She wanted a life—her life. Not the world her brother David had, where he was happy to live at home with his bride, where his life was determined by hereditary roles.

The bands around her lungs constricted as she tried to explain her need one last time, even though she now knew the answer would remain negative. The driving desire to be something more battered at her.

"I need to do something useful. I need to be able to leave these walls, and do things with people I choose to be with."

His eyes were now shadowed, gold ringing those green irises. She stopped. She'd learned very early on, the golden glaze meant building anger. She'd seen it before in Cressida's eyes, the night the vampire saved her. Not that she remembered much of that night.

"Miss Hope, I will tell you this once. You are a member of the nest. I am your Master. It is for a good reason that I say no. For your protection and that of all your kind and mine." The careful words cooled her fevered body, turning it to ice. "Now, I am not unkind or uncaring. I can understand your need and may be able to find you some employment utilizing your skills…within one of our companies. However, you will reside here until such time as I see fit." He stopped and Hope had the uncanny feeling that he waited for an outburst, but she was spent—exhausted by the brief, and impassioned pleas.

"You are also forbidden to make any attempts to seek employment either within, or outside the household, until I say otherwise."

Gracefully, the Master rose and extended his hand, gesturing to the door while all she wanted was to shrink away, even as she accepted the implicit dismissal with a feeling of anger. The cold feeling that invaded her body left her enraged. "I will see you tomorrow and I am sure I will have some more news."

Hope swallowed her argument. There was nothing to be achieved right now. No matter how much she hated this truth and his words, the argument had been lost—for now.

A swift move and he turned his back to her. She knew there was no choice but to leave his presence. Defeated, she stepped slowly across the plush carpet, curling her fingers into claw-like talons. Her eyes burned with frustration and she stalked from the room.

Perhaps her brother was comfortable with his life and situation, yet it would never be the one she would choose for herself. She stood beyond the door as it closed behind her. Shutting out of any chance to make any decisions for herself.

The story of her life.

She waited with eyes closed for just a moment, regained her composure before she opened them. No one had seen her and for that she was thankful. Hope headed toward the ornate staircase that would take her back to the floor where her suite awaited.

Maybe it was time to think outside the box, she told herself, as she placed a foot on the tread. Maybe that was the key.

It was only when she arrived back in her room that she realized she hadn't taken her oath of fealty. For her though, there was no escaping. She would need to talk to him again, see him. Perhaps next time he would listen and understand. For once, though, she felt no assurance that any positive outcome, even marginally, was to be had and that thought brought her no comfort.

CHAPTER THREE

*D*awn came as it always did. Light spilt through lace covered windows into a room heavy with dark wood antiques, the creeping warmth caressing her face as Hope woke. Dappled sunshine played over her body while she stretched and absorbed the heat from the brightening rays. Her eyes hurt and she rubbed them, making them feel worse. Grittiness scratched between her eyelashes, irritating her further. Her head was pillowed on large cushions and she watched as the gloom of night receded. Bird song could be heard in the bushes outside the window.

After returning home, it was difficult to reconcile the silence that surrounded her. The nest she'd lived in while attending college had always been busy. Full of hustle and bustle as others moved about their business. Laughter and chatter rang through the corridors, and the constant tap of feet on floors sounded like a drummers tattoo.

Unlike here.

Hope felt the cold emptiness keenly.

The manor they'd moved to after the attack, was stately and old, and so was the atmosphere—cloyingly so. Everyone spoke in whispers, and within her suite there was not a sound to be heard. Loneliness settled around her, choking her. This was not how she wanted to live her life: Surrounded by the trappings of position, without anything to look forward to, except more of the same—a life of dismal servitude to the nest was all that waited for her.

Today was the first day and she had no role. How to fill the endless stretches of emptiness had not been an issue for such a long time. Classes, assessments and social outings had occupied the past four years, but now a new reality stretched out before her, as did the rest of her life. Empty; painfully so.

She closed her eyes against the sudden burn of tears. What good was her degree if she wasn't allowed to use it? What benefit did a person enjoy in being an adult, if she couldn't make her own decisions about her life and how she chose to live it?

Rebellion warred with misery once more. She needed to find something to keep herself busy. The thought came swiftly, and she racked her brains seeking something useful to do. No doubt Master Xavier would, in due time, come up with something he considered appropriate. She snorted inelegantly at the thought. As if he'd any real interest in the day-to-day household routine. She settled herself. Now wasn't the time to cause waves. She remembered the words of one of the nestlings, a constant companion from years past, "More flies are caught with honey than vinegar".

Maybe she was supposed to grace his arm at a society function, or work with other nest offspring? Perhaps there was something she could do to show him? The thought tempted her. She turned it away for now, reaching for the alarm on the bedside table.

Even as she reached, she remembered the quicksilver feeling of attraction, the way her heart beat a little faster, and the mesmerizing pull of his eyes. She snorted again. Like that meant anything, except that she thought he looked good.

Disgusted with her thoughts, Hope rose, climbing out of the antique four-poster bed glancing once more at the bedside clock.

"Damn! It's seven!" She'd been so lost in thought, time had passed. The words burst forth as she scrambled out of the deep covers.

No doubt her mother would be downstairs in the dining salon with her father and brother. Hope knew from experience that she would be expected to make an appearance, and soon, otherwise it would be one more thing she would be brought to task for.

Her jeans and T-shirt sat on the end of the bed, where she'd thrown them the night before. Hope dressed carelessly, rushing to meet the commitments that felt strangling to her. She slipped her feet into light sandals, while she scooped her hair into a rough ponytail.

Perhaps she'd find out the plans for her future? There might be a slim chance her wants and needs would be included in the planning. Not that she held out much hope. Her father, James, was the Master's second—*Yeux Secondes* or second eyes. A human within the inner circle. His role, the one who watched over the nest, was to ensure its financial and legal security in this modern world. Something many Masters notoriously struggled with.

The problem with that was her father never knew exactly where the role within the nest and that of Father began and ended. Previously, it hadn't really bothered her, now after being away, experiencing other ways, her eyes had opened to larger opportunities. The tightly closed circle of familial responsibility choked her again, and she had to stop on the landing to drag in a cleansing breath.

Nests had an immense amount of power from the acceptance they'd achieved through the populace at large and the political associations, they'd groomed. There were legal protections, giving the Masters rights to make determinations of justice over their nests and, to some lesser degree, the nestlings within each family.

There remained some pockets of resistance; those who held to the religious hard line. They continued to label vampires as abominations in the sight of God, and that went hand in hand with their belief that those who served them were expendable.

Those factions continued to categorize the vampires as little more than creatures of the devil, sent by him to destroy all that was good, and, as a result, each nest was vigilant in guarding their holdings. Naturally, this encompassed the use of witches, and those with the skills of warding—the creation of magical barriers ensuring the safety of those within their confines.

In the early days, once the vampires had made their presence known, whole families had been destroyed in fires and physical attacks. Over time, members had endured ostracism and ongoing vilification, on financial and legal entities owned and operated by them. Some nests had fallen, and members had endured harsh and unfair limitations as a result of their known interactions with vampires. The vampires homes had become sanctuaries from the continued and relentless abuse.

Many nestlings of more powerful families saw their position as a badge of honor. Hope couldn't bring herself to feel the same level of satisfaction many had toward their social status.

It was a known fact that the annual requests for applications for placement in a nest each year far outstripped the positions available. It was rare for outsiders to be admitted, as each nest had limited resources. Many members came from families with years of service stretching over decades and some, as in the case of her family, centuries.

Added to that, far fewer attained the position of changeling—those preparing to change— and vampire. The few that were agreed to by the Council were coveted, and every applicant carefully examined before decisions could be taken first by the house, then ratified by the Council members.

She sighed, hating the situation and depressed state of mind she found herself in as she continued down the hall lined with precious antiques and carpets. Everywhere, the scent of the furniture oils and waxes permeated the air, and where previously she would have welcomed the scent, embraced the spirit of familiarity and comfort, now it smothered her. Her mind couldn't free itself from the implied responsibilities and ties that wound tighter and tighter.

Reaching the bottom of the stairs, Hope tugged on her hair, took a deep breath and turned left. She headed for the dining salon at the end of the corridor where the heavy doors were closed. Hope reached out to turn the handle, the sound of raised voices filtered through. She stilled. The unexpected sound held her in place as angry conversation flowed.

"She is to remain here. The Master was most clear about that." Her father's voice, though muffled by the oak of the doors, was firm and satisfied, and she waited to hear what more was said. All the while her heart sank.

"She needs something to do. Otherwise she will dig. If she finds out, then the nest could be placed in danger too." The anxiety in her brother's voice concerned Hope—after all what did he know about her that she didn't? "Your grandchild could be caught up in this, as well as Alexa." The cadence changed, become angry. "If need be, we will move to the gated apartments so I can protect my family." A loud thud, perhaps a chair being carelessly flung aside, resounded through the door, and she stepped back slightly. Her hair, in it's tail, whipped around as she checked both sides. No one saw her listening at the door. Hope heard steps and her heart rate increased, though, thankfully they stopped and in that split second she made a decision. They couldn't know she'd heard them. *Where to hide?* Hope looked around, before the voices started again.

"Damn it, the Master said she must stay here. His word is law. You know that, David. I will discuss the possibility of moving to the apartments if need be. For now, it is done."

Time to go. With that single thought, she willed her legs to move, touching the floor with only the balls of her feet, all the while hoping for silence.

The rattle of china clattered through the air, and she slipped back silently, finding the library door open and heading within before shutting it so that just a crack remained open, while she sheltered behind it.

A crash caming from the direction of the parlor had her wincing, realizing there was an incredible amount of force in the action. Yet, overwhelming feeling of relief flowed through her because whoever it was hadn't seen or detected her.

Holding very still, she spied her brother through the crack. He was tall and athletic. Good-looking, many would say, with dark hair and pale blue eyes. Today the only description that came to mind was... angry, as he stalked past the library door. The jacket of his gray suit fluttered with the force of his strides.

She waited.

Anxiety tied her stomach into knots, and her heart thumped wildly.

Hope waited a little longer, breathing as silently as possible, expecting to be caught spying on her own family, a new low she seemed to have sunk to. She castigated herself.

Silence reigned. Eventually, muscles held taut started to loosen, and she breathed the first full breath since hearing her father's angry voice. She moved toward the winged chair that Master Xavier had seated himself in last night, and lowered herself into the firm leather. Hope closed her eyes against the ever-present sting of anger, which rarely left her since returning home.

Was that her they discussed? What was the secret they were keeping, and why was it being kept from her? Thoughts raced around her brain, but she had nothing to hold on to. No scrap of information to decode the conversation or derive clues from it.

"Being back here is like being in a coffin." The words were spoken from between clenched teeth. The house was both suffocating and strict, when she wanted to stretch her wings and live.

Tears spilled down her cheeks, burning a path where they dripped, and she dashed the liquid from aching eyes, blinking rapidly to ease the discomfort while she looked in pockets for a handkerchief. Dabbing at her face and blowing her nose gave some slight relief. Her chest rose and fell as she fought back the useless reaction. "I'm stronger than them. I can cope and will find a way forward." The affirmation helped ease the anger in her chest and strengthen her resolve.

Until she knew what was going on, she needed to present herself as if nothing had changed. She rose and moved toward the door, cracking it open a little wider she peered out. No one was around. Quickly squeezing through the opening and heading down the hall back to the dining parlor, Hope knocked and waited for someone to answer.

Her mother sat at the table with her father and unsurprisingly, as befitted their status in a nest, they were both beautifully attired. Her father's black silk suit was immaculate and perfectly tailored as always, fitting him like a glove, teamed with a tasteful blue and white tie. Her mother wore a beautiful day gown of ecru silk and lace, her hair elegantly swept up into a chignon. Over the years, the blonde had become gray then white. As always, not a strand sat out of place.

A soft white hand raised her beautifully French manicured fingers, showing Hope the seat she was to occupy. Hope smiled, but it was met with a frown so she took her place quietly and wondered what her current infraction was.

"Hope, my dear, I hope you are not planning on dressing in that manner today. We will be meeting with Mrs. Atkins after breakfast to go through the weekly menus. Alexa will join us for lunch, and then the property managers and the interior decorator will be calling to discuss the new color schemes for the redeveloped apartments. Eat something substantial, and then you need to change." The cool words dashed any aspirations of appealing to her mother for help.

"I thought I might complete my unpacking..." The words died in her throat, as her mother looked at her, the pale blue eyes her brother had inherited were cold as they fell upon her, filled with disappointment.

"You have a position to uphold. It would be wrong if you were not available for the meetings or attired appropriately." Her mother lifted an elegant teacup to her mouth and sipped before continuing. "I will send Lisi up to attend to the unpacking and the arrangement of your suite." Her mother's voice, carefully modulated nonetheless, held a note of censure and Hope found herself nodding as she always had. Hadn't she expected this, though? The half conversation she'd overheard indicated she had a place and role to fill, whether she wanted to accept it or not. "Yes, Mother." She muttered the words through clenched teeth.

The clatter of the cutlery at the end of the table drew her attention. "Good morning, Father." Her words were spoken quietly as she glanced under long lashes at her father.

He nodded, draining the last of his morning tea from the exquisite pale pink and mauve teacup held in his hand. She knew it was an antique, carefully sourced to replace that which had been lost so many years ago. Everything they dined on, sat on or read was, she thought with more asperity than usual. Sometimes she felt like her life was caught in a time warp. Hope stopped and drew herself upright. This wasn't the time for self-pity or tantrums, she told herself firmly.

Her father rose after replacing the cup on the saucer. "Hope, I look forward to seeing you this evening. The Master has planned a dinner party for your return." The dismissive words brought her up sharply once more. Yet another time when she was being directed with her life, instead of making her own decisions. She gripped her fingers together, the sting helping to control her reaction. Her stomach churned and boiled, driving away thoughts of food and hunger. Her life had become an empty shell, and that was unbearable.

With a sharp and incredibly formal bow, her father left. When she turned back to her mother, silently sitting at the table filling a teacup, a feeling of disempowerment grew.

Moments later, Lisi entered the room to ascertain what she wanted for her morning meal, and all Hope could do was mutely shake her head. This was not an auspicious way to start the rest of her life, she decided.

CHAPTER FOUR

The black trousers itched, and so did the jacket over the light camisole. It only got worse as Hope idly listened to the drone of the housekeeper's voice—the nasal tones teamed with a touch of some southern dialect—discussing main meals. Elaborate French creations were suggested and discarded, while Hope listened without any real interest, gradually allowing her mind to drift away.

It was too hot to be in a suit, but her mother had insisted she dress appropriately to her requirements, having even gone so far as to shadow her back to the suite and choose something *befitting* her status. So here she was, marking time, sweating away in a meeting she had no interest in. If the truth be known, she'd rather have eaten something simple—bolognaise or even salads suited her for evening meals, and the same for lunch. As her mother had taken pains to explain while choosing her clothing, "We have a reputation to uphold." She also reminded Hope that this was the role she was brought up to fulfil.

Mrs. Atkins had been with the family since the fire and the events which changed Hope's life so dramatically. Not that she remembered very much.

A flash here and there. Sounds and smells came at odd times, each capturing a frame like a camera and shining for an instant, before retreating from her memory.

Swinging her feet back and forth beneath the seat, she watched her mother's lips move, fingers pointing to meal choices. Hope considered the boredom that would be her life from this point on, if this meeting was any indication. Indeed, there really was no need for her to be here —the few suggestions she'd made had been labeled inappropriate.

She could be going through her boxes upstairs, or looking for some sort of useful employment, not sitting here listening to the pros and cons of veal chasseur versus Parmesan risotto with green asparagus, Portobello mushrooms and truffle oil.

"What do you think, Hope? Should we consider the crème caramel?" Her mother watched her intently. *Damn,* maybe she'd noticed her inattention. Pulling herself back to the matter at hand, she looked again at the sheet. Ah, they were discussing the dessert for the fundraiser to be held in the next couple of weeks, for those affected by Brethren attacks. The end of the meeting was in sight.

"Crème caramel is probably good for wide appeal." Thinking fast had thankfully been a skill she'd learned at college. She glanced at her mother, hoping it would work. The tight white lines that appeared around her mother's lips told her it hadn't been fast enough.

"No, Mrs. Atkins, I think we might go with the sorbet in strawberry, green apple and lime flavors. Cooling and refreshing. Much more appropriate than raspberry or pineapple, don't you think?" Her mother's words were once more directed at the housekeeper.

"As you wish, madam."

Hope watched as the woman quickly scribbled down the options on the page.

"Mrs. Atkins, thank you for your time. We will meet again later in the week, unless there is something else you need?" The unspoken dismissal in her mother's perfectly modulated voice made Hope realize she'd wasted most of the meeting in the mindless absence of thought. She hoped her mother would not ask too many questions concerning the abortive meeting, otherwise there could be fireworks.

"No, madam. I believe this will be fine. I will send a copy of the completed menus to yourself and Miss Hope once I finish transcribing them. I will also arrange those applications to be handed over to you as they arrive." She moved her ample bulk, scraping the chair back on the newly polished wood floor.

The woman smoothed her rose pink and blue floral-patterned dress down, pushing against the wrinkles in an effort to iron them against their own will, while her feet were shod in comfortable and sensible low-heeled black shoes, polished to a high shine. Salt and pepper hair scraped back into an ugly bun and thick horn-rimmed glasses made her look anonymous and insignificant, next to Hope's perfectly turned-out mother.

Her mother rose, following the woman's retreat as Mrs. Atkins backed out of the room, then she firmly closed the door against the world, and Hope stood, waiting wearily for the outburst she expected, ready for the brief flare of anger that usually came as a result of her inattention.

"Well, Hope, I know you don't want to be here doing these things, but it is your role. Your future. At least show some respect for your position and pay attention. If not for your sake, then for that of the staff at the very least." The viperous attack took her aback, heat burning her face at the level of rage.

"Mother?" She felt shocked, stomach churning at the realization that the precious relationship she'd enjoyed with her mother was irrevocably broken. The anger on her mother's face, the way it twisted and the cold look in her eyes left Hope shrinking back. Never before had her mother spoken to her this way. Though there had been a distinct coolness in her attitude since Hope's return, this level of aggression was an unwelcome revelation.

"I never wanted you to go to college. By now, you should be looking for a husband within either this or an equal sized nest. Someone worthy, with skills and abilities that would enhance the nest's reputation and standing." Hope stepped back again, farther away from the icy blast that pummeled her emotionally. "Instead you continue with this...charade! Your head is full of silly ideas about having a career. You should be honored that you are a nestling of the biggest and most prestigious house, and you have a role to fulfill." Her mother pointed at Hope's chest, which now ached with the pressure building within it. "You have a status many girls would do just about anything to achieve. One that is unable to be matched by others."

Hope sat heavily. Sure, she'd expected her mother to be upset, but nothing like this. Never had it crossed her mind that her mother would react like wanting her own life was a cardinal infraction against the nest and a personal attack. All she wanted was to make decisions for herself. Not to have to sit in on meetings that meant very little to her.

"Mother? I'm sorry." The words pushed beyond the hurt, the slicing ache that attacked her chest. "I just… I can't do this. I can't be you. You love what you do. You do it so well. It's not for me though. This…" Hope gestured around the room. A veritable museum, with French rose wallpaper gracing the walls of the perfectly proportioned space, dark polished wood floors with fine Aubusson carpeting. Heavy green drapes hung over the French doors that led to a terrace where roses stood in geometric perfection. Paintings by old masters lined the walls. The Louis XIV desk and chairs, chaise longue, and gold and marble timepiece filled the mantle above the ornate fireplace all came together, creating a look of genteel finery. The crystal chandelier that dripped with perfect shining drops beamed light into the room. It was a cage, gilded perhaps, but a cage nonetheless in Hope's mind. "Isn't what I am.

"This is you. Not me." Her head moved slightly as she tried to make her point.

"No. This is you. This is your future. You will be taking over for me in the next few months." Her mother looked away, and a sensation of worry surged through Hope. "Your father has spoken with the Master. I… I can't continue doing this." Her face crumpled and for the first time, the strong woman she remembered from childhood seemed lost, while something sad rose in her face, and pain crushed Hope from within. "I wasn't going to say anything yet. My doctor has told me I need to slow down. I have…an illness. I need someone trained to take over the role as Chatelaine and Mistress to the *Yeux Secondes*."

The words hit like blows, another pain she couldn't contain screamed through her and her fingers curled into the palm of her hand, the blunt edges of her nails biting at the soft and tender skin. Her strong mother was ill? When had this happened? Why hadn't she known? She opened her mouth as her mother raised a hand. "We decided it wasn't right to tell you. I saw you in the meeting. I don't think you listened to one word. That has to change." The words were frigid and delivered forcefully.

In the back of Hope's mind an alarm rang viciously. She pushed it aside. Now wasn't the time to be second-guessing her mother.

"What about Alexa?" Her sister-in-law would probably jump at the chance to take over the position. That would free Hope up, and if her mother required care then she would be available. Surely that would be an acceptable outcome? Even as Hope thought it, she knew what her mother's reaction would be. It would be a shake of the head without a single hair flying free. "She could—"

"Alexa? No, the Master would not allow that. She doesn't have the knowledge and experience for the demands of the role, anyway. Let alone the discipline. She wants children and is in fact already expecting, from what I understand. That would get in the way of her learning how to handle a household and nest as diverse and large as this one." Her mother's words weren't unkind. Yet the tone they were delivered in, along with the hint of darkness lurking in her mother's eyes, just made Hope feel cold.

A bubble of fear rose in her chest, and she'd had to grip the arms of her chair tightly. "I don't want to do this." A feeling of being constricted against her will rose. It was if the walls were closing around her and soon there would be no escape. "I want a job, Mother. I want to do something with my degree. I want to be *something*. Not just someone who runs a nest. I want to live my own life!" Her voice quavered and Hope's gaze was met with a disdainful look and tense shoulders.

"You don't think I do something?" The cold anger in the answer ate at Hope. She'd overstepped the line and Hope bit her lip. There could be nothing more degrading than telling her mother that she did nothing—she could almost hear her mother's thoughts.

Coming home was supposed to be the beginning of her life, not a life sentence, she thought, self-pity dragging at her. She reached out toward her mother, seeking some form of connection. "I'm sorry, Mother. I didn't mean that as it came out. I meant; I just don't think I'm cut out for your kind of life. To be what you are and to do what you do."

Hope willed her mother to understand. Clearly this wasn't a prayer that was going to be listened to, from the set of her shoulders and the white lines around her lips. If only someone could or would understand. Instead her mother moved away, behind her desk. The physical barrier cut off any action Hope had intended, and the pain inside her grew bigger, suffocating her, until all that existed was a seething, frustrated mass.

"You may be excused for now. We have a meeting at eleven with the managers. Be on time. You may not care what I do, but I will be professional and well-mannered to the end. Remember, if you don't care about your reputation, I care about mine." Then her mother picked up a file and swung her chair around to face the window. She knew there was nothing else to do, so she turned slowly, picked up her papers and walked carefully toward the door. As she reached out, she cast a glance over her shoulder, the sight of her mother's back reinforced that it was time to leave. With a heavy sigh she left.

CHAPTER FIVE

*D*ressing slowly, Hope pondered on the day that had passed, stopping in the act of pulling the black and silver gown over her underwear- clad body: It started badly, and only got worse after the altercation in the parlor.

The meeting with the managers had made her mother angrier than she had already been. They'd discussed the ongoing issues with maintenance, managers and setting the increase in rental rates. Hope had watched with trepidation, her mother had been short and curt by the end, no doubt strung out by the varied problems that arose. By the time the decorators had arrived, her mother had been almost snarling in anger, and had ended the appointment with a request to meet in a couple of days, giving her time to consider swatches and layouts. Obviously, none had been what the woman intended.

Hope couldn't see herself continuing the program of rehabilitating the properties that had been targeted in the last few years by the Brethren. True, her mother had done an exceptional job, but she knew her attention to that sort of detail just didn't exist. For now, she would have to swallow her arguments until an opportunity came along to do something more fulfilling, and to prove to them that her place in life didn't include setting rental rates and choosing color swatches. After all, now she had the added fear of the news her mother imparted earlier.

Her stomach rumbled loudly in the empty room, the churn painful as the lack of food was brought to her attention. Lunch had been a cold affair, and Hope's appetite non-existent as the three senior women of the house had sat picking their way through a meal none of them wanted.

Alexa had been there with her blonde hair artfully tied back. She'd also showcased her willowy frame to perfection. Hope had been irked by her vaguely superior attitude as she wandered into the family dining room. As usual, Alexa was a fashion plate with her fitted hot pink pants and light cotton blouse, immaculate and much more suitable for the weather, while Hope, overdressed in her black pantsuit and heels, sweated.

Hope had moved the salad and cold chicken around her plate as she'd listened to a muted discussion of nursery design. Was mint more appropriate or should she steer toward cream with gold scrollwork? Her mother's replies, warmer toward Alexa than they were to her, reinforced the emotional chasm that now existed between them.

She'd made her excuses as soon as she could, and fled the room, though not before her mother had made the announcement to Alexa that Hope would be taking over the household in the next few months.

Alexa's eyes had narrowed, and for an instant Hope had seen dislike...no, hate spike through those cold blue eyes and her lips had flattened with distaste.

Now, standing alone in her room, she looked into the mirror, critically examining herself. Violet eyes, long blue-black hair fastened back in a faultless chignon. Classically simple diamond drops at her ears and throat, and the long black and silver gown made her look like an adult. Unfortunately, inside, where it counted, she felt like a lost little girl playing dress-up in someone else's life.

How was she to get out of this? Even as she pondered the thought, the phone buzzed and she reached absently to answer. "Hope here."

"Miss Hope? The guests are due to arrive momentarily, and the

Master is expected in a few minutes. Your mother asked me to let you know that you are required." The voice was vaguely apologetic, and she knew Gareth was uncomfortable passing along the summons. No doubt, the household had already heard about the tensions in the family. She felt a moment of embarrassment, her skin flared hot and she closed her eyes. It wasn't fair to live in a fish bowl like this and subject others to the angst within her family.

"Tell my mother I'm on my way, thanks, Gareth." She replaced the receiver. With a last look at the woman she saw in the mirror, the one with lost eyes, Hope turned away, her arches already reminding her she was unused to the high heels her mother had chosen.

Hope moved along the shadowed hallway and down the steps, slowly this time, fearing the evening ahead would be the usual dull and dry event her parents enjoyed. Then she brought herself back to where she was. It wouldn't be wise if she started the evening by tripping and embarrassing her mother any further than she already had.

Once she stopped and glanced around the foyer it was clear that her mother would insist she be with them to receive the guests in the ballroom. She moved in that direction, heels tapping on the floor as she entered through the open door. Her mother and father waited with David and Alexa. Both men looked fine in their perfectly tailored black tuxedos, while Alexa stood, her appearance ravishing in her midnight blue gown, no doubt chosen to accentuate her eyes, and cut low enough to show her shadowed cleavage, emphasized by the sparkle of jewels glinting like a million stars around her neck and at her ears and wrist.

Her mother, regal in a powder blue, two-piece long skirt and camisole-styled top, teamed with a light lace bolero, looked as fashionable and elegant as always.

Hope felt like an ugly cygnet beside them, and once more the sensation of being out of place swept through her.

"Hope. You're just in time. The Master has graciously offered to act as your escort for tonight." Her mother's voice was once more subtly censorious and she saw a glint of something in Alexa's eyes.

"Yes, you must have an escort, Hope. It's expected." Her brother repeated her mother's words as he looked at her, a hint of coolness in his eyes. A surge of emotions swam through Hope. Was she incomplete or less of a woman because she was alone? She'd never experienced this sense of loneliness before. Maybe it was because everyone seemed to be withdrawing from her? The question remained: Did she really need a man, a husband, to belong?

The sound of feet came from behind her and a scent redolent of male teamed with leather filled the air. The subtle fragrance warmed and reassured her, and she turned slightly to see Xavier, the Master, waiting behind her. His smile might have been considered slightly condescending, but languorous warmth still spread through her body. She gazed at him in silence. He held out his hand and she had no choice except to accede to his request.

Did she really want to avoid it? A new feeling rose in her chest, calling to a primal urgency within.

"Excuse me, Verity and James." He inclined his head slightly before continuing. "David and Alexa, may I have a moment with Hope?" It was, of course, a rhetorical question, as who would stop him anyway? He bowed slightly and pulled her away from the others. While they moved together through the bright ballroom to the doors beyond, the burning feeling of eyes watching made her back itch slightly.

"Hope, you look exquisite. Welcome home, officially." He smiled, and her stomach felt like it melted. He pulled her through the French doors, which stood open to allow guests to move around the gardens when the crush in the ballroom became too much. The smell of roses was heady in the night air, and the stars twinkled above. Soft tones of the band preparing caught her ears. All these things felt so far away and insignificant beside the man standing before her.

She couldn't define exactly how he made her feel, but new emotions pulsed through her at the look on his face, it held her in its thrall. She wanted to touch him, and this was a totally alien sensation.

The scary story told for centuries of the mesmerizing gaze of vampires was nothing but a fantasy. Here, though for one brief moment, she could almost believe it was true. Her heart beat faster and her mouth dried. And all she wanted was to kiss this man before her.

Of course, that sort of interaction remained forbidden to all except the one who would become his life mate—the human he would turn, and make his partner for the length of his unnatural life. A vampire might take casual partners, but that wasn't even something on the horizon for Hope. It would never be allowed by her parents and once more she chafed against the constant strictures and rules.

Even knowing all this, the urge to touch him called. Hope had to remind herself that he was beyond her reach, her dreams.

She curled her fingers against the want until the cut of nails in the palm of her hand stung, the pain holding her in place.

"Thank you, Master." The words settled quietly in the night.

"No, you do not call me Master. I am Xavier to you. Always Xavier." His smile was enigmatic, and in that instant, she wished she knew more about him. Those vibrant green eyes of his intrigued her—reminding her of deep pools and cool nights, and she wanted to dive into them.

Hope shook her head, clearing the sensual thoughts.

Flights of fantasy about the Master were not a good start, she told herself. She just wished her body would listen to her brain.

"Should we...?" The question trailed away, as she got the feeling that he too was in no hurry. How could that be? She felt breathless contemplating those thoughts. *Flights of fancy*, Hope mentally castigated herself.

"Yes, we should go in. The guests will be arriving, and we should join the receiving line." He indicated that they return to the room. She really didn't want to go through with the social farce. At this point there really was no other option. A loss of face now would have ramifications. She couldn't escape her role as a nestling and daughter of the *Yeux Secondes*.

A wave of his hand, a hand with long tapered fingers, indicated she should precede him, and obediently she moved into the room. "An old friend of yours is due to attend tonight." His words perplexed her. *Old friend? Who on earth could he mean?*

He slipped her arm through his as they reached her parents and she shivered. Before her, she spied David and Alexa at the start of the receiving line. She moved to take her traditional position. Xavier stopped her. "No, my dear, you stay with me."

Alexa must have heard that and for an instant a glare of arctic fury buffeted Hope, then was quickly concealed. Her mother's mouth tightened as she and her father resumed their places.

The first guest entered the room, quickly followed by others.

People she knew, some of her peers from school and other nestlings renewing their acquaintance, made light chatter as they entered the ballroom. Congratulations flowed, while here and there other Masters and Mistresses came to pay their respects to the newly returned member of the house.

The room filled quickly, laughter and gaiety the order of the day, when suddenly the room hushed. She looked up from greeting a nestling to see *her*.

There in the doorway was a person she would never have expected to see again.

Cressida.

Vertigo rose, swamping her momentarily and a memory bloomed, veiled like a looking glass obscured.

Hope shivered in the small room, her bare feet cold and sore. She just wanted to go home. She needed to go to the toilet, but it seemed important to hang on. She didn't know why she had this awareness, only that it had grown during her eight years.

The sickness had come upon her once more during the day, and she could smell the sourness beside the bed where the vomit lay in a congealed and smelly mess. It wasn't normally like this.

Then they had taken her. She wanted to cry for her mother or father. That seemed senseless.

If only she'd known that the nightmare, which spilled over into a daytime sickness, had meant danger. Always in the past, she'd known, except something about this time seemed different. Scarier than ever before. She hadn't told anyone about the dream. In the past they had smiled and patted her on the head, because it had meant the loss of a pet or something unimportant.

Her thoughts were muddled too. As if there wasn't yet a definite outcome. Silent tears dribbled down her face.

Hope didn't want to sleep, but the drowsiness tried to steal her from her current state of terror. It was an effort to fight it off and she clawed at her hands with blunt nails, fighting the grip of exhaustion. Instead, she thought about what she did know. She knew what they were, just as she'd known for some time the reality of what Cressida was. She was a vampire. They were too.

Hope knew Cressida was old and strong, but it didn't make a lot of sense. How could she know something like that? She couldn't ask, but somehow that truth was there.

The dreams that came in the night showed her pictures and stories. They always had. They always brought with them answers. For as long as she could remember, Cressida had treated her with care and attention, just as she would a spun glass creation. She'd dreamed of Cressida, sometimes scary things and sometimes of the olden days Hope loved to read about. There had always been blood. This time there was lots of it. A red tide of death.

It had been a red winding ribbon, reminiscent of the peaceful stream at the back of the manor where she lived with friends and family. Thoughts of her parents and brother swam through her head. Where were they? Were they okay? Would she ever see them again?

Hope brushed her hair from her face and yawned once more, pulling her clothing tighter. The throb of her bladder reminded her she'd been there for a long time. Surely they would come for her soon? Daylight couldn't be too far away. If only she had told Cressida that this would happen. But her dream hadn't come in a way Hope could understand.

She started at a crash above her head. She concentrated hard. Pushing aside the cobwebs of slumber that seemed to keep pulling at her—she was, after all, only eight—she listened closely.

Growling and roaring thundered through the house, Hope once more curled into a ball. This time the fear she fought washed over her as she squeezed her hands over her ears, trying to keep out the wild sounds from above. Unsuccessfully. Heaven and stars help her if it was another nest coming for her.

Hope looked wildly around, sought something that she could use as a weapon if they came for her. Nothing except slippers caught her eye. Slidding over to the small cot they had set up in the corner, she inched forward, her cold, bare feet moving over the concrete floor without a sound. Creeping, she reached for the soft felt footwear and picked them up, holding a trembling hand over her mouth so she wouldn't make a sound.

Two small white slippers stayed clutched in her trembling fingers. It would do. It would have to do, she told herself sternly. Hope moved to just beyond the door, as she'd seen them do in movies, and waited.

"Hope?"

The gentle query roused her from memories.

Age had not changed her, and for just a moment Hope felt suspended in a time long past. As a child, she'd felt a connection to this vampire Mistress who now headed the Council—the governing body of vampires and their nests. Hope watched the introductions of Alexa and David—Alexa usually sparkled, but before Cressida she was diminished by the vampire's innate grace and presence. Then Cressida moved on, before her mother and father who made much of their shared history, a kiss on the cheek and clasped hands. Finally, though, with one last fluid move, she stood in front of Hope.

"Hello, Hope. I am pleased to see you." The words were spoken in a kindly tone, a mere hint of a French accent colored the words. Hope felt a smile rising on her face, muscles stretching, and she breathed deeply. A feeling of well-being coursed through her, just as it always had in Cressida's presence.

"Xavier, you are lucky to have not just this nest, but Hope too. Now, let me take her for a few minutes so we can catch up."

"Of course, Councilor Cressida." He bowed urbanely and released Hope's arm, a limb he hadn't relinquished since they'd joined the receiving line, and for a moment Hope felt a keen sense of loss.

Cressida slipped her hand through hers, and propelled both of them toward the open door.

Hope contained herself until they had left the room, before turning to Cressida with a hug. "Oh, Mistress Cressida, it is good to see you. It's been a very long time." Hope let go and stepped back. Cressida took her hand, leading her across the slate tiles.

"Yes, child. I know. I have been looking forward to this for some time." Then she stopped. "I take it you have been given a role within the household?" Cressida's gentle question probed while she searched Hope's face for a trace of...something. Sadness? Happiness? Hope didn't know exactly what Cressida was looking for, as possible answers chased around in her head. Before Hope could answer, Cressida gracefully sank down to the stone seat, and patted the spot beside her. "Come sit with me for a moment, so we can talk freely."

"Ah, yes, I have. Been given a role, that is." The words were slow and she saw Cressida grimace.

"This is not what you want, I take it?" A sound must have given Cressida the answer she expected, as she shook her head. "I told them you would not be content with that. Your parents have never accepted what you could and would be."

Something was coming, something momentous and life changing, Hope was sure. She waited and before another breath Cressida resumed.

"Have they discussed that with you?" The words were asked casually, but Hope knew deep down that there was much more to the query.

"Well, my mother told me today that I am to run the household, and essentially I should find a husband..." The words trailed away as she saw the disbelief on Cressida's face.

"No! They never told you what you are?" Cressida's eyes flashed as she watched Hope. Anger crept over her face, accentuating feral lines that became apparent, replacing the beauty that had been there just seconds before.

Hope flinched at the ferocity in the tone, and the look on her face. "Is there something else I should know?" Maybe here she would find the information she needed to understand the strained relations between herself and her family.

"I made it clear to them long ago that you should be told... Damn! I will discuss it with Xavier and your parents. You were meant for more. For greater things." For the first time, Hope saw the cracked façade of calmness that Cressida habitually wore like a mask.

She looked enraged, and Hope felt concern for her safety, a feeling she'd never experienced with Cressida before. What had appeared with a flash slowly dissipated once more, as Cressida obviously controlled her fury.

Cressida closed her eyes and breathed deeply. When she reopened them, all trace of the vampire within was once more gone. A seed of disquiet had been planted in Hope's mind.

"I need to talk to Xavier, but not tonight. I would imagine he has not yet been told of your gifts. Tonight we celebrate. You've finished your studies and are back within the nest, and that is something we should all be thankful for." Cressida smiled, patting Hope on the hand, and she felt her world stop for just an instant, as pleasure flooded her system.

Then Hope regained herself, remembering the manners that had been instilled in her from her early teenage years. "Mistress, do you require nourishment?" she enquired. It was inappropriate for her as a daughter of the *Yeux Secondes* to feed someone from outside the nest, but she could arrange for a suitable donor if required. The Mistress smiled, obviously aware that this had been drilled into her.

"No, my dear, I have brought my own. However, thank you for the offer. It is kindly received. Now tell me, how have you found the manor? When Cyrus purchased it, he did show it to me, and I liked it. Naturally, there seemed something homely about it." Cressida smiled.

Hope laughed, remembering how Cressida had always found the old gray manor as homely, too. It had seemed ridiculous to an eight-year-old that the house, filled with draughty corners and hard stonework, could be welcoming. Now those memories simply amused.

Hope was about to answer, when footsteps alerted her to the presence of another, and Cressida smiled at her. "It is Xavier, come to rescue his damsel from distress." She turned gracefully toward him, with a small smile and not for the first time Hope was struck by the grace in her movements.

"Xavier, you and I need to talk. I think I will contact you tomorrow to discuss what is on my mind. Tonight is a time to drink, dance and make merry." She gifted them both with another smile, and Hope rose automatically. "Now I need to go talk with the other guests, children." Cressida stood, her movements regal and fluid, and she left Hope and Xavier standing in the cool breeze.

"It always strikes me as odd that she calls me a child, yet I am over four hundred years old." He delivered the words with a bark of laughter. "She looks little more than a teenager, yet she is older than I." He laughed again. "Come, my lady Hope, it is time for us to open the proceedings."

Hope allowed him to take her hand into the crook of his arm, where she once again felt that amazing sense of well-being and belonging. Together they moved back toward the doors and into the throng of well-wishers.

E arlier, he'd given in to the urge to take her aside, and heaven knew the need to kiss her had grown once they were on the terrace. *The scent of her fills my senses and her nearness...* Only the faint sounds of the arrival of guests had seen him stop before going too far, and committing the cardinal sin of leaning in to touch those lush lips of hers with his, of testing and tasting her, the way his treacherous body demanded.

Now, here they stood again on the terrace, with the scent of roses eclipsed by the fresh essence of Hope that filled him. At her nearness his body hardened. A special presence and quality about her filled his senses and made him want her more than he already did. It was more than the scent of her body. Not the whiff of copper that rose faintly from all humans, the scent of blood that always seemed to be around them. No, there was an indefinable quality to her, one he sensed on many levels.

He ached to test the suppleness of her body. In this case though, the only way he could meet that need was through one of the dances. Perhaps, if he was lucky, he might also experience it in the act of love-making, though she was still a virgin, he was sure.

He'd been Master of this nest for only a matter of months, so he'd never met her before last night. He'd joined the nest while she'd been away, attending college. Nothing had prepared him for the emotional rush he'd felt on first meeting her or again tonight.

Thoughts of her had dogged his sleep today, and he'd struggled to concentrate on anything else.

It was a state of affairs that he was wholly unfamiliar with. A single woman drew him in a way none had ever done before.

It upset his equilibrium. He'd tossed and turned all day, as thoughts of her had raced through his mind, calling to him. Pulling him time and time again from the drowsing torpor he usually experienced in the realms of sleep.

Now with his hand rested at the base of her spine, urging her to the crowded ballroom, he wanted to splay his hands over her body. The need to touch her silken skin pulled at him, and he realized he lightly caressed her through the gown. Warmth spread through him from the simple touch.

Xavier escorted her to the podium that had been set up for the evening. Speeches first, then dancing and supper were the order of events. He looked around, while Hope answered the few well-wishers that knew her well enough to call out. They were polite acknowledgments but not what he would call friendly acquaintances'.

That alone confused him. She was beautiful, clever and talented. So where were her friends? Times surely hadn't changed that much had they? Surely she didn't walk through life as a solitary being? Why weren't they here to share her triumph? He would ask later, he told himself; just as he would get to the bottom of why her family treated her like a pariah.

She climbed the stairs, her dress pulling tighter with each upward step and displayed the lines of her body clothed in silk. Firm buttocks and long legs, built for speed, as well as pleasure. His body tightened further as a rush of heat spread through him and Xavier had to look away from the sight. When he glanced back, she had turned around. She stood there, studying him from beneath long sable lashes that hid her eyes from his questing gaze.

Hope waited, extending her arm to him. A nervous smile was

present on her face, and he felt an answering one rise, his muscles moving involuntarily. He reached the top of the steps, taking her hand, warm and small, in his and he felt the flutter of nervousness in her tiny fingers.

She was not as unaffected as she tried to make out.

He nearly laughed out loud at the thought, before containing his mirth. Now wasn't the time. Perhaps later. Later he might consider how he would initiate the pursuit of pleasure with Hope.

Xavier brought his mind back to the task at hand. Turning to the microphone, he raised a hand before waiting for all to stop and give him their undivided attention. Chatter died away and the chinking glasses stilled. Everyone watched, and he felt pride once more that it was his nest that brought people out to celebrate, people who would usually avoid these receptions.

"Councilor Cressida, Masters and Mistresses, ladies and gentlemen, and, of course, honored friends. Tonight, we come together to welcome a nestling back to our fold. Hope has been away for several years, and returns to the nest from her sojourns into the dangerous world of college education." He waited while a ripple of laughter spread its way through the room.

"Nests are few in number and their members are precious to all Masters and Mistresses, especially considering the losses experienced by all of us. Most especially, we remember the losses this nest endured so many years ago." He waited, pausing while many nodded their agreement. "For that reason, among so many others, the safe return of every nestling is a time of joyous celebration and renewal. As each nest prepares to find fulfilling roles for each new member and those coming of age, so too does the nest prepare to grow once more as nestlings flourish. They form families who continue to increase the size of our nest and ultimately we, as Masters and Mistresses, petition the Council for the formulation of new nests, under the leadership and guidance of those who have gone before." Xavier stopped for a moment as a vision of Hope, next to a man, rose in his mind. She was heavy with child and the pain that vision brought nearly overwhelmed him. A deep breath later, he pushed the pain aside, while his mind scrambled for the thoughts that had scattered.

"The art of finding their role in protecting and helping the nest to prosper is one that we cannot take lightly." Many in the crowd agreed and he heard their mutters. "In the case of Hope, the nest has once more taken possession of both a fine brain and beauty." A few men chuckled at his words and he looked back toward her in time to see Hope blush prettily even and he grinned. "In Hope, we see that chance for the future of our nest, as she too takes her place and position. Please, join me in welcoming home our Hope."

He watched, as faces smiled in the crowd and cheers rose, meeting with his while he motioned for Hope to move forward and accept the adulation. He backed away from the microphone, feeling an awareness once more of the woman in front of him.

It was clear that she controlled the nervousness with an iron will as she plastered a welcoming smile to her face. "Thank you, Master Xavier. I too would like to thank all of you for your attendance tonight. Mistress Cressida, it is both an honor and a pleasure to have you here." He watched as Cressida accepted her words of welcome with a slight nod and smile. "Masters and Mistresses, long may your nests experience peace and prosperity. To my friends and family, there are no words that convey my pleasure in once more being within the folds of my nest. I thank you for your good wishes and constant support during my absence. I certainly hope to do the nest proud and become a member of good standing." With that she moved away from the microphone.

He waited one more beat. "Long may the band play and the food and wine be enjoyable. Eat, drink and be merry." A final loud cheer broke out as he joined her.

Short speeches were still welcome, he noted with a smile, turning away from the crowd. "Come, let me find some refreshment for you, Hope, and then we will open the dancing." When he glanced at her face, he took in the scandalized look there. What had he said to put it there?

"Xavier, you shouldn't do that. You're a Master and it is not appropriate that you should attend to me. Let me arrange it." Amusement warred with understanding, as he watched her move off the stage and arrange a goblet of wine for herself and the heavily blooded wine for him.

The amusement faded, Xavier sighed and followed her slowly. Sometimes he forgot, being a Master, that people expected to do things for him, which seemed rather odd even after the months of practice in the role. He would need to be patient in learning to be a Master, he reminded himself.

As Hope handed him the goblet, he smiled his thanks.

CHAPTER SIX

he music and the movements of the dancers built as the night wore on. Hope, unused to so much noise and movement, threaded her way through the crowds of dancers, their jeweled plumage glittering under the chandeliers. She headed deliberately toward the open door and the blessed coolness of the garden beyond. Her head whirled as the wine played its tricks on her senses and her stomach rumbled slightly with hunger. The small nibbles served had done little to satisfy her and she hadn't eaten much all day. Right about now, a hamburger and fries would be most welcomed, but she knew it wasn't in the least bit likely that any would be found in the manor.

Shaking off Xavier had been difficult. He'd been an attentive escort. His presence overwhelmed her, left her emotions engaged and off center where he was concerned. The longer she was in his arms during the obligatory dance, the harder she found it not to give in to the sensuality he exuded. Something she knew was completely forbidden to her.

Finally, she'd exited the room on the pretext of powdering her nose, and he'd obligingly let her go. Once she'd returned, it had been clear he was caught in a deep discussion with others so she'd skirted the room to seek the blessed relief of the garden.

The scents of perfume dissipated, replaced by the fragrant roses, while a small breeze swept across the overheated bared skin of her arms. For a minute she shivered as goosebumps peppered her flesh. She took a deep, cleansing breath, then another, letting it wash away the tension that wound through her.

Hope headed toward the far end of the terrace, seeking a quietly secluded seat where she could remove the torturous shoes for a short while, when she heard a noise. Or was it the absence of sound? The crickets that had been chirping earlier were now silent, and even the rustle of leaves had ceased. She cocked her head, listening intently.

Behind her, she sensed a rush of movement before strong, warm arms enveloped her. A soothing sound filled her ear, totally at odds with the hard body that pressed against her, causing all sorts of reactions to begin.

"Hope, you need to return inside now."

"Why? What's going on?" She turned her head slightly so she could see his eyes, golden and intense. She shivered again, this time from the frisson of fear that skittered up and down her spine. "Xavier?"

"Go inside now, child."

Cressida's here as well? That didn't bode well at all. She whipped her head around in surprise, searching for something, and felt the subtle pressure as Xavier pushed her toward the door, his movements a whirl of speed that disoriented her slightly, before shutting the glass firmly behind her.

She noted with shock that guards, both vampire and human, now stood within the doorways. A silent wall of sentinels, as hands pulled her away from the sight.

She'd already seen enough to frighten her. Each guard held a UV gun in their hand. Vampires who weren't invited were afoot, and something bad was about to happen. A fleeting thought battered at her senses, while visions streaked through her mind. Each moving faster than the last and she couldn't hold one long enough to settle on it.

She swallowed past a lump, and nodded jerkily before moving further into the room.

Those guards confined within had moved forward, closing the space between them and the glass, taking a defensive position—the personal bodyguards of the senior members of nests, were highly trained humans. Her stomach rumbled and churned. Fear filled her. What was going on?

"Come, Miss Hope. You must move to the center of the room now." Lisi, her maid and friend, had moved toward her and taken her hand. Lisi shook. A quick glance reinforced the fear as Lisi's skin turned white, not a trace of the ruddiness that usually filled her cheeks was discernible. Her bright blue eyes seem unnatural with the bright red hair, and that told Hope that the danger must be acute.

"Lisi? What's happening?" Hope made her legs move, though they felt wooden and heavy now that the first flush of adrenaline had seeped away.

"The Brethren. They know we have many of the Council and nest leaders here tonight. The guards got word minutes ago and are taking no chances, because they believe an attack is imminent." She spoke the words so quietly that Hope had to strain to hear them. "Thank heavens Mistress Cressida and most of the nest Masters and Mistresses had brought their own guards. They were planning the attack to kill as many nestlings and…" Lisi must have seen her reaction, as her voice died away when Hope took a look at her mother.

"Lisi, you may go." Her mother's voice was cold and dismissive. For just a moment, Hope wanted to ask her mother to explain what was going on, but the coldness she'd heard in her voice was repeated in her eyes. There would be no answers there either. *Ask Lisi later.* Hope made a mental note, and followed her mother to the center of the room.

The people inside were silent, and a pall fell over the crowd as they huddled closer together. The music ceased, and the nestlings jammed in groups throughout the room. No one spoke a word, and the atmosphere was cold with dread at what could happen.

A startling thought occurred to Hope. No doubt it was the knowledge all nestlings had: these types of attacks have happened before and would likely happen again. This wasn't the first time in their history. Not even the second. That this was a cyclical event—the war followed by peace followed once more by war shook Hope to the core.

A sharp and loud scream filled the air. She jumped. Her mother frowned at her, while a body hit the closed French doors with a thump—the door she'd just entered through, leading to the terrace and gardens beyond. She caught sight of a face, being towed backward, its mouth open wide as if shouting out. She couldn't tell from this distance if it was agony or anger, but the emotion was strong, making her ache and leaving her head pounding.

The wait seemed interminable. The occasional call and scream rent the air as the pervasive stench of fear filled the ballroom. She didn't see anything near the door again. Her belly continued to roil madly. Her father stood beside a guard, listening through a small earpiece and giving directions, she guessed from watching his animated arm movements and head shakes.

Finally the sounds quieted and an uneasy stillness filled the air, the queasiness in the pit of her stomach threatened to heave to the surface of the dance floor. Hope controlled it as best she could, one hand against the flat of her midsection, the other clutched at her throat as her head throbbed.

Finally, the doors opened and those who had fought, including the Masters and Mistresses of the nests and the guardian vampires, stepped back into the room. Many looked disheveled, some carrying injuries and torn clothing. Hope watched them return in silence. Many had been wearing evening gowns and suits that would only be fit for destruction, and each sported eyes which glowed a golden-red indicating a level of satiation. She gulped at the thought.

As they entered, she watched them scan the area slowly, and there was no missing the primal quality in their movements.

Cressida stepped to the front. "In light of what has just transpired, I believe it is time to retire for the evening. Please gather your guards. While the threat is past for tonight, I believe this is just the beginning of a greater campaign." Her steely gaze ran around the room, lighting on figures here and there. A quick nod and her personal entourage joined her, silently moving together to the center of the ballroom.

Then Cressida moved again, grabbing Hope's hand and she felt the chill of the vampires skin. A memory called, but she couldn't tell what from and brushed it aside. There was a glint in her eyes and a warmth Hope barely recalled filled her again. "We must leave now. I will be in contact." She smiled, softening the words before turning to James. "We will talk. You have not followed the instructions I gave you that night. It is now too late, and it is my prerogative to explain." Anger dripped from the words.

Hope watched the color leach from her father's face.

A quick small step would take her to him, but the cutting gaze he threw in her direction halted her movements, leaving her frozen once again.

With a quelling look back to her parents, then a regal nod at the others who surrounded her, Cressida turned and was gone.

Hope stood watching as the guests collected items, formed their small groups and took their leave. Some left silently, creeping out of the door with their party, while others left with low words of regret and a brief touch here and there. The sea of color and sound ebbed away.

Once the last guests were gone, Hope looked around. The detritus of the night was littered here and there. Abandoned glasses of champagne and plates of nibbles sat on chairs and small serving tables, scattered around the room.

The musicians had already left, and the army of nestlings who worked in the house descended quietly to complete the task of clearing away the evidence of the night. Trays and trolleys moved in silence, as others came with brooms and cloths.

She sighed, and turned to talk to her parents, but realized with a start that they had left the room without a word to her. She was alone once more. Hot tears stung her eyes, but she refused to let them fall. Instead she balled her fists. "Why? Why do they do this to me?" The whispered words had no answer and she angrily dashed the tears away.

Cressida's words played over and over in her mind, making her wonder at the anger she'd seen. Her father had obviously upset Cressida—something about not following instructions sat oddly, as he was nothing if not loyal to his nest and the Council.

The bravado of the moment melted away. The hour was late and she was tired. The possibilities of trying to work out what should or shouldn't be done confused her, and she knew it was time to retire. With a last look around, she turned to make for the hallway, when a hand shot out and she jumped with surprise, and a small dollop of fear. It went as quickly as it came, replaced by the feeling of warmth once more.

"Xavier! You scared me." She took a deep breath as the urge to put her hand to her chest rose. She controlled it with an effort, hoping to slow the mad beating of her heart.

"Cressida requested that we move you from your room to the guest suites below. I have already had your friend…Lisi? Yes, anyway, she has moved some of your things." The words were spoken with a stiffness of tone and his eyes glittered.

"What? Why?" This wasn't at all what she'd expected. Why would Cressida give such a direction, and to Xavier? He was the Master, and members of the Council rarely intervened in the day-to-day running of the households. Thoughts battled in Hope's mind. Why was she being singled out?

All thoughts and questions left her head as he tugged her along the hall to the door at the end. The one she'd always been told she was never to attempt to open. The one that led to the vampires' private quarters below.

When the nest had purchased the manor, they had been cellars and kitchens. She'd vague memories of watching the tradesmen come and go, day after day, as they prepared them for the new inhabitants, but never before had she entered.

He touched a point on the wall and a recess opened, hidden within the dark wood casing. The keypad came as a surprise—a high-tech security system was hidden within the wall. Of course, it made sense, but it had never occurred to her they would need something like that.

He depressed the keys and a green light glowed, a beep sounded, and the click of the locks filled the air as tumblers moved, unlocking the entrance. He reached out and pushed the panel open, she could see it led to a dark corridor beyond. She took one step forward, then another, and the passage closed behind her.

CHAPTER SEVEN

ope contained a shriek that fought to escape, her lungs burning from the effort. Darkness. It was the one thing she had dreaded since her abduction. Her hands moved forward of their own volition, while she shivered in the chilly atmosphere. The corridor was cool and the absence of light terrifying. Stone rough and dry caught her fingers and she tried to work out where she was. Xavier propelled her further into the dark, and she knew her breath was audible, the panting sounds filling the silence.

"Be careful, there are steps here." His voice at her ear made her shiver for a different reason and made the fear recede. She wasn't alone at least. In her mind, she knew her reaction was a mix of anticipation and panic, but there was also an indefinable feeling that whipped through her senses.

She shivered again, and an arm pulled her close, masculine and muscled. Warm.

The roughness of his coat grazed her arm and a sensual thrill filled her.

"Let's get you down to the chamber where there's some light." His voice was deep, and she could feel the vibrations on her skin. Her nipples tightened. It's just the cold, she told herself. She knew that was a lie.

A few more steps and Hope finally detected a glow. She moved toward it a little faster, catching her heel on the edge of a step. The stiletto hit the edge of an uneven tile, but in the dark she couldn't see. Hope pitched forward, wobbling, as her arms wheeled madly looking for something to grip. She threw her body backward, forgetting his presence for an instant, until his arms surrounded her, pulling her firmly against his lean, hard body once more. Xavier held her for a second longer than it took to find her balance, his hands splayed over her stomach, then they retreated once more.

"Just take a moment, Hope. Once you get used to it, you'll be fine, although maybe your eyesight isn't going to be much help in this environment. I will organize some lighting for you, so you can see where you are going tomorrow evening." His words centered her, and there was no trace of emotion that she could decipher in his voice.

They reached the bottom of the steps, the dim lighting revealing a long corridor. The alignment mirrored the upstairs layout, except, instead of heavy wood and cream painting, there were rough-hewn walls of gray stone, teamed with slate flags on the floor. Doors dotted left and right, and she craned her head to see within.

"These are the sleeping quarters of the guards. Our rooms are at the end through that door." He ushered her quickly along the corridor. The large wooden door at the end opened without a squeak, and led into a luxurious apartment, decorated in pale colors, so unlike the overpowering dark woods upstairs. She glanced around quickly.

"Wow! I never thought about your suite. This is lovely." Hope ran enchanted fingers lovingly over the light oak furnishings. A love seat sat on dark blue carpet. Exquisite paintings, she was sure were the works of old masters, graced walls covered in shimmering blue wallpaper, and beyond she spied a white cabinet filled with books. A large armchair nestled in a cozy corner.

"This is glorious!" The words were breathless as she looked around.

"Yes, from where I am standing the view is certainly lovely."

She heard his softly spoken words, and turned, only to find, instead of looking at the furnishings and walls, his eyes were deep pools of molten desire, looking at her. Something shimmered through her like quicksilver.

"Umm, where do I sleep?" The words were husky and she nearly closed her eyes, cringing at the double meaning. He snorted quietly, obviously having also come to that conclusion, but she looked away, refusing to give in to an emotion she didn't want to confront.

"Through here." Xavier indicated a door that blended into the furnishings, then he turned the small handle and opened it wide, allowing her to see inside as he stood back.

Hope peered into the room. Instead of the pale blues she'd seen within her suite, this room was decorated in gold and lush creamy tones that were warm and welcoming.

The bed was an antique carved four-poster of some dark wood, perhaps old English oak. She was bemused at the sight of such lush comfort and noticed the color was similar to the upstairs bedroom furnishings. That was where the similarities ended.

The curtains of detailed velvet were inset with fine lace, matching the coverlet, and the bed was piled high with what looked to be the softest fluffiest pillows. To the side was a boudoir chair covered in the same material as the curtains and coverlet, and at the end of the bed sat a bench, padded and inviting, before an ornate dressing table. She took another step in. "This is exquisite." She murmured the words as she took in the carved full-length mirror, and the series of doors along one wall.

"They lead to your bathroom and dressing chamber. I had all your clothing and personal items moved here, as soon as we became aware of the threat to the nest. Especially once Cressida made it clear your safety was paramount."

The words stopped her cold. She whipped her head back to him. "Why? Why just me, and not my whole family?" She urged him with every fiber of her being to explain, but he shrugged his shoulders.

"I don't know, but she said they would be fine. She is supposed to be contacting me tomorrow. For now, you are safe here." His eyes watched hers, the green of them reminding her of the river in summer, cool and enervating. Once more she shivered. He took a step back, breaking the spell. She swayed at the loss of the connection between them.

"My rooms are through here." He showed her back into the main room and opposite hers. "If you need me, all you need to do is call. I had a communications system installed here when I became the Master, so you will be able to be in contact with your family. Your computer is also being set up in my private office, through this door, and concealed behind one of the doors in your chamber is a multi-media entertainment system." His words made her feel as if she'd lost all the control over her life.

"Meals?" She hated to seem forward and rude, but now her stomach was churning with hunger.

"They will be delivered here by one of the bodyguards to ensure your safety, as your maid Lisi is only allowed to come as far as the secure doorway. I have arranged for guardians to take on the daylight vigil outside the suite, and they will ensure our safety."

They stood quietly for a moment and she nodded. "Right then. Maybe I should retire." She started to back away when he reached out and gripped her firmly.

"Once Cressida shares what information she has, we can talk more. For now, though, retiring is probably wise." He thrust a small tray she hadn't seen behind him into her hands. Food. She smiled ruefully before nodding her thanks.

Hope turned and walked through the door, closing it firmly behind her.

Hope woke, not sure what told her it was time to rise, but her body seemed to know it was morning. She'd fallen into a dreamless sleep, after eating the cheeses and fruits that had been delivered for her.

Her stomach rumbled as she glanced around the room. It was

luxurious, but it still felt like a cage, one she couldn't leave without permission. Gilded, beautiful and comfortable, certainly, but most definitely a cage and she was the prisoner.

Hope crawled to the side of the massive bed and swung her feet over. They touched the deep plush carpet, and she sighed as her senses went into overdrive at the feel of the deep pile. She made her way silently toward the bathroom door, and stepped through, looking around to see an enormous corner spa, deep and welcoming. In another corner sat a large open walled shower with an oversize removable head. The room was lit with subdued lighting, and she spied another door that opened into the toilet. Even vampires needed bathrooms, it seemed. Using the dimmer switch she turned the lights up slightly, enough to see comfortably, but definitely not bright enough to hurt a vampire's eyes.

Hope rushed through her ablutions, washing away the makeup she'd been too tired to remove when falling into bed the night before. She avoided looking at herself in the mirror hanging above the deep sink, knowing her eyes would look tired and shadowed.

As she headed back to the bedroom, she snatched her robe off the end of the bed. No way was she wandering into the main area without the added cover. Her pajamas might cover just about everything, and were way less revealing than a bikini, but she'd seen the glimmer of interest in Xavier's eyes the night before. Better to cover up and have a look around, find out the time and decide what to do next. Then she shook herself mentally. As if he would do anything, or show any interest in her. The thought was lowering.

The lounge room was deserted and she dragged in a sigh, thankful that being alone would give her time to take stock of the situation she found herself in. On the table she saw a tray, the highly polished dome telling her it was food, her stomach rumbled at the sight.

Lifting the dome she saw a bowl filled with muesli, a tub of yogurt and a medley of her favorite fruits. Beside it sat a bright red cooler box, and perched on that was a small kettle, a coffee plunger, a teacup and the necessary cutlery. Hope looked around, before opening the cooler. *Good*, she thought. They had delivered coffee, milk and bottled water. Someone upstairs had ensured she was adequately catered for. It was almost enough to make her feel comfortable.

Feeling happier, she collected the kettle and plugged it in, poured water into the reservoir and waited for it to boil. Coffee always made her feel better, so she prepared the plunger and ate breakfast while she waited for the hot drink. The rich dark aroma filled the room, and she inhaled deeply.

Coffee in hand, she headed into the office where Xavier had promised her laptop would be. A desk had been set up opposite what she guessed was his, and her small computer barely filled the tidy space. The room reminded her of his rigidly controlled behavior. It was a traditional manly office, with dark woods and heavy furnishings, though she suspected he didn't use it much. Right now, though, she wasn't interested in the surroundings or his use of them, as she headed over and booted up her computer.

It hummed to life and she smiled. She checked the time, waiting for the machine to make a connection to the Internet. Living out of town meant things like this took a lot longer. Just a little after ten in the morning and she grimaced. What on earth would she do with the day, waiting for him to rise?

Opening her email program, she sipped coffee as the messages downloaded. Nothing exciting, some spam mail, a few messages from friends who had reached their homes after leaving college, but nothing of any real importance. No one she felt a long-lasting connection to. She slumped back in the deep office chair. Now what? Maybe check the news, see if there was anything there, but nothing held her interest. She watched the time as she flicked around sites that caught her eye. Shopping sites didn't interest her and movies on the small screen just irritated her. She logged out and turned off the computer, feeling lonely.

She rose and made her way back to the main room. The door was just closing and she made to call out, but thought better of it. She knew Lisi wouldn't be allowed to enter, and the guards would be taciturn at this time of the day—they still struggled with the daylight hours, as the night was the time they were active.

A new tray sat on the table, and she wandered over, before lifting the dome and smiling. A burger and fries. She goggled when she saw that the drink was her favorite soft drink. Obviously, someone on staff remembered her predilection for junk food. She snickered. It was probably Lisi again.

Lisi wasn't that much older than Hope, yet she'd already carved out her own place in the world, coming into the household as a junior maid. Because they got along so well, she'd been given the role of looking after Hope's needs. Over the years they had become close, and even during her time in college they had corresponded. The memories made Hope feel a little homesick, which she reflected was silly, because here she was, at home.

Hope snatched up the food and retreated to the bedroom. Tears threatened but she dashed them away. There was no benefit in feeling sorry for herself. Even her internal thoughts couldn't raise her mood. She popped the food and drinks on a bedside table, and opened the doors where Xavier had indicated the multimedia unit was housed.

The first opened into a large dressing area, and she gasped at the space that lay mostly empty, with only some clothes gracing hangers in the center of the small room.

The second door she opened concealed a large television, DVD and speakers. Grabbing the remote, she headed to the bed and crawled onto it, crossing her legs as she reached for the food.

Flicking through the channels didn't really fill her with interest, and with a full stomach and boredom setting in, she dozed.

Xavier woke, unused to the sensation of instant awareness. The darkness around him was silent, and he remembered that Hope was supposed to be here. Why couldn't he hear her? He could tell she wasn't in the living area, no sound come from that direction. Sitting up, he lifted the covers off himself. He straightened the sleeping pants he'd worn to bed, they had twisted and crawled up around his body in an uncomfortable fashion. He usually slept naked, but with her staying in the suite he'd considered them to be unavoidable. He didn't want to scare her if she wandered in by accident.

The orders he'd given before retiring that morning had meant the guards would only enter the main room, not deliver his blooded wine to the bedroom. He brushed his tousled hair back as hunger pulled at him. He padded through the room toward the living area. On the table sat a tray. Obviously her evening meal, and his goblet of refreshment.

He frowned.

She hadn't come out for dinner, and that concerned him. Xavier glanced around. The office door was slightly ajar and he wandered in. She'd been in here. He could smell her scent, light and subtle, but it was slightly stale, and likely several hours old. He walked back to the living area and considered whether she would have tried to leave, so he moved to the door and knocked. It was opened by one of the guards on duty. "Has Miss Hope left the suite?"

"No, Master. Her meal was delivered about fifteen minutes ago by a guard, and I brought it straight in as you requested. Is something amiss?" The guard cocked his head.

"I don't think so." He moved back into the room, closing the door. Observing her door was shut, he considered whether he should invade her privacy. It was something that made him quite uneasy. She could be asleep or in the bathroom, not that he could hear any water moving. Or, something could be wrong.

After considering the food on the table, a lightning thought of poison assailed, he shook his head at the fanciful notion even as a quick hit of rage and panic rose in him. The food looked to be untouched, so that wasn't anything to consider.

Only one way to find out where she is.

He knocked on the door and heard movement beyond. He knocked again, a little louder, hoping for an answer. A muffled movement met his ears, and this time he decided her safety overrode her privacy.

Slowly he pushed the door open. "Hope?" He moved into the room, scanning as he went. She was asleep, curled on the bed, and the sight entranced him. He moved toward her, stepping lightly so he didn't surprise her. He was mesmerized by her ivory skin, and the dark hair that tumbled around her beautiful face. Her hair looked like silk, and his body urged him to reach out, to touch it once more. He dimly noticed that her robe was bunched around her waist, and a small amount of silky flesh peeked out as if daring him to see how soft her skin was. *Touch her while she sleeps. You are Master, and she is yours for the taking.*

He curled his fists along with his lips, and self-derision reminded him of his honor. *I am not an animal. I am not one of the Brethren. She is worthy of honor, and to defile her would be to discard everything I fight to uphold.*

"Hope?" He called quietly. No need to frighten her. Worried thoughts trickled through his mind as he called once more. "Hope?"

He watched as she murmured and moved on the bed, baring more of her midriff. His gut tightened, the heat of desire filled him, pooling once more in his groin. More skin bared, and her top lifted a little more while she stretched in the act of waking.

"Hope?" A little louder this time, and he recognized the strangled quality in his voice. He cleared his throat and her eyes fluttered once, twice then again before they opened slowly, it was, to him, like shades lifting off the most beautiful image in the world. Violet eyes blinked owlishly as she moved.

"Xavier? What are you doing awake?" The unconsciously sensual tone of her voice had his body tightening, while he fought for control. He closed his eyes and breathed deeply, but her scent invaded his mind.

"It is past six in the evening and you have been asleep." He wanted to wince at the banality of his answer. He inwardly shrugged it off. What else could he do right now, anyway?

"What? Oh, I didn't mean to..." Her voice trailed off and she looked at him. "There just wasn't a lot to do... Urgh! I feel woolly. I hate sleeping in the afternoon," she said, her voice soft and redolent with the remnants of sleep. A stray strand of hair flopped over her face. She brushed it aside, one finger hooking the stray tress behind her ear. His heart thudded hard against his ribs.

"Your meal awaits, sleeping princess." *If I don't get out of here soon, I'm going to touch her.* The thought shocked him. He'd never felt this level of neediness before, and he shied away from what that meant.

"Oh, right. Can you just give me a minute?" She scrambled off the bed, nearly falling in her haste. The robe tangled with her long legs. He reached out a hand to help her, but she moved quickly toward the bathroom, ignoring it, so he retreated back to the living room, giving her the privacy she needed.

Moments later, she joined him in the lounge area, and she lifted the domed lid. Her face wrinkled with distaste for just an instant, before, with a barely audible sigh, she picked up the meal and the cutlery.

"The food doesn't tempt you?"

"What? Oh no, it's just I am not the biggest fan of large meals for dinner." Her voice was low, and she glanced at him where he stood, reaching for the phone.

"Miss Hope would prefer something else for her evening meal. Prepare it and deliver it as soon as possible." He turned to see a shocked look on her face. He enjoyed it for just an instant, before moving back to her.

"Have I done something wrong, Hope? I mean, you are not pleased with the meal, therefore something else should be prepared." As he finished talking, the phone trilled and he idly lifted the receiver.

"There was no need. It was fine, truly." Her face was pale, and for an instant anger flashed through his mind, then he turned back to the phone in his hands. *Something isn't right here. I will need to talk to her about this after I see who is calling.*

"Master? James has said that is all that is available." The words were forcefully delivered by the housekeeper, Mrs. Atkins.

Caustic anger rose in his gut. He'd demanded a better meal for Hope, and it wasn't up to James to determine otherwise, or to countermand his orders. He opened his mouth to demand that James attend she when he continued...

"Also Councilor Cressida's assistant has called. She wishes you to come to her home tonight, to discuss the situation. She has instructed you to take Miss Hope with you."

He looked back at her. She sat, slowly eating a piece of carrot coated in some white fluid, nibbling on the end, but even to his eyes it looked less than appetizing. He strode over, his belly churning with anger, while he listened to the message blaring from the speaker. He gripped his goblet, quickly downed the blooded wine, then he put the cup down with a crash. Hope lifted her head, and looked directly at him.

"Come. Leave that. We have to meet with Cressida, we can find you something better on the drive." He grabbed her arm, marveling at the warmth and softness of her skin as he always seemed to.

It had been many years since he'd had a human lover. Maybe that was why he was so drawn to her? Something in him rebelled at the thought that it was because she was human, beautiful and young. No, he didn't want to know what the reality of this feeling was, yet he wouldn't label it as something so empty.

"I'm not dressed or anything." Her words drew him back.

"Then change, but be quick. We leave in ten minutes." She stood, and he watched as she disappeared through the bedroom door.

CHAPTER EIGHT

hey exited the stairs to the corridor. Her father stood there, waiting. He was as immaculate as ever, with the black suit teamed with a bright white shirt and conservative tie. His salt and pepper hair was cut close to his head, his face having undergone a transformation over the years. The lines around his eyes and mouth highlighted his chiseled jaw, now shaded darkly with a five o'clock shadow. Through the years, he'd slimmed to a streamlined shape, but he still exuded a power many men only achieved through bulk. His pale blue eyes were cold, and she shivered in reaction as they left her face and continued on to Xavier.

"Master, a moment of your time? I have prepared the statements for your perusal. The Iversten accounts have risen by fifteen percent..."

Xavier's hand flashed at her father. "James. I am displeased with you, but we have no time to discuss this. Hope and I have an appointment that cannot wait. I will attend you tomorrow evening. Give the portfolio to Javed, and he will go over it tonight with me when we return." The words were tight and controlled, but something glinted in Xavier's eyes.

Her father looked at her. "Hope, your mother wishes to see you..."

It was as if Xavier had never spoken, she watched Xavier's mouth flatten in anger. A tic at the side of his jaw started, and she would have stepped back if it wasn't for his firm grip on her arm.

"I have already told you, James, we have an appointment." This time the words were terse, and her father gazed intently at her, as if telling her of his displeasure. Confusion reigned. What had she done now?

"Father, tell Mother I will contact her in the morning. Right now, we have to go." She tried to soften the words with a smile, but the look her father gave her became a sneer. It slammed into her like a blow, and for just an instant she wanted to step forward and have him hold her.

Her father turned and walked away from her, and the thud of footsteps grew fainter as she watched him retreat. The action cut her. She gasped for breath at the physical pain it caused, shafting through her heart.

Xavier interrupted her thoughts. "Hope? Are you well?" The hand that held his shook slightly, and she gripped onto him, seeking assurance that this was a bad dream, yet it wasn't. She could feel the tensile strength in his grasp. What caused this madness between her family and herself? She slid her fingers into Xavier's grip and straightened her spine.

"Ahh, yes. Let's go." She tried to smile, even though she knew the failed attempt was noted.

Xavier didn't speak, and she was grateful for that small mercy, as he steered her out of the house, down the block steps. They crunched their way across the gravel of the driveway to the car that sat waiting. It was a monster, sleek and black. The windows were darkly tinted for safety reasons, and she noted that several other cars waited behind it. Their guard filed out behind them, flanking them in a formidable show of strength.

The air was still and heavy and she lifted her head, allowing her eyes to close so she could contain the pain and anger her father's treatment caused. The sweet scent of roses and jasmine filled her senses, and for just an instant a cool breeze filtered through the air, and then was gone, but the fresh feeling it brought helped to clear her mind. She allowed it to sweep away any trace of sadness or regret, before climbing into the vehicle.

Xavier slid in beside her, the files he carried tossed carelessly onto the seat. His personal guard and second, Javed, moved to the front with the driver, leaving them alone once more.

The first of the guardian cars pulled out. A boxy, black people mover took up position behind theirs, and memories of details long forgotten flittered through her mind. Each vehicle was heavy and built to the specifications of the nest purchasing them. The glass and bodies were bulletproof, and the engines had been replaced with faster heavy motors, allowing them to travel at speeds most humans were unable to handle. The tint on the windows was reinforced and carefully darkened, allowing the vampires within to seek shelter during the daylight hours, gave them a view of the world as they moved.

Each car was then submitted for testing by the traffic authorities and certified before being allowed on the road. They were also clearly made identifiable by the nest's coat of arms on the passenger doors. The registration plates were easily distinguishable by the red and yellow stripes.

Many of the militant humans argued it was unfair that vampires could drive these modified beasts on the roads, but the government had passed legislation to allow for this specialized certification some years back. Now most people just accepted it without question.

Hope leaned back into the luxurious leather seat.

"We will find a drive-through." Hope scowled but his voice was humor filled as he spoke. She wasn't some child who required cheering up. Once more Hope opened her mouth to comment, but a raised hand stopped her.

"I checked on your favorite dietary options while you changed." At his words she flashed him a look, he merely smiled back.

"I'm not that bad. I can eat normal food, you know. It's just heavy night time meals are..." She shivered in distaste, realizing that maybe she'd read the situation with the wrong attitude to start with.

If she was honest, it was probably a reaction to the altercation, if you could call it that, with her father. It left her edgy and off balance. It was also childish, she allowed privately.

"If I were you, I think I would feel the same." His grin was boyish, and for a moment she saw the man he must have been, so very long ago. She didn't really know anything about him, and suddenly the need to find out seemed so important.

"How did you become Master of the house?" Her mother had refused to discuss the matter when asked, and, given the situation, Hope needed to know as much as possible, so she could have some control over what happened to her.

He sighed. "It's a long story."

Hope looked at him. "It's a long drive. Please?"

Xavier nodded. "Okay, you know when you were abducted by the Brethren, there was a deal between Cressida and Philippe?" She nodded and waited patiently. "Well, there was an alliance formed. They both had the same sire, so it made sense for her to seek his assistance. In order to both rescue and protect you after you were located in the warehouse where you were hidden, she needed someone to take over the running of the nest as there were certain steps she'd to take. Steps that couldn't be taken without a price."

Xavier stopped and breathed deeply. "None of her personal guards who survived were sufficiently prepared to take over, so she made the pact with Philippe. I was part of his house back then, and I remember the night Cyrus was made aware of his promotion. He'd been Philippe's right hand for an extended period of time, groomed to take over running the nest."

Hope watched as Xavier turned away for just an instant as if revisiting the time once more. "Anyway, Cyrus and I were close, having seen nearly two hundred years of service together. I helped him to make the transition but...as he was groomed to be the next to make the transition within our own nest, it left a vacuum in ours. One I was sure I could fill. The nests are built upon a system of alliances. Some houses would seek their next Master or Mistress from others. It was a time of great upheaval in the houses. Such a thing had not happened since the Spanish Inquisition and when many came here."

Hope waited. This was a history she'd never heard, and it intrigued her. "So, how did you become the Master then?"

"Ah yes. Well, since the houses started forming these strategic alliances, the Brethren became more unsettled. More and more attacks occurred. One night, we were travelling with Philippe when our convoy was intercepted. We were flagged down to help a woman whose car had broken down—she was supposedly in labor. Philippe had a soft spot for children and babies so we stopped…" He sucked in a breath.

Hope extended a hand, seeing that the conversation was emotionally difficult for him. "You don't have to say any more."

Xavier held her hand and smiled. "You know, I probably do. I have pushed it away ever since it happened." His smile was strained, and it hurt to see him struggle for the words. A feeling of anger swept through her, but she waited in silence for him to continue. "Anyway, it was an ambush. Philippe got out to see what he could do, while we were busy with the vehicle itself. They had the new UV rifles. Others were waiting and they opened fire. Philippe was mortally injured, but we got them all. Captured them, and made sure they stood trial for the murder of Philippe and the other six guards lost that night.

"In losing our Master, the house had no head, so another was appointed by Cressida as the head of the Council as I wasn't yet trained. You did know she'd been a member of the Council previously, didn't you?"

Hope shook her head, there was so much information and lore that she didn't know. After all these years she still knew so little about them.

"Then one of the Councilors stood down last year, and Cyrus was nominated as the next to ascend, he requested that I take over the nest. I had been shadowing Xurian who'd been second to Phillipe you know, so it made sense. I knew how to run a nest. And here I am."

Hope was sure there was a lot more to learn, but for now she was content with the information he'd shared. It wouldn't help solve the problem of why the Brethren had attacked last night, but it was something to consider and file away.

She sighed as she looked out of the window to the city as they whizzed past. He looked so good in his black suit, cut perfectly and fitted to his muscular frame, and she wanted to turn back to gaze upon his beautiful visage. The scent of his aftershave, spicy and welcoming, filled her senses and she knew she was fighting a losing battle against her attraction to him—the one she'd been prey to from the first time she'd seen him. When she turned back it was to find him watching her; studying her with an intensity that made her quiver deep inside.

"Apart from that, Cyrus noted that there was a problem within the nest. The power imbalance, in my opinion, comes from so many changes in a short period of time—something that usually doesn't occur. To be honest, I have to agree with his assessment of the imbalance, but I'm still trying to get the business arm back on track. The nest had been doing well, until the last few years. Suddenly our financial reserves were dwindling no matter what we did. Investments that we foreshadowed were being picked up, before we could get them finalized." He sighed and leaned his head back.

Hope sat, quietly digesting what he'd told her. Something was wrong with the nest? For the first time, she realized it was rife—her father arguing the point with Xavier, the way her mother ruled the household. She looked out of the window and was stunned to see them pulling into her favorite takeaway restaurant.

The intercom buzzed and she watched Xavier open his eyes and straighten up, touching the speaker button. "Miss Hope, what would you prefer?" Javed's voice was filled with amusement, and she felt the heat flare in her face. Did they all know she'd a weakness for junk food?

She quickly made a suggestion for the order, and waited patiently for the knock on the door. A hand thrust a bag and bottle inside the vehicle, then it rocked slightly as Javed climbed back into the front. The engine hummed once more as they pulled back onto the road.

She sneaked a quick look at Xavier who watched her. His green eyes twinkled and his face quirked into an amused grin. "What are you waiting for?" His voice held laughter.

"Well, it's bad manners to eat in front of someone who isn't."

"Hope, eat your dinner before it gets cold, and we get to Cressida's." His voice was soft. "If it embarrasses you that much, I can turn away."

Hope knew it was silly, but the offer warmed her. "If you don't mind." She waited and watched as he repositioned himself, then quickly opened the wrappers and began eating. Burger first then the fries, as her stomach rumbled once more.

Embarrassment warred with hunger, when she'd finished Hope shoved the wrappers back into the sack, and wiped her face and hands with the napkin that had been provided.

"Xavier? I'm done." He turned back to her and she marveled at how such a big strong man—no, vampire—could move so gracefully. He smiled and reached out a hand toward her face. Hope sat still, wondering what he was doing. Her limbs weighed her down and an unfamiliar lethargy filled her.

"You have a seed right there." He touched her skin as he said the words softly. He moved his fingers against the side of her mouth, like the softest of velvets, then drew back, where they stilled before they touched her lips. His eyes glinted.

Her breath hitched in her throat and her heart pounded a fast rhythm. She wet her lips with her tongue, grazing him slightly. His eyes narrowed at the action, then slowly he leaned toward her. The whisper of his breath on her lips, so sweet and fragrant, sent her dazed senses into overdrive. Closer and closer he leaned, and she knew he was going to kiss her.

The phone buzzed, startling her. He pulled back, watching her, as he touched the intercom button, his chest moving rapidly. "What?" Xavier bit out the words.

"We have arrived at the gate." Javed's answer was terse, as if he realized he'd interrupted something. "Do you need me to do something for you, Master?"

"No, that's fine. Thank you." He punched the button once more and sat back, watching her intently, his eyes glinting in the low light, while the memory of the near kiss scorched her mind.

God, he must think I'm so easy. He's a Master and I'm the daughter of his Yeux Secondes. Nothing more or less. The internal reminder didn't help. She didn't feel any better about what had nearly happened. It just left her stomach churning even more, threatening to swamp her with the greasy waves of emotion. She felt bewildered and confused by her situation, her attraction to this Master vampire and her place in the universe.

CHAPTER NINE

Hope walked behind Xavier, his graceful gait filling her view. Together they passed fine paintings and antiques from wars long passed that reminded her of a museum. The entire public area of the house was filled with heavy dark wooden furnishings, and the familiar scent of lemon-infused beeswax filled the air. She was sure there was no comfort here in the formal areas, but if she knew Cressida, there would be hidden havens within the house. Rooms that would be welcoming and comfortable, probably painted in pale hues with light furnishings.

For an instant, the memory of the house she called home rose in her mind, and she couldn't contain the cold that infused her at the thought. The floor beneath her feet was slate and the tap of her heels sounded loud and echoed in the high-ceilinged rooms. She felt unwieldy hearing her awkward gait as it reverberated against the soft sigh of the steps of walking vampires.

When they had entered the house, each and every one of the vampire guards had been frisked—everyone, except herself and Xavier. Funny that. Hope snorted loudly. Xavier turned to look at her and smiled. She wanted to cringe, the heated red tide of embarrassment crawled over her skin again.

Instead of asking why they had gone through unscathed and unchecked, she accepted it. *You don't ask a vampire those sorts of questions.* She'd been told in the past, by those who didn't live inside nests, that asking vampires any questions was playing Russian Roulette. She'd come across that attitude regularly, but for the life of her she'd never understood their fear of nested vampires. It was the rogues you needed to worry about.

Several elaborately clothed vampires stood guard near a large wooden door, but instead of brandishing swords, they carried UV guns, and each wore a similar dark uniform with epaulets on the shoulders, jaunty berets on their heads and sashes running across their heavy chests.

The opening they guarded was dark and studded with gleaming silver. Hope grinned at the sight of the silver. Those who lived outside nests still believed that vampires had an allergy to it. Those within nests were sworn to secrecy about that false assumption. Instead, the deadly metal was copper. It reacted with something in their skin, causing burns on simple contact. For those who faced long-term contact, the result was horrific, including eventually eating through skin and bone, causing amputation and horrible poisoning. They nodded, and together moved to grab the shining silver rings that adorned the doors. They pulled and the entrance opened. Not a squeak was to be heard as the massive wooden hung door moved silently on well-oiled hinges.

Hope thanked the heavens she'd never seen it—the chatter from other nestlings had been enough to turn her stomach.

As she moved into the room, she found it warmer and far more welcoming than she'd expected. She noted the large round table in the middle, more gleaming dark wood and scented beeswax. The soft furnishings were powder blue this time, and with glints of gilding here and there, to take away the oppressiveness.

"Welcome, my child. Xavier, I am pleased you could arrange to get away so quickly." Cressida seemed to glide toward her. The grace in her movements continued to amaze Hope, as both hands were outstretched in welcome. On her face was a broad grin, and Hope accepted nods from the half dozen or so other senior vampires who remained seated at the table.

"Cressida, it is always a pleasure. However, you intimated that there was urgency to this matter?" Xavier's voice cut through the muted chatter.

She turned to him with a ready smile. "Yes, there is. Please take a seat." Cressida indicated two empty chairs beside her, then, smoothing down her immaculate blue skirt, sat slowly, as if gathering herself for the storm ahead.

"As you would be aware, Hope was abducted from the nest as a child. I spoke to James at the time, and told him he needed to ensure her safety and then once she was old enough, that he must tell her about her…situation."

Cressida stopped and looked at Hope, and, for just a second, Hope saw a quick flash of emotion in her eyes. Dismay? Pity? Concern? They were all there and others less easily defined as well. "You see, Hope is…a blood siren." She stopped.

Xavier sucked in air. "Blood siren? I thought that was a myth? How…?" He looked baffled.

Hope was even more confused. "What is a blood siren, Cressida? And why is this such an issue?" Hope could see that the genuine puzzlement in her tone caught Cressida off guard.

"Hope, dear, you have not been taught about the mythology of the siren. I particularly requested your parents not do so, until you had finished your school education."

A feeling of cold trickled down her spine. Could this be the answer to the abduction so many years ago?

"Clearly, however, they haven't explained anything to you since then. So, now I invoke my right to do so. During the centuries, we've had many sirens, both male and female. We knew they existed and they carried certain skills and abilities, however until recently we didn't understand exactly what made them special. That something existed in their blood. We knew that they were born with the ability to cure vampirism, and also to infect those who are susceptible. It's only been in the last thirty years or so, that we've acquired knowledge of how this has come to pass. As a body, the Council has made certain facilities available to doctors, to investigate what it is about the blood of these people that has been able to effect such changes." Hope waited for Cressida to continue, but she picked up her goblet and took a deep draught.

"Sirens..." Cressida stopped, then shook her head, before starting again. "As vampires we have a bi-polar outlook on sirens. At least, what we thought was the myth of them. For those of us in nests, we see them as having a place in how we came to be. Our mythology tells us that the blood of a siren made the first and most powerful vampire ever. With the help of science, we've come to realize that may not necessarily be so, but we still hold sirens as being sacred to us. To be protected at all costs. The rogue vampires though....They only see a weapon to vanquish the nests and a way to create more vampires in their warped image."

"Just before your birth, there was a breakthrough, that gave us a hint. We developed a test to sort those who were genetically capable of making the change to vampire. Resulting from that breakthrough, we tested every human in every nest, placed their blood in a specialized bank. Each new child born now has a vial collected before they are released to their home."

Hope blinked. She never knew any of this.

Cressida sighed, then continued. "When you were born we knew what factors to look for. We discovered there is a marker, a genetic...mutation in your blood that carries the virus for vampirism, though it is dormant until ingested by those either susceptible or already infected. Your blood is also volatile, inducing blood highs for some, which is why you have been so closely guarded in the past."

Cold. The cold trickle had turned arctic, as Hope sat still in the chair. She was a blood siren, able to cure and infect with the vampirism virus? Induce blood highs? Why hadn't her parents told her?

"Why did you...?" The words escaped and Cressida looked both embarrassed and annoyed. Hope shook her head, telling herself this couldn't possibly be true. She needed answers. "How did you become aware of this?"

"When you were just a baby, your blood was mapped as we do with each child born. It allows us to ensure that our records of births are accurate and to attribute them to the correct houses. It also means, when we have families with members of rare blood types, our medics have necessary stocks of their blood type available, to ensure the safety and security of each and every member of the nest. Well, that is how we managed to promote it to the wider public. The truth is, our concern over the situation with blood sirens had become untenable. We had already lost several, and we needed to find a way to assess every member quietly."

Cressida watched her as Hope struggled to understand the importance of the announcement.

"As you know, when we lose members of the nests, we make a sacrifice of blood. Usually we use the mapped blood as the sacrifice." She stopped, breathed deep and turned, pulling a sheaf of papers toward herself, flicking through until she found a page, mottled with age. Cressida pushed it toward Hope.

"When your blood was mapped, we instantly noticed the strange genetic markers. A sample was sent to the central testing facility and they had a susceptible member working with your blood. We were all unsure, until there was...an accident. That staffer turned within the week, but was unable to control his appetites. That is how we first became aware that you could be a siren. We ran every test to check the scientists could devise for the specific strain of virus that you carry. All three hundred of them."

How could this be happening to her? Pain, unbearable now, screamed through her. For so long they had kept this secret. Now, she understood why she'd been so consistently and heavily guarded. It didn't make the knowledge any easier to bear.

"We ran one last test, which was positive. An empirical test on a Brethren vampire. He was cured of the virus within days. That is how we knew definitively."

Hope clenched her hands tightly, seeking release from the words, but there wasn't any. This wasn't a bad dream. It was her life. "What does that mean for me, Cressida? What will you do with me?" Hope's voice wobbled a little.

"Child, we thought we had dealt with those behind the kidnapping, but, when we received the intelligence last night, we knew we hadn't got them all. Some of the information we have points to the fact that you were the one they wanted. The reason for last night's attack on your coming home party is tied to this, we believe."

Silence filled the room, while they waited for her reaction. She could feel the pressure of their gazes on her as she dropped her head. Waiting for the pronouncement of…what? Death? Banishment? Being treated like a science experiment and locked in a cage? Fear bubbled up within her.

"You will need to be kept under protection, which is why you were taken to the Master's suite. We thought previously that as everyone had been dealt with…caught…that no one would be aware of the situation. We didn't realize until then that there had been a group rebuilding their army, and looking for an opportunity to attack again." The words had Hope sitting back up, straight in her seat.

"We are also closing down the nest, for the short term, and consolidating nestlings to other manors in case the Brethren do something…inappropriate."

Hope felt even more puzzled, and lifted a shaking hand to her forehead. Her temperature going from freezing cold to raging hot and back again, she ached all over. "Why would you close the nest? What inappropriate action could the Brethren possibly take that would have an impact on the situation?" Situation was such a mild term to use given the circumstances, she thought with a touch of hysteria.

"Because they will attack the house and the units to get to you, Hope. If we don't reinforce the house, they will attack in numbers. If we do reinforce the house, we leave the other units depleted of security. Instead we will consolidate our resources to ensure everyone is protected. The guard at the manor is being tripled with my own and Cyrus' personal guards, but you will remain with Xavier under his protection until we can deal with the situation. We have our best operatives working on the case and we hope there will be a positive resolution soon. Until then, though, you will not venture anywhere he does not deem safe." The words were firm and infused with the magic endowed on Council members. Hope's body tingled.

"Xavier, she will be better protected with you. I think we need to move the majority of the nest members out of the house until we have dealt with this issue. Leave only the necessary staff and family members. I have also contacted the government liaison service, and you are authorized to use any and all means to neutralize this threat."

Cressida stood up and stalked around the table, the fury she'd kept hidden now released, and Hope watched, the feeling of being disconnected leaving her lost in the maelstrom of emotions. Fury, frustration, concern—all warred inside her mind. She understood that Cressida felt deeply about the nestlings under her protection. Indeed, Hope also knew she'd received special attention as a child from the Mistress vampire.

Cressida's eyes glowed and each step was jerky with suppressed rage as she spun quickly, her hair whipping with her movement. Hope could see the set planes of her face, white and sharp. Nothing seemed to make sense anymore, and Hope wanted to rail at the injustice of it all. She hadn't chosen this for herself.

"We thought that Estersham was behind it. Our best sources at the time told us he was dead and had been for centuries." Cressida dragged a hand through her hair as Hope watched. "Last night I received a message directly from him." She reached to the side and lifted a box, inlaid with gold, and walked back to Xavier. She all but flung the box on the table, where it landed with a thud. Xavier looked at Cressida then Hope before flipping the lid back to reveal a copper collar. Hope knew what it was. She'd only seen one before, in a glass cabinet in the house.

The collar was lined with black velvet, and this one still had the tattered scraps of the lining attached, though it looked battered and tarnished in the light. It was also engraved with the number three hundred and twenty-seven—the individualized number used for tracking vampires within the justice system. Usually the collars were buried after the vampire expired with whatever remains they found.

Hope watched Xavier close his eyes. His face was drawn and grim. When he opened them once more, a cold glitter shone. She shuddered, as a sudden chill invaded her body. Obviously, there was more to the story. Maybe he would tell her. One day. Right now, his fury was terrifying to see.

He was incandescent with rage. She could see that clearly and quivered in response. An enraged vampire is nothing anyone wants to meet. The thoughts echoed through her mind and she closed her eyes. What would happen next, now that she'd become a pawn in the game?

CHAPTER TEN

The trip back was silent and long. He heard Hope's breath and the beat of her heart, as she sat beside him. She'd been through an emotionally draining night, yet at the moment he could offer her no support, his fury at the revelations stripping him of the humanity it would take to help her come to terms with her own demons.

His emotions were turbulent. Estersham. How had he survived? The thought burned his guts like acid, churning and roiling in his stomach, eating away at him from the inside out. Estersham had been one of the most respected members of the Council before he'd turned rogue. Hell, he'd even been like a father to Xavier in those first years, taking him in hand as a young vampire, and explaining the rules of living in a society where your true nature must remain secret. It was Estersham who'd helped him to attach himself to a nest as a guard.

A dark event had occurred, changing Estersham to one of the most depraved creatures of the night. The kind that had been portrayed as the ultimate evil in the old stories passed down through the ages. He'd taken to feeding on the blood of unsuspecting humans, in the darkest recesses of the night, stalking them like prey.

If he hadn't seen for himself the changes in Estersham, he would have never thought it possible. His teeth were elongated and sharp. His eyes so cold and fearsome that they glowed red in the light of the lamps. The crimson stains of blood on his clothes. This was an Estersham he'd never before seen. Xavier had watched blood dribble down his chin, his face alight with glee, as he recounted murdering a family as they slept in their hovel. The horrifying image had haunted Xavier ever since. He also vaguely remembered his comments of the voice that spoke within his mind. Telling him that he was more than the humans who were cattle to feed upon.

The thoughts and memories that assailed him, of that hideous night when they had used the copper restraints, still made Xavier feel frozen. The memory of the mad way he'd fought, while the pungent smell of death hung in the air, stayed with him.

Xavier shook his head, trying to clear the memories away. It may have been over two hundred years ago, but it still felt like yesterday when Estersham had defied the rules, bringing them to the edge of discovery. The night he'd been found, the Council had sentenced him to death and, as they'd all thought, executed.

He cleared his mind of the memories, and focused on the task at hand.

The nest required protection. Its safety was of great importance, but paramount in his own mind was the safety of Hope. The thought of her being captured, taken and even hurt sent a shaft of pain through him. They would drain her dry, every drop would be used to either create new, first generation vampires with greater strength or to un-create nested vampires. That *she* was their ultimate goal was now clear. Without fully understanding his motivation, he knew that he would do anything, risk anyone, to ensure her safety. Not just because it was a decree of the Council. It went deeper than that. It was primal.

Xavier inhaled and exhaled, gaining control of himself before he set himself to the task of setting priorities: Move everyone possible out of the nest, arrange billeting for those they couldn't fit into the secure apartments, or who had no options, then transport them to their new abodes. He checked off each step mentally. He turned the plan over, searching for options of how to achieve the necessary outcome, as quickly as possible.

He closed his eyes and considered each nestling as he knew them. Some could be moved to the small hotel they'd just purchased, or to the apartments downtown. They weren't finished yet, but they could spare enough guards to cover the building.

Xavier ran through lists of Masters and Mistresses he could count upon to allow him to billet nestlings. Those with children, or the aged and infirm, would require particular care in their placement, then he could look at ways of grouping those who remained. The weight of responsibility for the care and protection of his people had never been so heavy.

Xavier let his mind drift to who could remain in the manor. Lisi, as Hope's companion, would stay within the house, and of course a cook and one of the cleaners. Her family would be there, though he felt a sense of disquiet, remembering the altercation with her father from earlier in the evening.

He reached forward to the button, and he began speaking to Javed about how they would enact the decisions of the Council.

The vehicle entered the drive, trees casting dark shadows on the gravel, as the powerful car pulled up smoothly. The motion woke Hope briefly. A door opened at the front and she raised weary eyes. Voices and movement pushed sleep farther from her mind, while the sensation of being lifted and a breeze roused her further. Hope blinked to clear the mist of slumber from her that had crept over her during the return journey.

"Where are we?" The words tumbled out groggily.

"Home, sleepyhead." Strong arms encircled her. Xavier. The scent of him filled her senses, and she felt the iron hardness of his body. Contentment filled her for an instant, before the gravity of his words penetrated her foggy mind. She tensed.

"Put me down. Masters don't carry humans into the house." Her words were agitated and she struggled against his hold, while the last wisps of sleep fled.

"Be still, Hope. Otherwise I may drop you." It wasn't censure in his voice, more amusement.

He thought carrying her was amusing? How on earth would she explain this to her parents, if they caught wind of it? Shame burned through her. "Please put me down." She stopped struggling, hoping he would accede, and she felt her face flame with embarrassment. Hope grasped him around the neck, pulling herself up slightly, so that she was at least able to cast furtive looks around her, about to breathe a sigh of relief, when she saw a padded slipper appear on the staircase straight ahead, followed by a leg and a dressing gown.

She closed her eyes. She knew those slippers and that dressing gown with the pink feather edging. She'd actually bought it for her sister-in-law last Christmas. Hope sighed. Nothing in her life at this point was going to be easy.

She and Alexa really didn't have anything in common, except that the woman had married her brother. And that made for strained relations, as she knew Alexa didn't accept that her role in the family and the nest was lower than Hope's.

"Hope? What are you doing? The Master shouldn't be carrying you around." Her face schooled into a picture of disapproval, and Hope knew the tale would be carried back to David and her mother. Yet one more infraction she would need to deal with.

"Master, allow me to help my sister back to her room." She scurried across the floor and reached out an arm.

"Thank you, Alexa. She will be remaining in my care." Xavier's voice was quiet but firm, a brief flash of annoyance and something else crossed Alexa's face, but once it was gone, Hope questioned if it was her discomfort around Alexa that caused her to see what didn't exist.

"It's fine, Xavier. Honestly, I can walk. Alexa, I will contact you and Mother in the morning." She hoped the tone of her voice would settle Alexa, yet her sense of disquiet grew.

Alexa stepped back, "Fine. I'm just heading to the kitchen for a glass of warm milk. Would you like one?" She indicated down the hall and much as Hope wanted to do something—anything—to mend the fences with Alexa, now all she felt was the dragging pull of weariness. Raising a hand, she tried to hold back a yawn, but it escaped. She clapped her hand over her mouth, but the sound alerted Xavier, who pulled her closer against him.

"Come on, time you went to bed, sleepyhead." He chuckled, and started moving again toward the specially reinforced door. Javed walked ahead of him, entered the code, then stepped out of the way for Xavier and Hope as the door swung open. They stepped over the threshold and down into the dark recesses. However, unlike last night, tonight, small lighting strips glowed at the edge of each step.

"This wasn't here last night." Hope wanted to bite back the inane comment, yet Xavier didn't act like he thought it was silly.

"No, I had them installed, so that you could see as you walked down the stairs." His thoughtfulness made her warm and gooey inside, and she sighed before impulsively shifting sideways to thank him. Her lips met his as the sense of electric surprise shot through her veins at the quick contact. He tensed, then pushed in firmly. Quick, but not hard or brutal. The feel of him left her disoriented briefly. He flicked his tongue against hers, and heat coiled in her belly. He pulled back.

"That was quite a thank you. I will have to do things like this regularly for you, I see." There was a grin in his voice, but beneath it lay an emotion that gave his words an edge.

Then he started moving again, while the memory of the kiss played over and over in her mind. Her dazed emotions were turbulent.

Hope's eyes opened once more to the shaded light of the bedside lamp. She was still clothed from the night before, in jeans and a white blouse, and she felt crumpled and sticky. She rose slowly and made her way to the bathroom, head aching and eyes gritty. Her body heavy with need. Hope stripped off her clothes, sighed as air slipped over naked curves. A quick flick of the wrists had warm water jets spraying over her body, causing tingles at each and every one of her nerve endings.

She closed her eyes and wished he was there...

Her back arched as she exhaled on a breathy sigh. Hope pushed against the hot, corded muscles of his body at her back, resting her head against his shoulder. Strong hands lightly rested on the sides of her hips, kneading her flesh. Her body heated and his breath moved the hair at the back of her neck, while she arched farther, silently asking for more.

A rumbling flutter began low in her belly. Excitement ran through her, her breasts ached for his touch. He slid his fingers sensually toward her belly and the other angled upward toward her peaked nipples. She moaned low in her throat, hearing him whisper, "Hope."

His touch was like wildfire, everywhere it went. Her body burst into flame, while she writhed against him.

He claimed her breast, lightly plucking the erect nipple between finger and thumb, playing her like a guitar. Her breath hitched in her throat.

Her knees started to buckle, but he caught her with a muscled arm, while he used his tongue to lave the side of her neck, and he closed his lips over her flesh. His elongated teeth grazed the sensitized skin he'd nuzzled, then he lowered her to the cool tiles at her feet. She felt the brush against her skin, exciting her further, and she knew he could smell the scent of her arousal, musky in the steamy area.

Oh God! He'd barely even touched her and she was going to explode! The tremors began...

"Xavier!"

She woke. She closed her eyes only to open them in an instant. Her heart was beating like a train, threatening to burst from her chest. She heard a rumble and the door crashed open wide. He stood there, face chiseled like granite, eyes glinting in the low light.

"What is it? Was something in here?" His voice was as hard as his face, and she could see his hands balled by his sides, and the way he shuddered.

"No, I... I had a dream. That's all..." What could she say? *I had a hot, sexy dream with you making love to me?* She discarded that immediately, but his nostrils flared. She could swear he actually sniffed the air. His eyes darkened further, and those beautiful green endless pools called to her. He jerked back slightly, then moved forward toward her on the bed. It was the movement of a hunter seeking prey, slow and determined. Her mouth dried, and she licked her lips.

"Were you asleep?" Now the pitch changed, became huskier. A half-smile lit his face, and now that need grew deep inside her.

"I just woke up, Xavier, so I guess you could say that," Hoping the faux irritation would side track him. *Don't let him know.* As quickly as the thought had come, it fled when he sat beside her on the bed, the slight dip rolling her toward him. Hope wasn't fast enough to catch herself and she tumbled against his chest. He leaned forward and her body touched his.

"You dreamed of me?" Her breathing became shallower, she saw awareness on his face. The question delivered, and delicious heat spiraled once more. She was aware of her own arousal, that her breasts were swollen and ready for his attention, nipples tightened and jutting against her clothing. Dampness gathered between her legs.

He bent his head toward hers and placed his lips to hers. She opened her mouth and welcomed him in. Melted against him. His beautiful lips moved across hers, while he invaded her mouth with his tongue and the unbearable ache grew inside her at his wonderfully spicy taste. She shifted closer, wanting to explore the heat that rose between them—needing to feel his body hard next to hers.

He kept his hands on the bed, he pushed harder and she moved backward and down to the bed covers. He reached into her hair, and the scratch of his whiskers rasped her skin. The kiss deepened, grew faster, harder and hotter than anything she'd ever experienced before. She grasped his shoulders, pulling him closer. He nudged his leg between her thighs before settling. She opened for him, uncaring now that he was the Master. All that pushed her on was the need for fulfilment.

A gasp and shudder escaped, and were joined by the motion of her head moving back and to the side. He slid his lips over her jaw and down the neck she offered to him. His warm hand touched her thigh, then continued to glide to the spot between her legs while she let loose a cry. He cupped her through the light layers of fabric.

Xavier pulled his mouth from hers, and, at her whimper, his teeth touched the side of her neck, grazing the soft skin beneath her ear. She mewled with pleasure.

Hope bucked beneath him, needing him to caress the hidden, tender flesh. She floated in the sensual world of passion. Eyes closed, and body straining for more of his touch, she wanted so much more. Then she registered he'd stopped rigid against her, his hand still covering her core, while she panted and writhed.

Xavier stood before moving away, and the need lanced through her again. A sound intruded. An insistent buzzing. Dear God! The phone was ringing. The noise was both insistent and ardor cooling.

Xavier looked back with eyes shining. "This isn't finished." With those gravelly words, he was gone. She could hear the sound of his voice, dim in the background, as she lay, still panting, on the bed. Her body felt tight and wired, her arousal uncomfortable. Her clothing disheveled and her hair...

She got out of bed with jerky movements. *This shouldn't happen. It couldn't happen. Perhaps I should contact Cressida... No...* She'd been most emphatic, and she couldn't ask to be moved. Just the thought made her lightheaded, and she swayed for a minute as vertigo hit. This was her mess to sort out. Right now though, she was still unbearably aroused, needing him and his embrace to set her free of the torture. Hope was in all new territory, never before wanting or needing this kind of intimacy with anyone.

She headed to the bathroom, stripping her clothes off once the door was shut, hoping that a bath would help her to cope, to maybe relax. To settle the chemicals coursing through her veins.

Her entire body still throbbed and the movement of her bra against her peaked nipples sent another shudder through her, making her catch her breath. Stripping off damp panties gently abraded the flesh that lay below, and she had to bite back a groan. She touched her breasts, grazing them and making lightning flash through her system once more.

A bath. Bubbles and warm water may help. She poured the mix in, breathing deeply. The scent of lilies filled the air, the water flowed while Hope watched. She slipped into the bath, which lapped at her skin. The sensual warmth once more roused her. She let her head sink back onto the bath cushion. She needed release. With that thought, she let her hand sink below the water and move down her body.

She cupped a breast and gently squeezed. Her body tensed in reaction, and a sound of hunger escaped. Her eyes fluttered closed as she arched backward.

She slid her other hand between the soft folds at her center, while the lapping of the water on her other breast pushed her farther along the path of fulfilment. She circled her areola, barely touching the skin of the distended nipple, and she slipped one, then another finger within her tight wet sheath.

Seeking the release she knew she needed.

She clenched, guessing that it was a poor imitation of what she really desired, but she urged herself on.

She rubbed in and out, using her thumb to find that most sensitive nub, her legs as open as the tub would allow. Rubbing harder and faster, her body undulated in the water. The lapping movement caused water to splash onto the floor, and her breathing came faster.

Hope pinched her nipple, then reached across herself to find the other giving it the same attention. Her breath caught and her eyes closed while she spiraled higher.

Water sloshed and lips opened over hers. In that moment of passion she returned the touch of mouth and tongue, uncaring of the consequences.

She felt the hand that covered hers, gently removing her fingers from her hot core to be replaced with larger, harder ones. The strokes now turned urgent, as she tried vainly to open her legs wider, tilting her hips upward, toward the man by the bath, thrashing wildly. The confident movement of fingers urging her on, while she knew instinctively to give herself over to the passion that now burned within her—toward Xavier.

He thrust his tongue within her mouth, in time to the finger, and he grasped her breast, kneading it softly, then rolled her nipple between finger and thumb. She moaned and shook with reaction as he pressed the small nub between her legs—teased it.

She quivered with sensation, chest heaving, as finally, with one last move of his fingers, he pushed her over the edge.

She felt the climax as his mouth left hers, and she dragged in deep breaths, eyes opening sightlessly. The rhythmic movement of the muscles between her legs clenched his fingers as the orgasm streaked through her body.

They stilled and she gripped her legs around him.

Claiming him intimately as hers.

"I told you we weren't finished." His voice was dark and full of promise, and she looked back to see him reaching for his belt. His shirt was already gone, lying in a heap, where it soaked up the water that had spilled over the side of the tub.

The rasp of his zipper filled the air. He slid black pants and underwear to the wet floor. His erection stood large and proud in front of her, and she gulped.

Before, when he'd found her in the bedroom, it had been the sudden thudding and rapid beat of her heart which drove him to enter without permission. Crashing through had been instinctual. The roiling emotions, primal and animalistic in intensity, had moved him toward her without thought. Once inside there had been no way he could turn back. He smelt her arousal when he walked back in the door. That musky scent had told him she was hot, and once he'd kissed her, his senses had narrowed. All he could think about was her.

Her arousal scented the air. His need to be with her took over. He needed to be with her, in every possible way. The need and passion had him so turned on, it had taken every inch of his willpower not to strip her naked and thrust within her body straight away.

Then the phone had rung, and he'd cursed it, as much as thanked some long-forgotten deity for the interruption. This number was one that very few people had, so he couldn't ignore its urgent summons.

The buzzing had cleared the sensual fog he'd been lost in for a few minutes. When he returned to the bedroom where he'd left her, she was gone. He heard the moans, the splashing water and his senses heightened further, knowing she'd been as aroused as he was. Heaven knew, he shouldn't have entered but his body had refused to listen.

Walking into the bathroom, he'd found her lost in passion, and he couldn't ignore the need that obviously rode her like a demon. Come whatever, he'd taste her, touch her. Be one with her.

And by God, she'd responded like he'd never seen before. Feeling her orgasm on his fingers had finally pushed him into making a decision.

Now, here he stood, watching and waiting for her answer to the unspoken question. His erection jutting proudly from the hairs at his groin, the seeping of his magic—imbued in him when he'd become a Master, left him tingling. He couldn't control the way it bled from his pores.

Her eyes shone like violet fire as she reached out with her soft, untrained, small hand, barely glancing his flesh. Slipping her fingers over the tip, capturing the seeping pre-cum that escaped. He watched, as she looked at it on her finger then brought it to her lips, flicking at it with her pink tongue. Then she smiled at him.

She rose in the bath, bubbles cascading over her curves. Her nipples stood erect, and one hand snaked back to her breast, lifting it to him as if in offering, while the other fastened around his proud length. Softly she pumped him, leaning against the wall and lifting one foot to place on the edge of the bathtub, turning toward him so he could see her glistening, dewy pink flesh.

He groaned and moved toward her. She opened wide to his tongue as it sought entry. He pushed her hand away, and he cupped her breasts, flicking at the nipples. She moaned, and he kissed her with every inch of passion within him.

. . .

She was so turned on. She didn't care about the rules that should keep them apart. Never before had she experienced pleasure so deep and she burnt. The feel of her fingers within her hadn't been enough, though, she didn't know why until he'd replaced them with his own. All she'd be aware of was that he too was aroused.

She felt it in the stiffness of his engorged shaft, and the seeping fluid that escaped the slit at the end of his cock, salty to the taste. She too was hot. Her overwhelming desire was for him to fill her in a way she'd never before experienced.

Hope yearned to complete the intimate act with him, and wanted him to feel the same soul-deep connection.

She writhed against the cold, tiled wall as she pumped him. Once his hand brushed hers away, she let it slip down her body, letting it move between her legs while she continued to explore his velvet covered hardness.

The feel of his hands on her breasts left her breathless, each breath harder to capture than the last. Each flick of his fingers at her erect nipples seemed to pull at something within her, making her tighter... hotter.

He removed his hands from her breasts, captured her waist and lifted her. Shock interrupted her pleasure momentarily, but he pulled her toward him and she smiled. She let go and he dragged her up against him as her body directed her to move and still more erotic actions. His sleek and hairless chest glanced against her nipples, and the reaction was electric, frissons of pleasure exploding over and through her system.

She swung her legs around his waist, while he staggered through the doorway. Hope felt the tip of his cock at her core. Unable to wait any longer, she pushed herself down onto him and groaned as she took him within her body. For a moment, sharp pain thrust aside the hunger and need.

"Be still, little one," Xavier murmured.

With her eyes squeezed shut, she complied and soon enough her body relaxed, and the sensation of stinging pain receded, replaced with the renewed flush of arousal.

She moaned as her hips moved under his touch. When she gazed into his eyes, they reflected the same fire burning within her veins.

Hope flexed her heels against his rock-hard buttocks and tipped herself forward, letting him settle deeper within her core.

"Oh, God!" She moved again, a subtle flex of her muscles, and she gloried in the pressure of his hands as they pulled her closer, while scorching mouths met and tongues tangled. Then they undulated together.

Firmer.

Harder.

Faster.

The sound of moans and cries filled the air as they continued to surge toward each other, the slapping of skin and the scent of arousal growing stronger with each touch.

Hope arched her back, the climax building in her body once more. She cried out, her muscles flexed and she felt him stiffen on one last hard thrust as he joined her, locked together in their private ecstasy. Her heart thudded, crashing wildly.

Slowly she slumped against him, winding her limp arms around his neck, collapsing on his shoulder, feeling boneless and replete.

She kept her legs around him, and nestled in.

He carried her to the bed and angled himself, and they dropped to the covers side on, so that they both lay entwined. Her eyes remained shut while she let her breathing settle, noting the soft movement of his touch gliding up and down her back.

"I've never done that before." She whispered the words to him and slowly opened her eyes.

His gazed back with haunting green eyes. "Then I am pleased you were with me." He leaned forward and kissed her softly on the lips, pulling the covers over both of them. She lay silent, listening to the beat of his heart beneath her ear, and drifted off to sleep.

. . .

He stayed still. The feel of her surrounding his flesh had been something he'd never experienced before, and that confused him. Previously, sex had been fun and even sometimes an athletic exercise. Being an immortal meant many partners and experiences, but he could honestly say he'd never experienced the like of this before.

Never the raging hunger for one person, driving everything else from his mind.

He thought over the phone call that had interrupted them, before flinging an arm over his eyes.

James had rung. Angry and upset at the decisions he and Cressida had made. He'd refused to acknowledge sending the nestlings from the house, even for a short term, was the safest and best option. Xavier made a mental note to discuss the ongoing issues he experienced with James with Javed. The *Yeux Secondes* was supposed to accept the decisions of the Master, ensuring the house and its affairs ran smoothly, but somehow along the way James had forgotten it wasn't his nest and he wasn't the Master. That concerned him greatly.

With a sigh, he let himself relax once more, breathing deeply, expanding his chest as he allowed the tension that had built within him to seep away. He'd told Javed to ensure no one else interrupted him. He grunted quietly, thinking about his responsibilities once more. Javed was making an excellent second, and he'd no doubt, at some time in the near future, he would be granted his own nest. For now, Xavier was thankful that his second would ensure his Master was undisturbed.

He smiled faintly. He could sleep, but when they woke, he would be ready for more of this experience, of loving Hope.

He closed his eyes, feeling the weight of her body nestled against him, allowing the unfamiliar emotion of contentment and well-being to spread through him as he shifted restlessly. Then, slowly, he cleared his mind and let the blessed oblivion of sleep claim him.

CHAPTER ELEVEN

She moved, feeling something hard and unforgiving below her head as she shifted again, becoming restless. An unfamiliar feeling of warmth surrounded her, enfolded her, and she snuggled down, opening her eyes then shutting them again quickly on realizing she wasn't alone in the bed.

Xavier's hands moved along her body and Hope registered she was naked, with aches in spots that hadn't ached before. Very naked indeed, with a hard male body sharing the bed with her. She swallowed hard, and the abrasions around her mouth protested. She moaned quietly.

Dear God! The erotic dream hadn't been a dream after all. Her stomach sank like a stone. She'd had sex with Xavier!

To compound her stupidity, she was still here, naked and in bed with him.

Hope opened her eyes with a small squeak of distress. She needed to get out of here, make sure she was dressed before he woke.

She scrambled to the edge of the bed, trying not to wake him. Quickly finding a cover to pull around her nude body, she attempted to clamber out. She nearly made it and was congratulating herself, when her foot caught in the covers. She almost tumbled off the bed when his hands clamped around her waist well before she made contact with the hard floor. Hope jerked with surprise.

"Good morning." His voice sent shivers through her and she remembered what he'd done with that mouth, just last night.

"Oh God!" The words escaped, and she felt a red tide of embarrassment crawling under her skin. She bit her lip hard.

"Not quite the reaction I expected." The words were tinged with amusement. He grasped her waist then pulled her back toward that hard, warm…and still naked chest. Her body reacted once more to the proximity, heating where they touched.

Awkwardness fought with need, and she moved against him. Arousal reared, clawing at her with desperation. Hope fought inwardly for control of her emotions, but it skittered away as she gulped for air.

"Uhh, Xavier? I don't think this is such a great…" She stopped, trying to find the words. "You know I don't …" Each sentence stuttered and died. What was there for her to say? *I think having sex with you is the worst decision of your life? Of my life?* She shut her mouth with a snap, because that was only true on some levels.

Each comment sounded either like she was a pitiable piece of humanity, or full of herself. *You're making such a hash of this.* She rolled her eyes at the useless thoughts crashing through her brain, and she struggled to find her equilibrium.

"Hope? There's nothing wrong with enjoying a physical relationship. Masters and nestlings have been doing it for centuries." The amusement she'd heard before was gone, and his words turned soft and even affectionate. She closed her eyes.

God, don't let me make more of a mess of this than I already have. If she were brutally honest, she'd tell him she wanted more than just a "wham, bam, thanks for the sex, ma'am" type of encounter. He was a Master, and she a nestling. With an effort she kept her mouth shut.

"Hope? Seriously, we have done nothing wrong." She felt him move, while uncertainty filled her. "I can go if you are so uncomfortable with this." The words were near silent, and he reached over, gently touching her shoulder.

Instinctively, her body curled toward him, and she gave in once more with a quiet sigh. She turned around, and attempted a wobbly smile when she saw the concern on his face. He pulled her close, back against him the sensation of warmth and belonging grew again. This time she leaned forward, allowing the sheet to slip, as she touched her mouth gently to his. In that instant, she knew: she couldn't fight this. Not when it was the one thing that made her feel like she was needed.

The slip of a hand against her skin teased her, together with the brush of a leg, and she sighed. He slowly pushed away the covers, revealing pale flesh. He looked at her, deep and long, then slowly swayed forward, until their lips touched lightly while the erotic pleasure spiked through her system.

With a gentle caress he touched her intimately. His fingers quested, grazed her core, and she writhed against him, seeking more of his magic touch.

He opened his mouth over a pink, peaked nipple, taking it into the warm, dark cavern, and he suckled at it. The long slow pulls on her flesh left her quivering with reaction.

Beneath her caresses, the corded muscles were warm and tight. Confidence growing, she slid her fingers over the flesh, while his gently slipped within her. Pressure, so intense, ballooned within her chest as she cried out, "Xavier!"

Hope bucked sightlessly, reaching toward him. She grasped his cock with her hand. The soft velvety flesh, rock hard in her grasp, and the abrasion of rough hair impinged on her mind for an instant, before it too was swept away by the tide of emotion.

He moved away. She moaned her displeasure and he chuckled, and shock waves battering her beleaguered senses.

Hope gave a soft, exploratory pump of his erection, glorying in his groan as she felt him swell further, the veins hard and pulsing under her soft caress. She lifted a hand and gripped his beautiful silky hair, twining her fingers in the length. Hope urged his face toward her breast once more, silently urging him to suckle. His lips touched her skin, and she voiced her delight.

Hot and wild emotions streaked through her. The primal needs within her demanding release as the fire inside her grew exponentially. Her veins carried the heat to every part of her body, and she gulped in a ragged breath.

She dug her heels into the bed as he pushed her back onto the pillows, but she had no awareness of his actions. Instead Hope allowed herself to be swept into a sea of sensation. He slowly, achingly, opened her legs, settling on his knees at her ankles, exposing her to his view. Xavier withdrew his long slim fingers from her burning center, the carnality in his gaze made her breath catch, while she waited dazedly for him to move.

Time slowed, and she felt more than naked. Discomfiture grew beneath his burning survey. Hope moved to cover herself, a hand fluttering toward her abdomen, but Xavier caught it, stilling the movement.

In his eyes she could read both need and wonder. His teeth elongated slightly during their tussle, and she felt herself dew at the thought of him latching onto her, drinking from her during the orgasm she knew loomed.

Xavier leaned forward. His hot breath whispered over her flesh, and another whimper escaped while he lashed her clitoris with his tongue. Her inner muscles contracted rhythmically. She fisted the sheet beneath with clenched fingers, while thrashing from side to side.

Her spine arched under his merciless ministrations as her body demanded more.

Even as her heart stuttered in her chest, and while her body finally released the pent-up tension, he drove her on. The seductive assault on her senses and the sensations wound through her once more. This time, though, Hope grabbed his arms, pulling him over her body, with a strength born of desperation. "Inside me... Oh God!" Her words were broken as his lips touched hers once more, and she finally felt him nudge her legs farther apart, as he settled himself between her thighs. The movements slowed again, while he stared into her eyes, entering smoothly, pushing and sliding to the hilt.

She rubbed against him. Her flesh sensitized in reaction to their intimate connection. Xavier moved and Hope met him, thrust for thrust, crying out as each action heightened the ecstasy building deep within her. He moved faster and harder, all traces of the urbane man long gone. She closed her eyes against the pleasure that raced through her.

His teeth grazed her neck and she climaxed, hard, in long squeezing pulls. He grunted and with a last tremendous thrust, crashed through her passionate daze. His release echoed with a grunting breath against her neck.

After long moments, the world slowed, and he collapsed upon her satiated. The beat of her heart slowly returned to normal, and the heat inside her melted away.

Hope opened her eyes to see him watching her. His eyes so green and deep, she could almost drown in their calming pools.

"Thank you, Hope." The words echoed throughout her.

"What for?"

"For being so giving in your passion. For sharing yourself with me." He smiled, the crinkles at the edges of his eyes telling her of his pleasure.

"I should be thanking you. You're a very giving lover." Hope slid her hand up and down his spine. She was embarrassed on one level, with her words and actions. At the same time she had a hunger to let him know how much he'd given to her. How deeply she'd felt the pleasure.

"Then we shall have to thank each other." He kissed her on the tip of her nose, then pulled her into his arms and she nestled against him quietly, letting the calm fill her once more, before she finally let the embrace of sleep take over.

Stress. It had to be the stress of living in secure quarters with the enigmatic vampire Master. Not having any contact outside the walls, unless Xavier allowed it, weighed on her and she nodded her head and rubbed the toothbrush vigorously over her teeth. It had made her feel abandoned by her family. As if everything that came before had been swept away, rather like an evolutionary change. The thought echoed in her mind and she dismissed it, aware she was being dishonest with herself.

The toothbrush clattered to the sink and Hope leaned both her hands on the counter, looking into the mirror. "Be honest with yourself, Hope. You wanted the sex. You both wanted the sex, and you agreed to it. You were a full and willing participant, knowing it would strain things further. You knew that when you started."

Even as she looked at her face in the mirror, she could see him in her mind's eye. Beautiful. Masterly. Sexy.

And, oh God, such an amazing lover.

She leaned closer, noting two small grazes barely discernible on the side of her neck. Maybe if she changed to one of the peasant tops, she could wear a ribbon and cameo around her neck to hide the evidence—just in case they ran into her family.

Satisfied with that, she hurried into the bedroom, pulled open the doors to the dressing room and hurried in. Drawers faced her and she quickly stripped off the satin dressing gown and began hunting through chests filled with clothing to find a matching bra and panty set. Her fingers closed over scraps of cherry red material. She'd never worn them before—they had been a gift from one of the nestlings she'd lived with during college, a reminder that she was an adult and able to make her own decisions.

They had chuckled that she always took the safe option. She smiled at the memory. That couldn't be said anymore.

Her mother would be horrified with her choice of underwear. Hope smiled sadly. *She doesn't need to know.*

With a jolt of defiance, she pulled them out, dressing in the wispy fabric. The snug panties were little more than a lacy triangle of red netting dotted with tiny kisses at the front and barely any back. The bra was even less, covering just over her nipples, and small kisses dotted the material. She could see her shadowed breasts just behind the naughty images, in the floor-length mirror, and for an instant her body quickened while she imagined Xavier's reaction. She smiled.

There in the cupboard lay a lightweight red peasant top, and she considered teaming it with the black figure-hugging hipster jeans. Perhaps if she wore them with her favourite heeled boots, and pulled her hair up? Once that was completed, she looked at herself critically in the mirror, shaking her head while adding a ribbon choker, hiding the small graze at her neck.

Better to wear the hair down.

Hope grabbed the hairbrush and was taming her long, black hair when Xavier walked in. She stopped, watching his reflection in the mirror.

The grace of his stride, the hidden muscles under his clothes dried her mouth as she felt the pull of his presence. He came to a stop behind her, pulling her back against him with a soft smile.

"You look lovely tonight, Hope." He lifted a hand and ran a gentle finger over the choker she'd chosen. "I didn't hurt you, did I?" The words were low, and his eyes, green pools of forever, reflected in the glass before her.

"No, Xavier. I just thought it might be wise with my parents, that's all." She placed a hand over his and turned her head, swiftly kissing the warm hand where it lay on her shoulder, thanking him for his concern.

"Yes, that makes sense. Come, we have work to do, and we do have a timetable." Once more, her stomach bottomed at the thought of what her parents' reaction might be when they saw her with him. She couldn't hide out here all night, her conscience reminded her.

He wound his arm around her waist, grabbing her attention, and pulled her toward him. "First, another kiss." His lips met hers. Tenderly. He lingered for an instant, and the fire streaked through her once more, then he pulled back. "Tonight, I would like to share your bed again, if you will let me."

A thrill of exultation warmed her from the inside, sweeping away the coldness that had filled her since rising. "Yes." The words were a whisper against his lips, and he kissed her once more. Another warm touch of lips, and her stomach quivered with anticipation at the long night that was yet to come.

Moving quickly up the dimly lit steps led them to the secured door and out into the chandelier-lit hall, then into Xavier's office, their feet tapping on the cold white floor as they went.

"I had a computer set up for you in here. Your degree in information technology will be very useful to us later. Right now, I need you to go through the list of nestlings and consider who would be better in which other nests, as you know them and the others quite well, don't you?" Xavier stopped suddenly, and Hope nearly collided with him.

"Yeah, I guess so." She nodded absently, her mind already racing, cataloguing those she knew.

"Good. I have a list of how many each can take, and I will also arrange for some to be transferred to the new apartments." He pointed to a desk that had been set up just to the side of his. A steaming cup of coffee waited for her beside the monitor, and she smiled again at his thoughtfulness.

"Right, I can do that. How many apartments and bedrooms are available in the building?" She seated herself at the computer and turned it on.

"All the information is in the folder Javed is about to bring in." His words were short and vague, and she glanced around to see he'd moved silently into the seat opposite her, and had turned on another computer. A bright red folder was clenched in his hand, and for the first time he seemed tense.

Not long afterward, Javed came into the room, and she raised her head to watch him. "Xavier, James would like to see you, if you have a minute? And here is the information you requested for Hope." The words were unhurried, but the look on his face told Hope he'd already had a set-to with her father.

"Give the folder to Hope, and tell James I will see him in a few minutes."

She smiled at the absent tone in his voice, imagining her father's reaction to being brushed off.

"Of course, Xavier." Hope heard Javed walk toward her, turning quickly, in time to see him hand over a thick folder with a broad wink.

Hope smiled her thanks, then turned back to the computer, thankful the vampire guards had welcomed her into their ranks so easily. She opened the folder, seeing lists of the nestlings, and, noticing tabs, she flicked to the next set of lists, which were the details of the empty apartments. Another tab caught her eye—the details of the numbers of nestlings each nest was willing to billet. The enormity of the task was clear. It had never occurred to her just how many nestlings lived within the manor grounds or were attached to the household.

Closing her eyes briefly, Hope breathed deeply, clearing her mind of everything around her. Now, with a renewed sense of focus, she reached for the coffee and started work.

He was aware of her, the tapping of her fingers on the keys, the flick of pages while she moved between the lists. Even while he fought the awareness, he read through the information that had been recovered so far from the testing on the collar. The copper had undergone carbon dating to check its age, although he was sure it was the collar that had been fitted to Estersham. The numbering was the same and so was the lining and the collar itself, right down to the small dent on the clasp. That, and a gut feeling kept telling him that it was the real collar. If that was so, why hadn't Estersham died? Who had betrayed them? And whose ashes had they retrieved?

The thoughts chased around in his mind, and his stomach roiled at the truth.

Someone had known, and that someone had betrayed their oath. Worse still, that someone had been human.

The two rogues they had captured from the battle at the party had given up very little information. They were little more than drones, sent into battle with the vague promises of a standing in the new order, and had only seen the leader from the back, never having been considered important enough to address him. Not a lot to go on, and once more the feeling of anger clawed at his insides.

They would make another move soon. He could feel it in his bones. If it was Estersham, then he would be cunning, just as he'd always been—a brilliant strategist. Xavier just hoped the bloodlust had taken the edge off that inventive mind of his.

He allowed himself to recall his strongest memories of Estersham. The Estersham of his experience had treasured grace and culture. He'd been a man given to deep thinking, and with a thoughtful nature, but all of that had been shattered when he'd succumbed to the imperatives of the virus and the taint of the blood drop. It had wiped out his ability to be human...and humane. It had left little more than an animal behind. A brilliant animal, Xavier conceded, capable of thought but still one who accepted the will of his primal urges.

The struggle was one all vampires faced. The dark hunger they lived with on a nightly basis. It forced them to seek sustenance in the form of blood. For centuries they had been little more than ravenous animals, though over time they had come to realize that it was the action of taking blood from the source, especially through to the last drop—what they called 'the death drop'—that pushed them to need more. Increasing the hunger until it finally overwhelmed and stripped away any sense of humanity they struggled to retain.

This was why they now lived in nests, with donors who willingly gave their blood, which was carefully decanted into blooded wines. Never would any nest-based vampire take the death drop. Once that was ingested, then the barriers they each erected over many years deteriorated. Each final, ecstasy-laden drop stripped from them another link of civility that kept them from being little more than animals.

Most newly turned, though, retained enough humanity and morality to be able to survive the call for some time, so long as they remained satiated. It was only as they grew older, required less sustenance, that the danger really showed itself. He closed his eyes, willing the chilling thoughts away.

A knock on the door interrupted his attempt to refocus. "Come." He knew who it was before the door even opened.

"James, please come and be seated." He directed James to the chair opposite his desk.

The man strode forward. As always, he was immaculate. For the first time Xavier could detect a coolness in his manner.

"Master, I am concerned that Cressida has somehow confused the situation. Hope is nothing more than my daughter. As such, I feel it would be inappropriate for her to remain in the secured living quarters. Her room can be made ready immediately, and she can be returned to her family." The words were curt and short.

The lack of concern that James exhibited for Hope's safety puzzled him. Surely, he would want her to remain in the secured living zone while there was any hint of danger? It was obvious he doubted the threat was real… Either that, or he just didn't care.

Xavier watched silently as James spied Hope, noting the way her slender shoulders tensed. She continued working on the computer. He could hear the increased rhythm of her heartbeat, it left him angry and edgy.

James opened his mouth, as if he was about to say something to her, and the hot thread of anger that had welled within him at James' outburst, grew hotter. Xavier knew she would not defend herself once he started. She would accept the castigation James would throw at her, as if she deserved it.

She was upset, he knew. The scent of her anguish filled the air, astringent and biting. And he didn't like it. Not. One. Bit.

"James. I have discussed this with Cressida and the members of the Council. Hope remains with me, until the threat is past." He delivered the words in a calm and reasonable voice, despite wanting to bellow them. His anger raged, but he fought for control. Mastered the emotions and seethed silently. The constraints of his position rode him hard.

James opened his mouth, obviously to rebut the statement, and Xavier's fury grew once more. Before he could think, he'd leaned forward, placing both hands on the desk. He watched with satisfaction as James took an instinctive step backward.

"I have said all there is to be said. If you have a problem with my ability to lead the nest, then you will need to take it up with Cressida personally. However, I have her support on this. Understand me well… Cressida is seriously displeased with your inability to follow her instructions, and, I assure you, I am also not impressed."

The man flinched slightly, and Xavier felt a small kick of triumph. "For now you are excused. But…" The words hung in the air between them, and James was white with anger, the lines deepening around his tightly clamped mouth, the barely controlled shaking of rage mingling with fear, the scent filling the air. "You will never again correct me. I am the Master here. Oh, yes. And I will not allow anyone to harangue Hope either." He waited a moment, letting his words take root. "If I get even the slightest whiff of that, I will show you how I deal with recalcitrant nestlings." He paused for a second. Waited some more. He saw James' nervous eye movements, trickles of sweat dripping down his white face which meant he was considering just what discipline might be enacted. "You may go."

James backed away from the desk.

He caught the flash of hatred in the eyes of the man he'd just dressed down. Xavier understood his reaction. James, after all, had just been humiliated in front of his daughter. The woman he treated lower than dirt, and that didn't bode well for Hope, leaving him feeling worried about an undefined retaliation. The man left the room and Javed moved in, closing the door quietly behind him, while Xavier considered options and plans.

"Xavier, do you think that was wise?"

"Perhaps not, but I had to make those points. Now, in future, I want you to liaise between James and myself. He was, shall we say, annoyed with me, and I was probably a bit more…forceful than I should have been." He grinned slightly and looked at his friend, before letting the bravado leach away. "I think we need to let the situation settle somewhat now." He stood, pushing back the seat and scanning the room silently. "Hope? It is time to head to the offices downtown. Grab your bag and meet me at the door."

He watched while she rose unsteadily, only a silent jerk acknowledging his request, and he felt suddenly angered that she'd witnessed the scene. It was wrong, and he'd given in to an urge, best restrained in future, he reflected. "Hope?"

She didn't turn toward him, instead kept her head low as she answered, "I'm fine. Just give me a moment and I'll be ready." She scuttled out of the room, and he watched her go.

"Javed, follow her, but don't interfere unless she is waylaid." The disquiet he felt rose inside him. He watched Javed move quickly and quietly, as if he too expected something to happen.

Something about the relationship between James and Hope was wrong, he acknowledged again. He needed to know more, but right now he'd bigger issues to deal with, ones that required his full attention. Xavier reached out a hand and lifted the receiver to demand a driver.

She hurried out of the room, not caring where she was going. Anything was preferable right now to Xavier seeing her cry.

Hope felt the harsh grab and pull of her arm. She whipped around while *he* dragged her to the corner of the corridor close by the secured doorway.

One look into his icy blue eyes and fear filled her.

"What did you say to him?" Her father's voice sounded both remote and filled with hatred. Hope shuddered as a trickle of cold dread snaked down her spine.

"Father? I didn't say anything. Cressida told him that I am a blood siren and that I need to be kept safe."

His grip bit into her tender flesh, and she had to fight to hold down a yelp of pain, even as she pulled away. Her heart pounded.

"You slept with him, didn't you? You're just like we were told. A slut. You disgust me." The words stripped away his civilized demeanor, and wounded her like a dagger to the chest.

"Father? I haven't done anything wrong. I'm not bringing the house into disrepute. I'm doing what Cressida—" She entreated him, but it seemed to only inflame the situation further.

James growled. "Garbage! You don't deserve to hold the name of my daughter. They were right all along. Bad blood always tells!" James flung her from him and she flew across the room, hitting the wall with her head and an elbow, the immediate pain stunning her, and she slid to the floor.

Quick steps hurried down the hall then Javed was there, helping her up. Her head spun and her arm ached, while her vision blurred at the hot burning tears welling in her eyes. They weren't just from the physical and mental pain, but overlaid with rage at the way she was being treated.

"You will never touch Hope again. Do so, and you will find Xavier will, at the least, expel you from the nest, if he doesn't choose something more...final." The same careful touch continued, helping to steady Hope as it steered her toward the door, and the buzz of the electric locking system. In the dimness of the stairwell, dizziness hit, spinning around her, causing her to miss the steps. A sensation of being lifted and carried to the stairs intruded dimly. She barely noticed Javed calling Xavier as he set her on the chair. The intercom system pinged while she huddled miserably, but she paid it no attention, lost in a world of swirling emotions.

Hope roused when Xavier laid a gentle hand on her moments later. She registered the shaking touch, and she ached to relieve his concern. "I'm fine, Xavier." She said the words, but knew they were untrue.

"I never thought he would do this. How could he?" Soft touches soothed her, brushed away the disheveled hair from her hot forehead, before moving softly through her hair to check the back of her head. He gently probed, finding the spot that ached the most.

"Oww. That hurts." More tears escaped from between tightly clenched lids, and dripped down her face. "I'll be okay. Just give me a few minutes." She scrubbed her hands over her face, before silently hunting in her pants pocket for a tissue, coming up empty.

A wet cloth was pressed into her grasp, and she grabbed it, welcoming the soothing coolness with a hiccupping sigh.

"Xavier, I'm sorry. I didn't expect this, otherwise I would have protected her." Hope heard the anger in Javed's voice, but couldn't rouse herself right now, so she let the conversation swirl around her. Seeking blessed oblivion for just a few minutes longer, while the fear settled within her gut.

"No, Javed. I knew that there was an underlying anger, I just didn't expect this. Contact the office and tell them we won't be in tonight." His voice was tight, and she choked back a sigh, pulling the cloth from her face.

"You need to go in, and I think it would be best for me to get away from here for now." She pushed out of the seat, against the hand he held out. "Just give me a minute to wash my face properly, and tidy myself up." Hope rose, unsteadily, ignoring his support, leaving the room with as much dignity as she could muster.

Reaching the bathroom, she tossed the washer into the sink, before running the cold water, and pressed the wet material against her puffy eyes. A quick glance showed them watery pink, tear tracks through her minimal makeup left trails down pale cheeks, and hair in disarray.

Nothing for it but to fix the mess, she reminded herself, carefully drawing a brush waiting by the sink through her hair, avoiding pulling too hard on the sore area.

Cosmetics spilled from the bag she rifled through, while Hope hurriedly repaired her face as best she could. She gave a quick shrug as she accepted her fate, and made her way back to Xavier who waited in the lounge.

He looked at her, and the frisson of emotion that whipped through her senses made her tingle. "I'm ready."

He nodded and took her hand, carefully holding it like it was made of spun glass, and bent to kiss it, before tucking it safely in the crook of his arm, as he walked out of the room with her.

CHAPTER TWELVE

The arrival at the office was almost anticlimactic after the shocking events earlier in the night.

The heavy vehicle wound its way through dark streets where little traffic moved. Most people avoided this time of night, their fear of vampires and other supernatural beings caused them to continue to dog those hours. Only humans with a purpose made their way in the night, usually street walkers and their pimps, supernatural beings and their helpers, and of course those who warred with them—hunters and religious zealots.

Xavier expressed his concern with soft queries and touches— gentle touches that left her aching at the unfairness of her position. Once the vehicle drew to a stop, he opened the door for her. She stepped out and looked up at the shadowed building. She'd never seen it at night, and the neon lights on the building reminded her of the icy blue of the Christmas tree lights they usually decorated the grounds of the manor with. It was breathtaking to behold from below.

Together, they rode the elevator to the forty-third floor. The tall structure in the heart of the city was glass-walled, so the view was awe-inspiring. The lights shimmered and flashed as she watched quietly.

Hope fought to control her emotions. Agitation at the way her father had acted, loss at the special affinity a child should have with a parent and anger that he hadn't taken the time to listen before lashing out warred within her. All she could do was control the anger that burned, harness it, until she could deal with the consequences—and when she didn't feel quite so shattered.

The bell dinged and the door opened smoothly. The anonymous metal and marble reception area that she'd never liked was gone, and in its place was a cool and quiet haven. The plush carpeting in sea tones of green was welcoming and cooling. Relaxation chimes played through hidden speakers, and a young woman manned the pale wood reception desk with a welcoming smile.

"Good evening, Master Xavier." The melodic tones almost sighed, and Hope knew that this young girl was so much more than she looked. A quick flash of teeth confirmed it. She was a vampire.

Another quick glance at the woman poured into a pale green suit reminded Hope of her current untidy state of being. At around five foot with platinum blonde hair, the only way to describe the vision was a pocket goddess. An unwanted emotion wound through Hope.

"Catriona, how is your evening going?" His words were jovial, and something nasty snaked its way through Hope. Jealousy. A hot and caustic burn filled her belly.

"It has been great. And I just got the best news. Councilor Cressida has given permission for me to change Emily. Now we can be together forever." She grinned broadly, her pale blue eyes flashing with excitement.

"That is excellent news indeed. Any plans for when?" He leaned forward, engrossed in the conversation. Hope had read it wrong, was left reeling as realization dawned. Since when was jealousy, especially of the misplaced variety, part of her makeup?

"I was thinking perhaps when we take vacation. Sir? I wanted to ask, is there any way Emily can move into one of the nest apartments until it happens? Now that she is officially credentialed, she is unprotected." The words were hesitant, but Hope saw Xavier smile.

"We are having a move around of the nests, so give her address and contact details to me, and I will see where we can make a spot for her."

His grin was genuine as he grabbed Catriona's hand and squeezed it. They obviously had a great employer and employee relationship; still, she felt dirty and small, smiling blandly as Xavier introduced her. "Now, you don't know Hope. She is going to be under my protection, and will be given entry privileges at all times. She will require a desk in my office and a computer. Can you arrange equipment to be brought in as soon as possible? Until then, she is going to use my laptop, and will also require full tech privileges."

"Certainly, sir. I'll get onto both those jobs right away. It's a pleasure to meet you, Miss Hope." The words trilled with an odd hint of an accent, as her fingers flew across the keyboard, obviously attending to the requests immediately.

Hope followed Xavier down the hallway to another door. When it opened, she gasped. The office was twice as big as her father's, located opposite, she remembered. "It has been so long since I have been here, but honestly, whoever did your refit did an amazing job. I love the colors. And Catriona is perfect for your receptionist. It's fantastic news about her partner, too."

"Yes, she is perfect for the role. She's been waiting for her partner Emily to be credentialed, but there have been ongoing issues for the last twelve months. I talked to Cressida a few weeks ago and somehow it happened." Hope saw that he watched her reaction. She knew what credentialed meant. 'Authority to Turn' was the term most used within the nests.

Hope nodded absently and she looked around, taking in the workspace, desk and the expansive view.

"Enough about that. If you're tired let me know. If I can't get out of what I am doing, I have a small bathroom and bedroom off there." He motioned to a door behind his desk. "If you need to rest before we leave, you can go in and sleep. And that is an order. Now come and sit down, and I'll get Damon to get you something to drink. What would you prefer?"

"Coffee would be great." She sat down opposite his desk, waiting as he hit the intercom and requested her drink. Once he finished, he fished out another folder, this one she'd seen before. It contained a detailed list of apartments and a set of blueprints, showing the layout of each individual floor of the buildings, where they would need to re-house the nestlings. She grimaced at the enormity of the task. Xavier pulled the file Hope had been working on from his briefcase.

"I'll need you to start ordering the beds, furniture and any other equipment for the apartments. They need to be suitable for the members we put in each apartment."

"Xavier? They won't be the ones my mother was planning on." She held her breath waiting for his reply, her stomach knotted.

"Probably not, but I want you to go through anyway. This should only be a short-term measure, but I want them comfortable for the time they're there." He smiled, and she relaxed once more. "There are websites and phone numbers for the various suppliers we deal with at the back of the file. Get them furnished and ready for the members to move into, preferably by the end of the week. If you have to pay premium, do it. There are lists of order numbers you can use. Just jot down the companies against the items. Furnish as you see fit but if you don't know what to do, just ask."

He looked back to the screen, not dismissively, just letting her know that he had other tasks to complete. "I have some investments to go through, and reports to read. Then a couple of phone calls. A few hours should pull us up."

As he finished, a knock on the door sounded, and within minutes, a desk, office chair, printer, computer and file trays were in place.

Hope logged onto the computer and started.

She swung her head around and was surprised to find Xavier looking at her. "Something wrong Xavier?"

"I was watching you work. Your concentration is amazing. That wasn't why you turned around, was it? Are you feeling okay?" His words were soft, and he peered at her intently.

"Yeah, I'm fine. As I was going through the apartment listings, there is a small, single bedroom one. Do you want me to allocate that to Emily?" He smiled and she warmed inside.

"That would be perfect in most circumstances. Thank you for thinking of Catriona and Emily like that. However, in hindsight, my preference would be to have her move into the manor. While we vampires are a conservative lot, I believe it's time to do something more. It's rare to find a same gender relationship, so we don't automatically consider their needs, but times are changing." He laughed ruefully.

"No problem. How do you want me to proceed, then?" Hope's pen hovered over the pad she'd been using for making notations.

"Hmm, maybe we had better move her stuff immediately. We can have it stored, and she can be moved into Catriona's suite in the secured zone. How quickly do you think you could organize it?"

"Well, surmising she's available, we can have her in there tomorrow night. I can send the movers to work during the day, and have your own men move it all tomorrow evening."

"Do it and I'll let Catriona know."

She turned back to the screen and completed the request.

"Send me a memo to forward to Catriona. You do know how to use the interoffice memo system, don't you?"

She smiled at the expression on his face. *So it had just occurred to him, had it?* "Yes, I worked here in the last school holidays before college." She flicked the memo across to his workstation and went back to her task.

Tiredness dragged at her and her head throbbed viciously. Even as she fought the drag of sleep, her arm and head ached. There was no way she would tell Xavier. One last page of ordering to complete, and she would quietly creep to the bathroom and wash her face. Maybe she would find some painkillers in there. She snorted silently at the ridiculous thought—painkillers in a vampire's bathroom.

He must have seen the slump of her shoulders, or heard one of the sighs she tried to hold in, because the next thing she knew, he spun her chair around, and lifted her into his muscular arms.

"What are you doing?"

"Taking you home. I'm finished and you, my love, look done in."

"I still have…" The words trailed away and he grinned.

"Damon will finish your ordering. The billeting lists you can continue tomorrow night, and Javed will start the move for those you have organized tonight." His voice was firm as he carried her down the corridor. He stopped at the reception desk.

"Is Emily ready for the move?"

"Yes, Master Xavier, and the movers are already there packing up. Thank you again so much…"

"It wasn't me, Catriona. Thank Hope here."

Hope squirmed at the glowing look on the woman's face.

"Thank you, Miss Hope. I appreciate your thoughtfulness." Catriona beamed at her.

In her exhaustion, all Hope could manage was a quiet nod and a smile. She let her eyes close and her head lolled toward Xavier as they started moving again.

"The car is ready for you downstairs and Javed says he has everything under control." Catriona's voice washed over her as the ding of the elevator called.

CHAPTER THIRTEEN

ope slept, and Xavier concluded it was no wonder. With the changes to sleeping routines, the fright and injuries earlier and the shock of finally knowing exactly what she was had caught up with her. Not to mention the exertion from the night before. He grinned wolfishly, remembering her uninhibited response.

He held her close, looking down at her as the elevator came to a stop. The subtle darkening of the emerging bruise on her forehead angered him. He would need to take disciplinary action against James, but that wasn't urgent right now.

Finding Estersham and neutralizing him was.

Long strides brought him out of the elevator toward the opening doors and he could see Javed holding the car door wide. Carefully Xavier climbed in, cradling his precious cargo tightly against his chest, so she wasn't jostled and wakened.

The door shut and he felt the motion of the car as Javed clambered in. The car engine revved and they were moving.

He watched her sleep, inhaling her subtle scent, lost in thoughts of how amazing this gentle woman was.

An explosion snared his attention. The second blast went off, making the car shudder. The intercom buzzed. Hope roused and he reached over to open the communication between himself and the front of the vehicle, pushing hair from her face as he answered, "What's going on?"

"One of the cars has been…blown up, we think. The bang, then a black cloud showed at the same time as we lost it on the radar and intercom. We are taking emergency action now." The vehicle jerked slightly, pushing them back into the seat of the car.

"What about the others? Have we lost any others?"

Another explosion had the car slewing to one side. Hope held onto to him tightly, her eyes wide with fright. He held her closely against the shuddering.

"It looks like another one is gone, Xavier. We're going to have to go to air mode. It will get us off the bridge and give us increased maneuverability."

A whine rent the air, and the car jerked again. The forces pushed him farther back into the seat as they rose from the ground.

He looked out of the darkened window. Two smoking hulks littered the bridge below, flames licking at the carcasses. Then the vehicle banked sharply. He swore savagely, gripping the door handle. Someone would pay dearly for this.

"Get into the seatbelt, Hope, then hang on." He growled the words, and dropped the screen between them and the front of the car.

She scrabbled at the belt, white-faced, the rapid bumping of her heartbeat told him she'd a fair idea about what had happened. He released the intercom button.

"Xavier? I've called for back-up. Two more cars are en-route and I have requested air support from the government. They are scrambling the mini-jets right now. Their ETA is about three minutes." The whining of engines made it hard to hear.

Another loud bang reverberated from below. Something whizzed past the conveyance, as fury roiled in his gut like an angry pot. It licked and burned, and he dug deep, restraining the urge to attack. He had Hope in the car and her safety was paramount. Nothing would happen to her. He wouldn't let it.

He watched as the driver and Javed quickly conferred, the sound of screaming engines making it almost impossible for him to hear, even with his vastly superior auditory skills.

Another bang and they banked again. Javed turned back to him, his eyes wide. "We need to get down. Our stabilizers are damaged, but Christophe thinks he can get us closer to the center of the city. Hang tight. It's going to be close." The car grew sluggish under the constant onslaught.

The vehicle dodged and wove up and down. As they got closer to the city, the weaving seemed to settle a little. They dropped slowly, but the vehicle was badly damaged. Smoke now invaded the passenger area.

He was aware of Hope, quiet but obviously terrified, and he pulled her tight against him, while she twined her fingers with his, seeking comfort.

Her human frame was infinitely more fragile than his, and he kept her close in case he needed to act as a buffer between Hope and a hard landing.

He watched the ground rushing up to meet them. His grip on Hope tightened. She shook. He wanted to tell her it would be all right, but he wouldn't lie. It could still go very wrong. He held her tight, and watched the drop slow down, but not enough.

"Hold on. It's going to be a hard landing." Javed's voice rang through the cabin, as Xavier curled his body around Hope, covering her head as the car around them exploded.

Hope opened her eyes to the smell of burning rubber filling her senses. Her arm and leg hurt and something heavy lay across her. Xavier.

"Xavier? Wake up, Xavier. Something's burning and we have to get out of here." She didn't know what it was, but the instinct to hurry was something she couldn't ignore.

He groaned, and she pushed ineffectually with one arm. The other she couldn't use easily, and the pain that rushed through her sucked the breath from her body.

"Come on, Xavier. Wake up." He groaned again, as if in response to her harried words. He opened his eyes, slowly, and she pushed again. "Xavier, we have to get out." An edge of hysteria colored her words, as big greasy waves of fear tumbled around in her stomach. He blinked once then again. Xavier moved to the side and a weight lifted off her leg. He clambered to his knees.

"Oh, God. Shit. You're hurt." The words grated out as he reached toward her. A trickle of blood snaked down the side of his head, but he ignored it as he looked around.

The door buckled inwards, the dark upholstery pushed out of shape filled the area around them. It was hard to move without knocking something. She tried to stay still as the unwelcomed pain in her leg consumed her.

Xavier pushed on the twisted metal. It gave with a groan, opening slightly. Hope watched as he pushed again. It gave a little more. He turned his back to it, looking at her with an unspoken question. Hope nodded. She was still with him. She waited as he turned back to face the door once more. His movements were jerky and awkward, yet he gave one last tremendous heave. With a groan it gave and light spilt into the wreckage of the vehicle, as did more smoke.

Xavier reached for her, carefully lifting her in the cramped conditions. She cried out. The pain left her wanting to retch. Bent over nearly double Xavier covered her protectively and pushed his way through the misshapen opening. He headed to the sidewalk, scanning the area before laying her down on the concrete. Tears dribbled down her dirty cheeks, and he wiped them away with care.

"Where are Javed and Christophe?" Hope said between coughs as more smoke filled her lungs.

"I don't know, but I have to see if they got out." He straightened, and she could see the tattered remains of his clothing. Cuts and scratches oozed and the grazes on his face worried her as billowing gray clouds covered him, hiding the damaged skin from her view. "Will you be all right for a moment?"

She nodded and he moved back to the vehicle. She couldn't see, as the dark fog became increasingly dense. She coughed again. Her ribs ached from the involuntary action. She flung her good arm around her chest, seeking some surcease from the throb.

Then she spied it. Red and yellow flames, dancing through the smoke, and she knew they were in more trouble.

Fire.

"Xavier! Xavier!" The blackness grew larger in the sooty haze, as the flames grew, and licked at the back of the vehicle. "Xavier! The car is on fire!"

She screamed to him as he emerged, Javed in his arms and a grim, pained look on his face. Blood ran down his cheeks and a gash on his forehead was laid open to the bone. Her stomach churned and roiled, and she fought to contain the nausea. "We have to get out of here. The car is on fire."

"I can't put him down, but we have to get you to safety." The anguish in his eyes tore at her.

The sound of rushing feet came from beyond the smoke. "Damn it!" Xavier placed Javed next to her quickly and turned. His eyes flashed golden and his teeth descended—ready to fight.

Hope wanted to cry. To scream. To rage against the fates for not only putting them in this life-threatening position, but also for hurting Xavier.

The noise was hideous. The black smoke choked, while the leaping flames licked at them from the wrecked vehicle. A feral sound escaped from Xavier, just as the licking of the flames seemed to ratchet up. The heat generated by the fire made her skin feel like it was shriveling against her bones. Fear left her shaking.

Hope grabbed Javed with her good arm, bringing his supine body closer to hers. She looked around for somewhere to hide, but the billowing cloud of black hid everything from view.

She coughed, chest screaming as the paroxysm continued. *This isn't how it was supposed to end!* The words echoed in her mind and her eyes burned. *Dear God! And Xavier? What would happen to him?* She felt the trickle of tears, scalding hot running down her face. She focused on

Xavier's taut back, and suddenly noticed the tension drained away from his posture.

The outlines took form. Her breath fled, as finally they were revealed—other vampires from the nest. The fire was still too close, and… "Xavier? Where is Christophe?"

He turned and she could see the naked grief on his face. He shook his head and looked away—back toward the others.

Pain lanced through her heart because he rejected the comfort she could offer. There was no time to contemplate their situation. Not now. They still had to survive this inferno. She thrust the hurt aside as they moved swiftly. One picked up Javed carefully, pulling him from her grasp, and Xavier leaned back toward her. He bent with a small groan of pain and slid his hands underneath her, careful not to further injure the limp arm or the leg.

"Xavier. No. You're injured." She held on, though, not wanting to hurt him more. She cast a last look at the fire before closing her eyes.

Red-hot pokers of pain shafted through her each time she coughed. She bit back cries of discomfort, knowing all they would do was torment Xavier with the knowledge of the injuries she'd sustained.

They moved through the shadowy gloom of smoke, and toward the night. The smoke choked her and stung her screaming eyes. The strength of Xavier holding her tight against his body reminded her that they would get through this. She tried to think how long they had been under attack then waiting. It had felt like forever, yet instinct told her everything had happened within a very short amount of time. Long minutes passed, ones she would never forget.

They emerged from the smoke. The side of a building was just beyond them, when a rumbling sound started. Xavier ran, as did the others around them, and this time the jostling grabbed her breath, seared her from within, and the gray she'd kept at bay seeped into her vision as she fainted.

A sense of weightlessness and dim conversation interrupted the nothingness. Movement and people talking impinged then floated away. Lights flickered briefly before darkness descended again.

She wanted to sleep, but something woke her, touches and probing.

His voice guided her through the darkness. Xavier. It wove through the dreams, sometimes distressed and other times startlingly angry. She reached toward the voice. It pulled at her.

She woke.

Eyes opened to the light. A dim glow shone in the room. She was back in her bedroom in the secured quarters. She mentally catalogued her injuries.

Her arm ached, but while it pained her to move it, she realized that she once more had motion. Her leg and chest still hurt, along with other aches and pains, though the agony in her chest had settled to a dull ache, except when she coughed. At least the vicious stabbing was gone. Her leg seemed unresponsive—immobile.

"How did I get here?" The words rasped from between chafed lips. It sure didn't sound like her voice, and her throat burned.

"You're awake." Xavier leaned in, and she grimaced at the gray tone to his skin.

He smiled, and ran an unsteady hand over her forehead. She watched him, as the lines of tension smoothed out of his face. "Do you remember the accident?" His words were soft.

"Yes. How is Javed?" She moved, no more than a small jerk, but she hissed as pain hit again. The last sight she'd had of the swarthy guard was him in the arms of another, and she certainly had no memory of him regaining consciousness.

"He will be fine. He woke earlier and has been fed. By tomorrow he'll be as good as new. You, on the other hand, dislocated your shoulder, broke your leg and suffered extensive bruising to your chest and ribs." Xavier lowered himself until he perched on the edge of the bed. His eyes closed, and when he opened them again they gleamed. "You should never have been hurt." The gentle words filled the hollow space in her chest.

Hope raised her arm. It ached, but she could now at least use it. She touched his face lightly, letting her fingers still on his skin. "It's okay, Xavier. You did everything you could. You shouldn't be angry at yourself. You didn't drive me into danger."

He averted his eyes, dealing with some emotion that caused him pain. "Hope... In such a short time you have become...important to me." He turned back to her. "I don't understand how this has happened, but I need you as much as I need blood and oxygen. I will not lose you." The words were forced out, and she saw that he hated to admit this weakness.

Xavier's gaze dropped and he plucked idly at the covers on the bed. Her chest tightened when she saw his discomfort.

Emotions she'd tried vainly to ignore reared their heads. "Xavier... I don't know what is happening either. I'm kind of lost here too." Her words were thoughtful and he leaned forward.

The touch of his lips upon hers were soft. Emotion swelled and she waited for him to move away, but he didn't. "Stay with me?" The words were out before she could call them back.

He nodded. "I'll stay, but I need to have a quick shower. I haven't had a chance yet."

She looked down, and noticed she was in a bra and briefs. The cute, sexy red set she'd pulled on earlier. He smiled at her when she wordlessly asked him with her eyes. "I thought you would be more comfortable." With that he winked then turned, soundlessly walking to the bathroom, but she noted he left the door open.

Sounds of running water lulled her back toward the call of sleep. She let herself go.

CHAPTER FOURTEEN

The dream crept through the night, filling her with a cold sensation as the sepia-toned scene appeared before her. She watched the movements. The fire and a child removed from the house. She knew the child was her. Her stomach churned, as it changed to the room where Cressida had found her, cold on the cot in the otherwise empty room, still as a statue.

Then Xavier. She saw him dressed in old-fashioned clothing, with laced ruff at his wrists. His speech so different, but his dear face the same. Another man. Tall and blond—a foil against the dark-haired man who'd caught her attention. There was something wrong with this man, though. Something in his eyes was cold—so cold.

She needed to warn Xavier, but he looked through her. She put a hand out to touch him, but instead of solid muscle, she met empty air and she heard a keening sound, knowing dimly that it was coming from her.

The scene changed again. A car then smoke. A face watching and laughing in the shadows. Blond hair again phone in hand. She heard his quiet mutter of, "It's done." He'd orchestrated and viewed the action she concluded.

Once more the scene changed, a building and a gun raised, but before a shot could be fired on the three forms, more came from within the gray mist.

The building was tall. She knew without conscious thought that she'd seen it before. An explosion and it was gone. Billowing smoke filling the air, as a rain of paper and debris fell to the ground and she could see bodies strewn everywhere. The hideous, grisly sight made her feel sick. There on the ground, dead, was Xavier. Blood seeped onto the pavement beneath him, and she ran to him. She wanted to scream her despair, but she couldn't. Someone grabbed her. The laughing man held her, mocking her—and them.

It was Estersham. She was sure. She turned—

"Wake up, Hope. It's just a dream." She was held in a strong grip. Xavier restrained her gently, as she woke from the nightmare. Sobbing. Hope sucked deep desperate breaths in, filling her lungs. She shivered as the cold of the dream still held her in its awful grip.

"Nooo..." She wrapped her hands around him, turning a little, awkwardly and painfully. "He won't take you. I won't let him." Her broken words filled the quiet room.

"Who, Hope? Who won't take me?" She snuggled awkwardly, trying to exact more warmth for her chilled body. Xavier was her rock. Xavier was her anchor in this world, where she was lost and alone.

"Him. Estersham." She snuffled and hiccupped in his arms. The bare skin of his chest under her head, as he rubbed gently, sent warmth flowing back into aching limbs. "He wants you dead. I saw it. Blood. On the ground. You were dead." She felt scalding tears rolling down her face, dripping onto his chest, where they pooled. She knew the words made no real sense. She needed to clear her mind, but fear held her in its desperate grip.

He continued to rub her back while she settled. "Do you want a drink? I can get you a bottle of water if that will help." His quiet words calmed her. The storm inside her began to abate. She hadn't had an episode this strong in a long time. Usually, it was something less important.

Her premonitions, though she shied from that label, usually

warned of an accident that led to broken bones or a lost pet. Occasionally they were about more important aspects, such as the passing of an elder. Tonight, though, she knew it was a warning. That it could have been a premonition scared her.

Different. This time she'd seen the muted gray tones of times past then the future. She knew it instinctively.

"Yeah, just water. Thanks." She waited while he slipped out of the bed, his nude body dappled in the shaded light of the lamp. The muscles of his back rippled, and she lay back. Something about Xavier sang to her, on every level. She cared deeply already. She really didn't want to, but she did.

He returned, twisted the cap off the water and climbed into the bed before he handed it over. She drank deeply, sating the thirst that raged. The after-effects of the strong emotions left her wrung out like a dirty dishrag.

"Now you need sleep. I'll hold you and keep the nightmares at bay." His words lulled her as he pulled the bottle from her hands, tucking her into the bed comfortably. She wouldn't sleep, she was sure. Even with the thought, the heat in the air sapped her energy as efficiently as the nightmare. *Thank God for air conditioning.* The last inane thought fled as she closed her eyes, trusting Xavier as sleep reclaimed her.

He followed her with his eyes. Her bruised and battered face glowed white in the dim light, as she rested. The nightmare had exhausted her resources. Being brutally honest with himself, it had given him a fright too. Her thrashing had woken him, and when she'd cried out, he'd wished it was possible to fight the demons in her mind. He wasn't gifted with that sort of ability. Even with that knowledge, he'd wanted to crush the thing that caused her distress. Distress was too mild a word, though.

The previous night had reminded him just how fragile a human was. It was only when the nest doctor had pronounced her broken leg the worst of her injuries that he'd relaxed. Javed had been injured too, but his sleep would heal him when combined with his recent feeding.

Christophe had been lost to the nest, as had the others from the vehicle detail. All up, the deaths numbered five. Five excellent guardians, his psyche added.

It was a low point of his Mastership, but one they would avenge. In the coming evening they would hold a memorial for their lost warriors, but for the moment, his focus was firmly on Hope.

He reached for the cellphone. Cressida had said to ring if she experienced nightmares. He'd thought it overkill. Now he realized they were precognitive events.

He tapped on the screen, and it immediately went to voicemail. He left a short message, looked at the phone and turned it off. No sense having it ring and wake her. She would wake soon enough.

Xavier reached over, placed the device on the bedside table and curled around Hope, noting that she no longer shivered. Her skin had been icy cold when she'd woken, but he still pulled the covers more firmly over their bodies. He lay still, listening to the quiet sound of her breathing. Then he let the silence eventually lull him back to sleep.

CHAPTER FIFTEEN

The sound of voices woke her. Grogginess weighed her limbs and mind down as she fought through the layers of sleep. "Who is it?" Her slurred demand must have caught whoever it was.

"You're awake. Good." Cressida's voice filled the air. "How are you feeling?" The genuine concern in her voice filtered through the sleepiness that fogged her brain.

Hope levered up on one arm, realizing she was still in the bra and panties Xavier had left her in from the night before. She grabbed at the sheet, hauling it up over her chest, feeling awfully exposed. "I've seen better days, but I'll live, thanks."

"That's good." Hope watched as Cressida walked around in a circle, as if unsure where to begin. Finally she stopped and looked squarely at Hope. "Xavier told me you had a dream. Can you tell me what happened in it?" Cressida's face was kind, but it didn't soften the blow.

"Why?" The strangled word escaped tight lips. "No. I really don't want to talk about it." A bubble of fear grew in her chest. *I don't want to think about this. Please don't make me relive it.* Even as the thought grew, she realized the futility of the desire.

"It really is important. You know that. And if we know what you saw, we might be able to stop it before it occurs." The pleading in Cressida's voice confused Hope further. She wanted to tell Cressida, but the fear of revisiting it, of it actually coming to pass terrified her.

She squared her shoulders. Cressida and Xavier needed her to be strong. It was time to act like an adult. She wasn't a frightened little girl anymore.

"He died. Xavier. There was blood. And a blond vampire I've never seen before, yet I knew his name in the dream." Her stomach cramped, but she looked directly at Cressida. "It happened when a building was blown up. The blond vampire had others there, and they were smiling. Many people died. Xavier died. I couldn't stop it and *he* laughed."

"Do you recognize the building or any of the others?" Cressida sat down on the edge of the bed, her fair features creased in thought.

"No. I think I'm supposed to know the building. It is important for some reason… I just don't know what it is, though. Being in my dream, I guess, makes it important. You know that's how it works. It's rarely easy to understand the first time. Or even the second…" The words trailed away.

"I'll have Xavier run you through a gallery of known buildings, blood testing centers, main nest buildings and offices belonging to our allies as well as our own. In the meantime, the doctor tells me your leg is broken. Even with your fast healing, which is a by-product of your siren blood, we're going to require that Xavier work from home. We have some theories, things we can do to help us track down the perpetrators." Cressida nodded, her face grim, working through the list she no doubt had in her mind.

Hope waited in silence, watching the woman before her. "I need one of our scientists to come take a sample from you. I have an idea, but it may take us a couple of weeks to follow through. Are you happy for us to take some blood?"

Hope nodded, wishing that solving the altercation could be that simple, but knowing it would only answer a few of the questions they had. "Yeah. Just let me know and I can be there."

"They'll come to you. At this time, we need to keep you as safe as possible."

Until now, while she knew they wanted her, she hadn't worked out that the attack was a means to get her. "Are you sure it was me they wanted?"

"Beyond a shadow of a doubt, child. You are their primary target right now." The words fell like stones, crushing her as surely as boulders. Her eyes stung.

"Why? I mean. How could this be?"

"Well, you know that you're a blood siren. To hold you is the greatest power a vampire can have. You are the ultimate weapon. He can create armies with your blood. And because we now know that vampirism is a virus, we have learned that he can un-create others with your blood."

For a moment Hope sat still, watching Cressida. Then Hope stirred restlessly, thinking over the words, acknowledging the unreality of the discussion.

"Added to that is your ability to see things that could be. With that combination, you're very attractive to Estersham." She smiled at Hope, but that didn't dispel the fear Hope felt, or the lump that was lodged in her throat.

"I don't want to be a weapon, Cressida, I just want a normal life. To find a lifetime partner of my own choosing. To have a job I chose. To have a family." Her words broke at the end and she sniffled.

"Hope, some of those were never on the cards for you. And I can't undo the fact you have only just found that out. These are things you should have been made aware of years ago." The words were sympathetic, and Hope knew Cressida was doing her best to offer comfort.

"What we can do is find the threat and deal with it. The best way is for Xavier to protect you, and for my people to work on finding them, and making sure that the appropriate action is taken. A vampire war would destroy the relationship we have with the governments, so we want to avoid that at all costs. It means people would fear us, and forever affect our way of life, one that we have come to rely on."

Hope heard the words, but they didn't ease the pain.

"It would impact on every human that has been associated to a nest. We have oaths to fulfil to humans and nestlings. This is the only way." Her tone was firm, as she laid a hand on Hope's trembling one. "You are strong and we will protect you. That is the only comfort I can offer right now." With that Cressida stood up and walked from the room without a backward glance.

CHAPTER SIXTEEN

For Hope, the next few days passed slowly. Sitting in bed, with a computer on a hospital table, gave her things to do that involved her brain and hands—most of the time anyway. After the first few days, crutches arrived and she could hobble slowly between the rooms.

Hope continued to work through the lists of nestlings, arrange for their moving and other tasks Xavier set for her. He'd moved his main staff, Damon and Catriona, together with Emily into the house so they were safe, and he could continue to work without leaving.

It palled. Very quickly. The lounge had been cleared of furniture and temporary workstations set up, so she could participate and be involved. She still hated the necessity of having to hide.

No one talked about the attack. The night after, a memorial had been held. A chaise had been set up for Hope on the terrace and Xavier had carried her up, a team of vampire guards flanking them. Because Christophe had been a young vampire, a turned nestling, there had been blood to give as an offering to the fire built on the gravel drive. The others were older, so blood offerings weren't available. Instead, there were photos given as tokens for the dead.

Many of the vampires wore Christophe's favorite color, bright purple, and even Hope had joined them with a loose purple tunic Xavier had ordered for her, that had been delivered just in time. The entire household mourned the loss of the five.

The keening of those who knew them best had been hard to ignore. It was the first vampire memorial she could remember. Her parents had not wanted her to attend the one when she'd been kidnapped, as there had been so many lost and, in their minds, she'd been traumatized enough.

Life had to go on, as Xavier commented when addressing the house. The observance of death must be balanced with that of life. How she wished that were true, yet the most overwhelming memory of the memorial was her parents, her brother and sister-in-law...the representation of her old life. They had refused to acknowledge or even talk to her. She felt, in her own way, that it represented a kind of death—the loss of her family.

They stayed at the other side of the terrace, keeping their distance, talking among themselves and from time to time dropping cool looks on her. They'd made no move to join her, and that hurt beyond anything else. Hope knew Xavier was aware of her emotional pain, but he'd said nothing either.

After the memorial had ended, he'd carried her back downstairs to the secured area, ordered a meal and had given her one of the sedatives the doctor had ordered. Each night she'd slept in his arms and woken there too. He'd been attentive, caring and understanding. Yet the pressure within her started to build.

She didn't have a quick temper, more of a slow boil, and, like a clock, the timer was ticking. She felt cooped up, though everything she wanted was available, drought to her bedside and the lounge. Even her favorite foods were delivered.

There were also nourishing broths and nibbles from carrot sticks to savory tofu dishes and custards. It irked her, being locked away, feeling like a prisoner, with no hint of parole.

Bathing was handled by Lisi who was granted unprecedented access to the secure living quarters. Yet the people she'd thought would want to see her made no appearance or contact. She wanted to go outside, to breathe the air. To feel free of the constraints Xavier had instituted. She might be well aware, they were for her safety, but they chafed badly.

For two weeks, Hope seethed, letting the emotions roil and grow inside her. Anger and frustration became her constant companions, as day segued into night. Her leg grew itchy in the cumbersome cast while she waited impatiently for its removal, unable to do some of the simplest things she'd taken for granted previously.

She woke, held tight in his arms, lying quietly until she opened her eyes. Looking up, she could see the ceiling. A ceiling she now knew very well and was quite sick of. "Xavier? What time is it?"

"Early yet. Only about five o'clock. Why?" His tone was puzzled and still sleep fogged.

"I want to see my parents." The demand echoed through the quiet room. She could almost see it falling like bricks, as it registered in his mind and her petulant tone too.

"I don't think that would be a great idea right now. How about I go order you some breakfast? What would you like?" His face became shuttered, as it had done more often in the last few days.

He pulled the cover away as if making to get up, and she could see the blue striped pajama bottoms he'd worn for the last few days.

"I don't want breakfast. I want to see my parents." She knew the tone was childish, but it was time for something to give. She needed to know what had changed between them, and what she could do to bridge the chasm. "Ask them to come down here."

"No."

"Oh come on, Xavier. I haven't been upstairs in nearly two weeks. If I can't go up, they can come down." She wheedled, but he was unbending. His face could have been cast in granite.

"No, they are not allowed into this area. They have never been. Not even for you will I allow it." He didn't face her.

She slumped against the pillows. "Xavier? I need to see them." She sighed the words, looking away briefly.

"I can't allow that, Hope."

Frustration like a burning tide swept through her. "So, I'm to stay here, like a prisoner in a gilded cage? For how long? Until I die? What if I don't want to stay?" Her own voice turned cold. She watched as he made his way toward the door. "Xavier? When? When will you let me go?"

"I can't, Hope. Don't expect me to give you an answer to that. I can't." He'd reached the door and gripped the wood edging tightly.

"Can't or won't? I won't stay in hiding forever. Don't expect me to either." She grabbed a pillow and threw it, seeking a way to relieve her feelings of anger. The frothy pillow bounced and rolled off the end of the bed to the floor in silence. She looked at it. What was she doing?

"Feel better now?" His mild voice broke through the silence.

"No. I don't." She hung her head, shamed by her childish behavior, but the pressure inside her needed an escape before it choked the life from her. "I need to know what has happened. Please?" Angry tears pricked her eyes. Why was he being so obstinate? "I need to find out what's changed. Why my father reacted like he did." She gulped as emotions almost overwhelmed her. "Why my mother hasn't made an effort to contact me. Can't you see? It's tearing me apart." The tears trickled down her face, a hot wet river. Her chest heaved with the effort of containing her emotions.

He turned around, hiding his eyes behind closed lids. She could tell her pain was hurting him. "I can't allow that. Having Lisi and Emily is pretty close to breaking the rules. Catriona is taking Emily to the safe room tonight, for the change, so that will no longer be an issue, but I can't bend the rules any further. I had to get a dispensation for those two." His voice was strained, and when his eyes opened, the green in them was tired and pale. "I may be the Master, but I have to abide by the rules too. If I could do what you wanted, I would." He sounded beaten. The lines that bracketed his mouth told her of his struggles. The ones she'd missed, while feeling miserable and sorry for herself. He was suffering too.

"Xavier? I'm sorry... I didn't realize." Hope squeezed her eyelids shut, lifted her hands and scrubbed, but the tears ran down her face still, shattering her brittle composure.

She was so hurt, confused, desperately in need of reassurance. For weeks she'd been accepting of the soft touches invalids received. She needed more. Not sexual, but reassuring and reaffirming.

The dip of the bed told her he'd returned to her side. Strong arms encircled her, and she slowly let the tears flow. "Why? Why don't they want me anymore? I mean, they weren't demonstrative or emotional or anything like that, but never cold like this. Even when they were cross with me as a child, they made sure I knew they loved me. I don't understand. I don't know what I've done wrong." Her words were muffled against his shoulder, as shudders racked her body.

"I don't know either. There's much more to this than meets the eye, but I know this is something we need to look into." He kissed the top of her head, rubbing soft hands over her back. "Right now, you need to know this isn't about you. I can assure you that you aren't unlovable and that it isn't anything you've done. You've done nothing wrong. It isn't your fault, and we will get through this." He whispered the words against her hair, his arms tight around her, holding her close against his bare chest.

She inhaled the scent of him, it filled her senses. She opened her mouth over his skin, allowing her tongue to peek out and take a quick taste.

He sucked in a breath. "Honey, if you keep doing that, I'm going to want to go all the way. And that might hurt you. So, maybe now isn't a good time. Right?" He started to pull away, and she could see the erection tenting his pants.

"You won't hurt me. We can be careful," she pleaded, but he pushed her farther away, making his point firmly.

"I'll tell you what. When the doctor gives the all-clear, I'm yours." He smiled at her.

His eyes glittered and those sexy lips of his curled at the corner. A flicker of flames licked at her belly. *The doctor is here today, so just you wait!* She let the thoughts fill her with anticipation, but didn't say anything. Just smiled and he looked at her. Suspicion was clear in his eyes, as she grinned wider.

"Now then, young lady. You seem to be healing quite well. Have you been getting around, using either crutches or a cane? You're young and healthy enough." As Hope nodded, he continued. "Master Xavier is also hoping to arrange for a physiotherapist for you. I know one attached to a friendly nest. I will pass it by your Master, and we can go from there. Though in the period your nest is in shutdown, they may prefer to consult via the Internet. Any questions?" The doctor started packing away his torture equipment, and wasn't looking at her. Hope considered that a good thing as her face turned red.

"Yes, doctor. There is something I need to ask. Umm… Is my leg well enough to stand up to…you know…activities of a personal nature?" *God, how embarrassing this is*. At least she didn't have to worry about birth control. Her face reddened at the thought of what they had done, and how regularly before the incident. Until she had something in writing for Xavier, he wouldn't countenance a return to the intimacy they had shared beforehand.

"What? Oh, well as long as you are careful. No hanging from the chandeliers, of course, but with appropriate care, yes, that should be fine." He looked at her, and she wanted to shrink into the sheets. His face glowed with interest, and she could almost hear the questions bouncing around in his head.

"Umm… CanIhavethatinwriting?" Her voice was little more than a rushed whisper now, and he smiled. He had to be at least sixty with a shock of white hair. *It's like talking to my grandfather*, she thought. Except hers would have been horrified in this instance. The doctor continued to look, and her face flamed. The longer he watched her, the broader his grin got. All Hope wanted was to find a crack in the floor to crawl into.

"Yes, of course." He pulled a notepad and a pencil out of his long jacket, licked the end and started writing. "Whom shall I address this to?"

A twinkle shone in his eyes, and Hope felt like a naughty teen caught doing something she shouldn't. She had to stop from squirming.

"Err… Just 'to whom it may concern' would be great, thanks." Hope watched as he finished the note, and handed it over. She grabbed it quickly, and shoved it into the drawer beside the bed. "Thanks so much. When should I see you again?"

The conversation retreated to neutral topics, and she felt some of her embarrassment ebb away. He took his leave, the door shutting quietly behind him.

She scowled. That had been an ordeal, but at least she got the note for Xavier, which she retrieved from the drawer, scanning it quickly.

'To whom it may concern,

Miss Hope is now well enough to resume an intimate relationship. However, it is my opinion it should be neither physically taxing nor uncomfortable.'

Swallowing a strangled gasp at the humor, she held it tightly in her hand, before rising as carefully as the bright cast would let her. She was attempting to make her way to the bathroom—a slow and steady task—when Xavier opened the door and entered silently.

"What are you doing out of bed?" His demand was tempered only by his smile.

Once more she got the flutter of butterflies deep in her belly.

"Going to the toilet. I think I can manage that on my own these days." Hope's grumble was met with a small chuckle, as he reached out a hand. She looked into his eyes. He must have seen something in hers that told him she needed this small bit of independence, and withdrew the hand slowly, letting it drop. Hope let go of the breath she hadn't realized she was holding, before continuing her painful hobble past him, reaching from one piece of furniture to the wall, and slowly toward the door.

Just as she reached it, Hope turned and held out a hand, the one holding the missive. "Here, you may want to read this." He took the paper from her hand with a quizzical look, and she moved again, shutting the door behind her.

Everyone was finally gone and the lounge was quiet. Hope was tired, but happy. She was moving around, with the crutches firmly under her arms. When they'd first arrived, her steps had caused mirth and merriment among all watching, but she was now used to them and could maneuver smoothly around the room. Each time Xavier looked at her, the heat in his eyes stole another little bit of her heart.

Dinner had been silent. For Hope, it had consisted of grilled chicken with assorted vegetables, followed by chocolate mousse to celebrate her all-clear from the doctor, but her appetite had been nonexistent, and she'd sipped on the water Xavier kept pushing her way. She would have preferred a nice white wine, but the one time she'd suggested it, she'd been met with a short 'no'. She didn't ask again, knowing he was concerned she would fall and reinjure herself. Something she wanted to avoid also.

Xavier sipped his blood wine slowly while Hope ate. His eyes practically glowed and the heat grew inside her belly. She was sure he was mentally undressing her, and she warmed at the thought. His gaze dipped down into the valley between her breasts, displayed in the hot pink camisole he'd ordered for her, and she watched his eyes as they travelled over her body, feeling a tingle as her nipples tightened with awareness. Only one word described how he looked at her. Hungry.

Finally Hope pushed the plate away. The mousse was hardly touched, but she couldn't manage any more. She hadn't tasted any of the flavors she usually savored. No. All she'd done was watch Xavier gazing at her, becoming more and more aroused. Each time her lips closed around the spoon, his eyes had darkened further, a flush cresting his cheeks, and she knew his thoughts.

She squirmed, wanting to run a hand under the band at her neckline. Sometime in the last while, it had grown tighter, and she felt choked by it. A single trickle of sweat moved down her spine. She shivered, and it cooled her fevered skin.

She gathered the crutches near, popping them under her arms, and pushed herself up. Xavier was there, pulling out the chair, steadying her as she positioned herself. He splayed his hand against her belly. Her flesh quivered in response.

"Xavier..." The words died on her lips, as his found the back of her neck. She leaned forward slightly, while he slowly inched his fingers across her stomach, over the silky fabric, where they sought entry to her flesh.

The shock of his touch against her skin caused her to quake. Hope arched back slightly, nearly losing her balance with the crutches. He disentangled himself before scooping her up. The crutches fell to the ground, forgotten with a thud.

"Xavier." She moaned. His lips found the sensitive skin at her throat. The bed gave slightly underneath her, as he slid down with her to the covers. The touch—his hands—inflamed the desire that had been licking at her since the doctor left.

"Tell me how to love you. Tell me what you want." His guttural words filled the air.

She reached out blindly. "Just love me, Xavier. That's all I want." Her eyes fluttered closed. He settled his hand around her breast, softly kneading the flesh, but not touching her distended nipple, even though the light cover of her top. She ached inside, and only Xavier could fill the need that rippled through her.

He placed warm hands under the waistband of her skirt, working on the elastic. She shivered in reaction, lost in the sensual web he wove.

He found the indentation at her waist and flicked in and out of her navel, while the other hand slowly pushed the camisole out of the way. Up, up, up it crept. He sought the band of her bra. One that wasn't there.

"Each time I looked at you, I burned at the thought of your beautiful breasts hidden below the silk, but no bra to get in the way is very sexy. Did you wear the panties I bought for you, though?" His tone was harsh, and she cracked her eyes open to see his face, set with need.

"I…ah…had Lisi go shopping for me. I…" He touched and tortured her flesh, as she tried to answer him. Thoughts fled as he pushed the skirt slowly down her hips, to reveal the green panties beneath. He sucked in a breath at the sight of the lacy thong that covered very little. The thong matched the color of his eyes.

He slipped a tantalizing finger under the elastic at the top of the lace, lightly stroking the treasure that lay hidden below, and Hope reached for his hand. "No, Xavier. Not yet. Please?" Her words were broken, her body alive with the need that was driving her insane.

He pulled his hand back, and reached for his shirt. She watched as he slipped one button, then another from the holes. Her heart rate increased, as inch by beautiful inch his chest was revealed to her. How she wanted to run her hands over the hot planes.

Hope tugged her top over her head, as Xavier grasped the waistband of the skirt she'd worn. He pulled down, careful to avoid knocking the cast and quickly stood. He flicked at the fastener at his pants, a ripping sound, as the zipper opened to reveal the sexy green boxers below before they slipped to the ground. Then he stepped out of them. She itched to grab the band and yank it off him. "Come here, Xavier, and let me help you." She sat up slightly, crooking one finger. He smiled. Her body and breasts were tight with a burning need. She was almost naked, only covered by a scrap of lace, which hid nothing from his heated gaze. He looked her over. Up and down, and she shivered once more, as the sensual tension settled within her.

"I hoped you would." He flowed toward her, the satin tented over the erection hidden beneath the cloth. Xavier reached the side of the bed, and she slipped questing fingers under the band, feeling the hot throbbing flesh against her skin. He sucked in a breath, and stood still. He became rigid beneath her ministrations. She smiled before carefully peeling the boxers from his body. Her gaze soft as she looked upon the body she uncovered, starting with the strong powerful thighs, trim stomach and thatch of hair around his erect shaft.

A quick smile in his direction, before letting her eyes wander once more down his body. The satin boxers lay pooled at his feet, sitting over the black shoes and socks that he still wore.

Xavier turned and slowly sat down upon the bed, next to her. Pushed the boxers off with a movement of his feet then followed quickly with toeing the shoes off. She stared at his black socks. "Oh my, Xavier. Socks on in bed?"

He growled, and she giggled at the sexy response. A strong, handsome man in bed with her, and she laughed again at the silly thought.

"Well, you're still over dressed, though I do like those panties. Maybe we should get you some more of them." His voice deepened, as he leaned over to lightly kiss her. Letting the touch linger.

Xavier tugged the light material at her waist, pulling it from her body. She went white hot, his careful caresses along her sensitized skin leaving licking flames in their wake.

Once more, his lips touched hers. She closed her eyes, allowing the pleasure of him, naked and close, to flash through her system. She arched toward him as he grasped the swell of her breast.

Xavier had moved, letting his mouth wander slightly from her lips to her jaw, and Hope shivered at the sensation of his hot breath caressing her skin. Each new touch stoked the fire deep inside her.

A quick wriggle and she moved so he could settle himself against her nearly naked flesh.

She gasped. The feel of him was electric, and she bucked slightly, feeling his engorged head rest at the juncture of her thighs.

"Hope, you feel so good. Now I want your breasts, to hold them in my hands. I'll watch your beautiful pink nipples tighten while you wait for me. I want to suck them into my mouth." His words excited her further, while the sensations of him running his fingers over her firm flesh set off fireworks on her skin.

He bent forward, but instead of kissing her nipples, he grazed his chest across the sensitive skin. Leaned into her and kissed her with heat and desperation. She felt him tremble with desire, and she ran inquisitive hands up and down the skin of his back.

She grabbed him close and held him tight, seeking an intimate connection, then he shifted and pulled up. He breathed heavily, telling her wordlessly that he was as hot as she was, and she moved upright, following him as best she could.

His shaft jerked when she touched the tip with her finger, running it down the long, hard length of him, while he settled back on his knees, one hand around her bare ankle, slipping the leg farther apart and baring her for his gaze.

Looking at her, his face was a graven mask and in his eyes glittered with a need she wanted to fill. He reached out a shaking hand toward her, running a finger up her core. Each pass burned, each touch deepened. Then he placed his tongue to her skin and lapped. She writhed beneath his ministrations, bucking wildly, until Xavier placed a hand on her belly.

"Not yet." The tip of his tongue found the sensitive nub and flicked. She shuddered with the sensations as he slipped one finger within her wet opening, the touch leaving her gasping. He continued the motion, in and out nearly pushed her over the edge, while she gripped the sheets beneath her.

"Xavier… Oh, God… Xavier…" She gasped, and squirmed beneath him, but he continued onward with the erotic torture.

The liquid heat pooled inside her. He stopped sucking to look up. "Do you want more?"

"Please, Xavier. I just want you." The words were barely coherent and he gave one last lick, removing his finger then replacing it with his mouth. Letting his lips settle around it, he sucked. The carnal act stole her breath.

Once more, he teased her with his mouth then tugged away. Again his finger slid deep inside her finding the spot that made her gasp. He pumped her sex gently, while he positioned himself, then moved his hand away, only to replace it with his engorged cock.

She sighed at the feel of him embedded fully within her. He moved, and she met his thrust carefully.

Xavier reached over her, grasping a pillow from the other side of the bed. He slid out of her and she mewled at the loss of his weight, his touch, but he looked up, his eyes glittering with need. Then he positioned his hand under her, pulling the pillow beneath the cast, and swiftly returned to her. Once more, he filled her to the hilt.

She wound her good leg around his hips, levering into him, and pulling him as close as possible.

"Don't want to put any pressure on your leg." His words whispered against her mouth, then their mouths met. She met his thrusting tongue with her own, and let it dance against his. She could taste muskiness in that sweet wet cavern of his mouth—her taste.

He pumped her slowly while he worked her nipples into tight buds, she let her hands roam his body.

"Oh, Xavier, more. Please!" She begged. He shoved harder and faster within her. She writhed beneath him, feeling the increase of pressure building, low and deep in her belly.

He pushed into her, her body tightening. Glorying in the weight of him above her, and how he moved within her quickly, she orgasmed. A keening sound erupted from her throat.

The rhythmic spasms of muscles clenching and releasing flashing through her body like quicksilver. He flexed one more time, and she felt him stiffen, gripping tightly to her hips. His pulsing release, deep within her, filled her with satisfaction.

Their bodies stilled, locked together. She opened her eyes to see his dark hair pillowed on her breast, where he'd slumped against her.

Breath slowing... as did beating hearts.

She closed her eyes. Dear God. There was no way she could give this up. Not the sex, but the sense of connection she felt with him. Of rightness. He was the Master vampire, and she was what? His girl-friend? His lover? She loved him. A tear trickled seeped out of the corner of her eye, as the truth occurred to her.

She. Loved. Him.

Oh, Lord. Please don't let that be right. Please no! Don't let her have made that mistake. Even as the thought flashed through her, she knew. She'd tumbled into love with a Master vampire.

Her.

The one the bad guys wanted.

The one her parents didn't want.

She bit her lip hard and more tears pricked and rolled down her cheeks.

"Hope? What's wrong? Did I hurt you?" He lifted his head, touching his hand to the trails of wetness on her face. "What? Do I need to call the doctor?" He was half rising, as she grabbed his hand.

"No. Nothing is wrong. I'm just being silly is all." She swiped at the tears, sniffing inelegantly. "I just… Before you I never knew that I could feel so much. I want to thank you for that."

Inside, though, she screamed out her frustration. *I want to tell you I love you, but can't.* It wasn't a fair burden to share, and she knew he'd already taken on the responsibility of keeping her safe. So instead she leaned forward, touching soft lips to his. "Thank you." Keeping control of her emotions, though, left her stiff, and she saw the questions in his eyes.

Knowing you're a fraud offers no peace. Her honest assessment of her actions left her feeling cold and lost.

They settled down, with Hope caught up in Xavier's strong arms. She listened to the sound of his breathing, evening out as she lay still, looking at the wall, hoping for the welcome oblivion of sleep.

CHAPTER SEVENTEEN

The dream came again, this time darker and more intense than before. The thick fog lifted as they appeared in front of her, the atmosphere both chilling and foreboding. She shivered. Everything seemed muted and tinged in gray, like old photos. Men dressed in black trench coats stepped out of the fog, but she couldn't make out their features. On an instinctive level, she knew smiles adorned their bloodied faces, but she couldn't see them clearly. The drips of blood trickling down their chins chilled her to the bone. The building behind them, a hulking mass, continued smoking, as remains littered the ground. Bodies. Blood. Everywhere.

The copper tang filled the air, souring her stomach. The scent was making her ill.

She could see them once more. Xavier, with his blood seeping into the sidewalk, his eyes blank. Javed, a few feet away, lying still on the ground, his eyes dull in death. She rushed forward, but strong arms caught her. One of the black trench-coated men. "No!" she screamed. Her heart breaking as she surveyed the surroundings. The carnage before her, the scenes of the dead and dying and the sounds of anguished moans overwhelming her. The blond man stepped forward. The one she knew was Estersham.

"It is time." He moved closer, and she knew she was about to feel the sting and tear of his teeth…

"Hope? Wake up. Come on."

She thrashed as the remnants of the dream filled her with sickness. The tang of bile present in her mouth and on her tongue made her throat burn.

She was clammy and cold, even as Xavier held her close, hauling the covers around her.

"It was the same dream, but different. I don't know why, but it was." She shivered uncontrollably while she thought of Xavier, lying dead on the concrete. "There was smoke and bodies, and I'm sure I know that building… I don't know why! He shot you." She wailed the last words, hands raised in supplication.

Gently he rubbed up and down her back. She hiccupped, and gratefully accepted the warmth of his body touching hers. He kissed the back of her neck, reassuring and warm.

She slumped back against him, and the nightmare receded. "It's trying to tell me something, and I don't know what. I don't dream like this a lot anymore…and it was never like this."

She shuddered as her mind cleared. "I did up to the point when the nest was breached. Not much since then. Now they're back and I can't interpret them. The only thing I know is they can't have you." She gripped his hand, brought it up to her mouth and kissed it softly.

They stayed together while the day wore on. Eventually they dozed, still wound around each other.

****

Xavier watched as Hope picked at her breakfast. She was pale, her eyes tired, and dark circles ringed them. She hadn't slept properly since the last nightmare, spoke little and seemed lost, her movements listless and painful to watch. He wanted to do something for her, but didn't know what and the frustration rose once more.

Yet, even for that, she turned to him in the night, soundlessly seeking his embrace. The longer she suffered, the more difficult it became for him to watch. He breathed deeply, letting his lungs expand in preparation for the discussion he was about to open. This could be his last chance, and it frightened him as much as the knowledge that her dreams were tearing her apart.

"Are you going to eat that, or just play with it?" He used a languid hand to point to the meal, while his efforts to continue to act unconcerned tore at him. Her pushing and playing with her food had become a daily occurrence. He wanted to jump up and pull her into his arms, but he held himself in place. This had to be done.

She jumped at the blunt words. If possible, she paled further.

"I'm really not hungry."

He felt as much irritation as worry. She pushed the plate away. "Actually, I think I have some work to complete..." She started to rise from the table, maneuvering the crutches into place.

"Stop. Hope, we need to talk, you and I. Need to work out where this situation is going and what needs to be done." He'd been thinking it over, balancing the issues inside his head.

In the half standing position, she waited. Head bowed, and he felt like a heel, kicking her while she was down.

She quivered, then stood waiting. In the last few days, nothing else had worked to make her understand she wasn't to blame for any of this, and he knew he needed to get through to her. *This has to work.*

"I really don't want to talk about it." Her voice was uneven.

He felt worse, as the knot of uneasiness grew in his breast, but she had to work through the issues, otherwise she would become ill from lack of sleep and food. *If nothing else more sinister,* he told himself.

"Hope, you have to talk about it. Bottling these sorts of issues will tear you apart. I don't want to see that happen." He injected as much warmth and concern into his words as he could.

The look in her eyes was wild in the half-light, then her face hardened with anger. "Why? Why don't you want to see that happen, Xavier? Because then you might lose the warm body in your bed of a night? The sex on tap?" The bitterness in her voice shocked him, as her chest heaved brutally.

He slumped back heavily into the seat. As soon as the words were out of her mouth, she stopped. The shocked look on her face coincided with a pain in his chest. Her ugly words sliced into him sharply.

Did she really think that of him? That he thought so little of her? That emotionally and personally she wasn't important to him? The words flew around in his brain. He'd both proven and told her that she was essential to him. So, what had he done wrong?

"Oh, my God!" She closed her eyes and crumpled into the chair. "I can't believe I said that." Hope dropped the crutches to the floor, the clatter echoing through the silent room. Her head dropped forward slightly, but he could still see one hand clapped over her mouth, and she grabbed at her stomach. "I didn't mean that. Honestly." She lifted her head as the words tumbled forward. A red tide climbed her porcelain skin. Her face was a picture of shock and horror.

He hurt in the region of his heart, and wanted to rub it away, but knew it would offer no surcease from his anguish. He ached for her in a way he'd never before experienced. It had been him, alone for a long time. He'd had friends, some closer than others. Estersham had been significant in his second life as a vampire, at least until he'd gone rogue. Yet, no-one had meant quite so much to him as Hope did. He was confused about how to deal with the emotions that swamped him.

Before him was a broken woman, her hands shaking and her skin parchment white as she struggled to deal with her fears. Xavier's heart squeezed once more at her pain.

"I don't know what I'm saying anymore. I can't sleep. I can't eat and I feel like I'm going mad! I go to sleep knowing what I'm going to see. Knowing that they're there, waiting for me. Ready to show me something I don't want to happen. Something I don't want to see. And most of all, I don't want you dead." She shook, hands clenched tight.

This time he rose, going to her.

Xavier knelt on the floor beside her and pulled her into his arms. "Hope. None of us can change what has happened, but if we can work it out, we may be able to change the future. You said, after the last dream, it had changed. If we could work out why, we might be able to change the outcome. To do that, though, we need to know what happened, and be able to break it down. I know it's difficult, but we can do this. Together."

His words were soft, but he was sure they got through to her. She stood there, eyes tightly shut as she retreated within herself.

Gradually the tension surrounding her melted away and she reached out, gripping him tight, as if trying to crawl inside him, and he held on. The horror and fear in her eyes haunted him.

"Okay. I'll try." The words were tiny, but there was purpose and commitment in them, and they soothed the ache inside him a little.

Something moved through the air. A change in himself, skittering just beyond the reach of his mind and senses, but he felt an uneasy ripple in the back of his mind. Something indefinable.

Her stomach cramped. Had she really said those horrible things to Xavier? The look on his face when she'd said them haunted her. She felt sick just remembering.

He'd wanted her to talk about the dreams, not about their situation. God help her, she just wanted to forget the nightly horror. Each time she closed her eyes, though, she could see the scene in front of her. Smell the smoke and copper tang of blood. Her stomach churned harder, and the sick taste of bile rose in her throat. The unpleasant sensations were her constant companion these days and she knew her lack of hunger could be attributed to that. Her refusal to share the constant churn had been out of concern for Xavier's piece of mind.

"Xavier, I've tried to make it go away when I'm awake. It won't. It's always there, and I don't know what to do. The images haunt me." She closed her eyes, scrubbing at the itchy, aching orbs with the heel of her hand, gritted from lack of sleep. The lump in her throat, constricting and burning her.

"I can't understand what you are going through. I can say with certainty that something you said or we did changed the future. The future you saw in your dreams the first time."

She waited for him to continue.

"We need to work out what, so we can stop it from happening. You need to tell me everything you know and saw. Every detail, no matter how small or insignificant it may seem." He grabbed her hands.

She realized just how cold she was. "Do we have to do it now?" Her voice was strained, as if she'd been screaming. Her throat ached, she wanted a cool drink to clear it away. "Can I grab a drink first?"

Hope watched as Xavier checked his watch. "You know what? It's going on four in the morning. I think we should try when we wake up tonight. I'm also going to try to arrange a visit upstairs for you tomorrow. Maybe that will help a little. I know you're feeling stressed with everything, and being down here for weeks hasn't helped." Hope knew Xavier was seeking some way to relieve her distress.

He smiled, and she saw the strain lines bracketing his mouth and eyes. "What is it they call it? Cabin fever?" She laughed, knowing her answer to his question was quivery and damp sounding. "I'll have your parents lined up for nine—that way we can do them first, then come back down here and go through your dream. Does that work for you?" His voice was soft and coaxing, and she found herself nodding in agreement to his plans.

She knew he was humoring her, and she worked at pasting a smile on her face. He slipped soft arms under her legs. "Xavier? What are you doing?" He hefted her in his arms.

"Taking you to bed. To sleep." The words were firm, but caring, and she had to swallow the feeling of inadequacy and guilt that filled her.

She'd been so wrong with her accusation, and he needed to understand her apology was sincere. Sometimes facing up to being more than just rude was difficult, and this was no exception.

"Xavier? I was wrong. I shouldn't have said that before about a warm body. It was low of me and I didn't mean it. Not really." Her chest hurt as she pushed the words out. *God, I hope he understands what I am trying to say.* She could only hope that she hadn't damaged what they had growing between them.

He stopped in the doorway. "You may not mean it now, but maybe you did at the beginning. You wouldn't say those words if at some point you hadn't thought them. I'm sorry if I ever gave you the impression that you weren't important to me." He stopped, closed his eyes and swallowed.

She searched his face, the sensation of guilt pulsing stronger than before. "Hope, I don't know what to say, other than I don't make a habit of sleeping around. Those who do share my bed are valued and important to me. You are important to me."

The words were said slowly and she thought they were rather like a vow. He looked at her with eyes that glittered, and she read the sincerity in those deep green pools. He leaned his head forward and softly, achingly, kissed her on the lips. Light, but full of what she hoped was promise.

CHAPTER EIGHTEEN

*H*ope woke with a start. The room was quiet and she was alone. Her lips trembled. *I am so dumb. Xavier is pissed off with me, and I'm here on my own. If only I had kept my mouth shut, instead of letting it run off without thought.* A tear trembled from the corner of her eye. It plopped onto her cheek, before running down her face. Hope sniffed, scrubbing the silent tear away. "You are such a fool, Hope. Xavier is a good man and you had to speak without thinking, spewing your angry and thoughtless words." She mumbled, as she pulled a pillow over her head, hiding from herself and the emptiness in the room.

"Who are you talking to?" Xavier's voice filtered from the bathroom.

Her body froze in shock at the sound of his voice, and she let the pillow fall to the bed.

He hadn't left. He was still here. Triumph roared through her system. Energizing and cleansing and she smiled, wiping the last of the teary remnants away. That feeling was swiftly followed by remorse, that he'd heard her comments. She closed her eyes. "I was just talking to myself."

Soft fingers trailed up her arm and she jumped. "Hope, you aren't a fool." She looked up at him, surprised by his words. She hadn't heard him approach, but in the weeks they had been together she should be used to that.

"You are one incredibly sexy lady, holding up in an impossible situation that very few people would even understand, let alone have to endure." She watched him as he smiled, grabbing her hand and pulling her upright. "Now, incredibly sexy lady, it is time to dress. Tell me what you want and I will be your personal slave." He grinned at her, the infectiousness in it catching her, making her heart skip.

"Maybe the long black skirt and the ruffled white blouse, do you think? That should keep mother happy and still be comfortable enough for the weather."

In all honesty, the meeting with her parents frightened her. How would they react to the undeniable relationship between herself and Xavier? She oscillated between the 'knowing they wouldn't accept it', and 'I'm an adult and this is my choice' options. In the deepest recesses of her mind, she quaked. These were her parents, and their goodwill was so important to her, and she badly wanted them to accept that she loved Xavier. Her original concerns rose once more, swamping her. When had it all started to go wrong?

Xavier came back into the room, holding the clothing she'd requested along with lacy scraps of underwear. A broad grin on his face, and he handed the bra and panty set over.

"Hang on, these aren't mine." She pointed to the underwear.

"Yes they are. I had Lisi pop over to the mall and pick them up for you, together with some other bits and pieces." His grin got bigger—wolfish even. She grabbed the bits of cloth from his hand, blushing. Basic white, sure, but the tiny panties were little more than a triangle of silk and elastic, and she rolled her eyes. He winked and she stood, placing one foot after the other into the skimpy bottoms, and started to pull them up.

The bra next, little scraps of matching silk, underwired for some hopeful support. The balconette bra slipped over her skin like the caress of Xavier's hands. The cups barely covered her nipples, and she looked down at herself, then back to him. His eyes twinkled and she groaned. "How am I supposed to carry on a proper conversation with my parents, when I keep thinking something is going to fail?"

Xavier moved in close, placing his hands on either side of her face. "Because you know it delights me to see you displayed for my eyes, and because you know, no matter what they say, you're beautiful to me."

His scent filled her senses, increasing her heart rate to a rapid tattoo. He kissed her, softly to begin with, but she leaned closer to him, opening her mouth to allow his tongue access. The kiss grew hotter, and she moaned.

He carefully pulled away, saying in a hoarse voice, "We had best get ourselves ready for the meeting." Xavier looked at her, and she could see he was just as affected by the scorching heat of their passion. It felt good, knowing he not only wanted her, but was unafraid to show it. Xavier left the room, and she watched the movement of his body until he was out of sight.

With a sigh, Hope grabbed the bedside table and hopped into the skirt he'd left on the floor. Pulling it up and fastening the zipper, she then slipped her one good foot into a light sandal as she grabbed her crutches. She hobbled into the dressing room with the blouse in hand.

Once in front of the mirror, she took a look at herself, the black skirt all but hid the hot pink moon boot that now replaced the ugly cast. The little skimpy bra covered her nipples but not much else. She gazed at herself objectively. She was slim with small pert breasts, lightly flared hips and flat stomach. Her long black hair was straight, but the blue highlights shone under the lights, and she critically scanned her eyes and skin.

Hope shrugged, though—nothing he hadn't seen before and wouldn't see again—and decided against the makeup she would usually apply.

She tugged the top off its hanger and started to pull it over her head. She slipped one hand through, pushing a crutch to the wall, relying on only one, and was just getting her head through when she lost balance. Hope shrieked as she started to topple, throwing herself onto the uninjured side, when warm hands grabbed her.

"You're a menace, you know. Can't even dress without causing yourself another injury." The voice was heavy with laughter, and she relaxed.

Xavier to the rescue again.

She limped into the room. Xavier had offered to help her once they had climbed the steps from the secured living area, but her stubborn will told her she needed to do this under her own steam. And she had, but was paying for it now. Oh boy, she was puffing by the time they reached the office, felt the trickle of sweat that snaked down her back once more, and knew it wasn't the closeness of the atmosphere that caused it. The door clicked closed behind them.

A chaise lounge had been carried in for her comfort in the old-fashioned room, and she gratefully headed toward it. Xavier was right beside her, and as she raised her leg, he was there with the pillow, thoughtfully propping it in place, then taking the armchair beside her. Locking his fingers with hers in a show of what? Solidarity? Right about now, she didn't know or even care. He was here with her, and that was what really mattered.

She rested her head for an instant, closing her eyes and gathering her emotional resources for the ordeal ahead.

"It will be fine." His words were sure, and she took comfort from them, before sucking in a nervous breath as the knock on the door sounded. She spun her head around, and saw he was watching her.

"Ready?" His eyes were deep pools she just wanted to drown in. She pulled away, lightheaded from the broken connection.

"Yeah." She breathed in the air trying to get some distance between them, but Xavier gripped her hand tighter. She sighed, understanding he was making a point, both to her and to the household.

"Come." He spoke the word in his displeased tone. The weeks of togetherness had taught her many of the subtleties and nuances of his voice.

The door swung open. She could clearly see her parents, neither appeared happy to be there given their stiff body language and cold faces. The disapproval in their manner sent chill waves across the room.

Hope grimaced as they saw her holding onto Xavier, but right now, he was a lifeline for her, as the arctic blast surrounded them like a heavy cloud, freezing her insides. She could clearly see the flat lines of their mouths edged with anger, and she silently sighed.

"Please be seated, Verity and James. Hope has been very despondent the last few days. Her concern over the..." She watched as he let his voice trail off, and his face turned hard. "...encounter you had with her, James." Xavier stopped.

Hope could see a banked anger in her father's eyes. "Mom? I haven't heard from you. I tried emailing, but didn't hear back. I even left messages on your answering machine. Why didn't you try to contact me?" She held herself still, waiting for an answer.

"What? That's a silly idea, Hope. You took off, immersed yourself in some..." Verity's arms flew around in elegant wheels, "dangerous and reprehensible carry-on, and now it's our fault?" Her mother's voice rose with disdain and anger. Hope wanted to cringe away, but this was a discussion they had to have. "You cause all these issues, and then expect us to accept the blame? Hope Elizabeth, we never raised you to be self-indulgent." Watching her mother's flaring nostrils, Hope wondered if the woman should get so upset with her illness. "Sending you to college was a mistake. Cressida insisted, but I always knew you would get ideas above your station." Her mother's voice was shrill, her chest heaved. Something inside Hope broke under the barrage.

"I didn't do anything. I just want—" Even as she moved to talk, her father rose menacingly. Xavier growled, but James kept coming. Before he could reach her, Xavier was there in front of her—a physical barrier, between her and her parents. Hope realized then that was all there was to be said. They were together now, and either her parents would accept that fact or not. Their cool demeanor answered one of her questions.

"Stand aside, Xavier. This has nothing to do with you. It is a family issue." The voice was hard. Cold. Forbidding.

"No, James, I won't. Hope is now under my protection."

Her mother gasped. Hope closed her eyes. There was no way they would accept that, the knowledge hurt her. "You will never raise a hand to her again." She shivered from the chill in Xavier's voice.

"Master Xavier, I don't see how this has anything to do with—" Her mother's words were also cut off, and Hope's eyes snapped open in time to see his face, angry, now looking back to her mother.

"No, you don't. Hope has done only as she was instructed. Nothing less and certainly nothing more than has ever been expected from her, but I cannot fathom your behavior. Surely you can see she has been hurt enough by your coldness? Can't you see just how miserable she has been? She just wants her parents there for her."

Her father sneered. "What? So we can watch her display herself for you and any other, in the hopes of somehow debasing herself, in order to achieve a nest of her own? We warned Cressida this would be the outcome, but she wouldn't listen to us."

"And I was quite right too." Cressida stood in the doorway, anger on her face, eyes glowing red. "I told you to tell her, James. You didn't." She stalked toward them, her words colder than ice, and a vicious look on her face. "Why is that, I wonder? What made you keep such a secret from her?"

Her father stepped back, away from the quietly advancing vampire.

"If you question any more of my decisions or those of Xavier...and yes, even Hope now..." Cressida stopped and looked at James.

Hope saw that sink home, the paleness of his face, the quick flick of his eyes to her, and back to Cressida.

"Yes, Hope is now untouchable. You will pay for your disobedience. Verity...my surprise at you knows no bounds." Cressida stared hard at Hope's mother. "As a mother, how could you forsake your child? Your own flesh and blood? Your only daughter?"

She hadn't found out what had caused the rift, the reason for the meeting. With Cressida's pronouncement of her status as an untouchable, she now had been named unofficial partner to Xavier, something sure to pour hot oil on an already smoldering fire.

She winced. Not the outcome she was looking for, not by a long shot. She had to try, just one more time.

She knew objectively that any relationship under normal circumstances would be forbidden between herself and Xavier. Perhaps because of her status of blood siren she was in some kind of no man's land, but no doubt her parents felt that the rules governing vampire and human relations should stand.

"Cressida? Can I speak to my parents alone for a minute? Xavier? Please?" He turned and scrutinized her, deeply, as if he was trying to read her very soul, but he must have seen the entreaty, as he slowly stepped back.

Xavier glared at James before nodding stiffly. One hand extended to point at James' chest. "Touch her and I will rip you apart, bone by bone. Are we clear?" Then he strode off, anger radiating from each footstep. Hope wasn't happy about the situation either, but the answers were important. She wasn't sure how or why, but the undeniable truth was, they were. To her, even if they weren't to anyone else.

The door shut quietly behind Xavier and Cressida. She knew there wasn't long, and that he would be listening through the heavy wood, but she had to do this alone—for her own sake.

"You slut!" The cold words flew from her father's mouth.

Her mother grabbed his hand as he made a move toward her. "Don't, James. No matter what we know, she doesn't deserve that." Verity shook her head.

Hope ached, taking this small action to indicate that there was at least some small spark of parental connection hidden deep within her mother. "Mother? What happened? I don't understand. I went to college, and when I came back you didn't want me. What did I do?" Her words trembled, and she knew the hurt in them was there, for everyone in the room to hear.

"Do? The college romps? The flimsy underwear in your drawers?

You came back, and panted after the Master like a… Like a cat in heat! You disgraced us in front of our friends and peers." Her father's words hurt, sharply stabbing at her psyche. "You wanted nothing to do with your birthright, and then you sit there, as if someone treated you badly? Good Lord, you think you are something more than you truly are." Her father looked at her disbelievingly. "Then you order us to be here, to attend to your ridiculous accusations?"

Hope was stunned. *College romps?* She'd attended two parties held by her carer's daughter. Nothing romp-like about those. And the underwear? What did they think she'd been? A pseudo call girl? They had been gifts, not of her choosing.

"I never—" Hope tried to defend herself.

"You prostituted yourself while away, and expect us to watch you do that here? I don't think so. We heard about your wild parties and behavior. From this day forth, you are no longer our daughter." With that cold pronouncement, her parents turned away.

She sat there, stunned and shattered by their words.

The door crashed open and Xavier barged in.

"Get out! Pack your things and leave the manor. I will arrange an alternative residence for you, but from this day you will never hold the position of *Yeux Secondes* in any nest!" Xavier's face was a mask of fury, his eyes glowed golden and his body shook as he contained his anger.

Her father swept from the room, and her mother scuttled beside him like an obedient puppy. The part she'd always played, just the same as the cold front she'd shown staff.

Hope willed her mother to look back, to say something, anything to make the situation right. The door crashed shut behind them and her hopes were smashed.

Hope watched as Xavier strode angrily around the room, dragging his hand through his hair, which now stood spiking on top of his head, his face drawn with tension and anger.

Feeling like it was a bad movie, Hope tried to ignore the ache inside. She couldn't stem the scalding, silent tears rolling down her cheeks, while she clutched shaking hands, tightly holding on to any form of control she had left. No matter how hard she wished she was imagining the situation, it was real.

A sob erupted, her chest heaving with the force of her emotions. Another sob ripped free and the torrent released. Xavier moved to her, cradling her in his arms, his quiet words and soft touches a balm, while she let the floodgates open, lost in a world of misery.

CHAPTER NINETEEN

avier was furiously angry. As angry as he'd been when he'd first become a vampire, the heat inside him wanting to shred through the civilized veneer he'd spent hundreds of years perfecting.

James had crossed the line with his accusations about Hope, which finally pushed him to have James and Verity removed from the house. The remaining problem, though, was that he no longer had a *Yeux Secondes*, and he needed one. He couldn't possibly run the nest, continue overseeing the investments and protect Hope all at the same time. There was the added factor that he knew her father had been skimming income from the nest. Before everything had blown up, he'd been ready to move against James.

The house was in a state of division with those loyal to James and Verity, and those loyal to the Master and his nest, adding to his problems.

David wasn't ready, but really who else was there? And for that matter, he wasn't sure he could even trust him at this point, his wife almost a carbon clone of Verity. What was her name? Alexandra? No. Alexa.

Something about her sat wrong, but he needed someone to take over from James, and David was the only real contender right now.

He sighed, but even to himself it sounded harried. He'd dig deeper. Only time and information would clarify what it was about the whole situation that stank of a wider conspiracy.

Alexa would have to take orders from Hope, whether she wanted to or not. He wasn't sure how that would work. She'd seemed cool toward Hope, and he thought that maybe he should have Lisi act as some sort of go-between. Offer Hope a break from dealing with the emotional ties of her family for a while. He filed that thought away, and watched her as she tried to find some inner balance.

Hope was a mess, huddled in the corner, her face white. The rage within him, that her father's and mother's comments had raised, threaten to drown him once more. How could they say those things? No one spoke to Hope like that! Not to the woman he loved.

Xavier stopped, inhaled, while he gripped at the bridge of his nose and closed his eyes. The revelation had just rocked his world off its axis. He tried to block it out, but it remained, settling in his chest, warming him through to the core. Cressida had stopped him coming in to intervene, until it had reached a point that he could no longer ignore. With this new understanding of his emotions, he knew why he'd reacted the way he had beforehand. Right now, he had other more weighty concerns than his own emotional ponderings.

God knew if she would be up to the discussion they were due to have about the dreams after this debacle. She was so stressed, she might shatter at a wrong comment. He could see it in the rigid way she held herself, the distance in her eyes. The way she skittered back each time he reached out to soothe her.

He swore viciously in his head, but refused to give in to his anger. She didn't need to deal with any more drama right now.

Cressida rested a hand on his shoulder. "Xavier, take Hope out. Make sure you are well guarded, but let her have some time away from here. I will oversee James and Verity's removal and arrange for David to assume the mantle of *Yeux Secondes* temporarily. Give her a change of scene for a while. Somewhere safe and secure, but get her out of this house for now."

Cressida's words were gentle and understanding, and he turned to see worry on her face. "I don't know if we should. Honestly, Cressida, this whole thing seems off." In the back of his mind he knew someone was passing on information concerning their movements. It had to be someone from within the nest.

Would this time be any different? Could he keep Hope safe, if they left the grounds? Cressida was right, she needed to get away to let some of the stress wash off.

"I agree. But she needs to be away from here now, to recoup. Take her to my home. You will be safe there. I have the grounds heavily warded, so only those invited by me can enter. Hope needs time to heal, even if just for a little while." With those soft words, she reached into her pocket and held out a small talisman. "This will get you through the wards."

He wrapped his fingers around it, squeezed Cressida's hand in mute thanks, then turned back to Hope, who remained seated on the chaise lounge, just as she'd been when her parents had been ordered from the room. His heart thudded, and he wanted to offer her anything that would heal her. If this was the key, then he'd take it.

"I'll take Javed with me, as well as our guards." He turned away, grabbing papers from the desk and shoving the laptop into a bag with fast jerky motions. "Cressida, could you arrange for Lisi to pack Hope's things? Maybe tell them I am taking her to the country house. That way, we might be able to buy some time to get to your estate safely."

Cressida inclined her head, then turned on her heel before heading to the door. She stopped and looked at him. "She is worth so much more than rubies." Then she left him standing, watching Hope in silence.

Sitting in the car beside Xavier, Hope registered the cold, yet she still had a sense of being displaced. Her eyes ached from the crying jag, but she ignored them. Xavier had tried to grab her hand, but she'd pulled away, needing to retreat within herself.

She refused to think of what her parents had said, but as they had rounded the drive, her mother's car had pulled up to the side of the house beside her father's. She'd caught sight of the suitcases being loaded. The lump in her throat grew big enough to choke her. They were leaving.

She closed her eyes and feigned sleep. The sound of the motor running as the car ate up the distance kept her thoughts company. She knew Xavier watched her, but she wanted distance right now, so she could think over what her choices were, or at least what they would be, once they found and dealt with Estersham. Once they dealt with the person within the nest carrying information. Once the rogues had been neutralized and were no longer a threat to the nest.

The trip was swift and within no time the vehicle stopped, but she still had no answers to the questions that kept occurring to her. She opened her eyes, saw Xavier pull a talisman from his pocket and reach for the door. What was happening? She gripped his hand, opening her mouth to ask.

He looked at her, smiling. "It'll be okay, I just need an opening in the wards to let the vehicles pass."

Her stomach flip-flopped. He would be unprotected, and she reached to undo her belt, but he stayed her hand. "No, you stay here. I just need to get the three vehicles through, then I will rejoin you."

She felt sick. Lost in her own little world of misery, she'd forgotten the risks he was taking to protect her.

"But, Xavier..."

"No. Stay there in the vehicle. This will only take a few seconds." He closed the door behind him, and she stared forward.

A cool, heavy, fog-like entity settled over the inside of the old stone wall adorned with an ornate metal gate, and she guessed it was a kind of magical warding. The gates opened, and she watched as he moved forward, gripping the talisman, while they widened enough for him to hold the item in the gray substance. A movement near shrubbery caught her eye, but she ignored it, gazing instead at Xavier.

Then the veil shifted, forming an entryway, just wide enough for the vehicles to pass in single file. He turned back with a slight wave, and Hope observed fascinated as he all but glowed in the heavy clouds. A phenomenon she'd never seen before, or even heard of.

The vehicle roared back to life, an insistent throb beneath her body as it moved, while the crunch of the gravel barely intruded on her survey of Xavier. The car slowly inched past, and she turned so she could continue to see his actions.

The second car moved beyond the fog, entered the grounds, and kept going on Xavier's hand movement, past the car she sat in, then the third inched forward, entered the drive and slowly moved past.

The movement near the shrubs caught her eye again. A figure cloaked in a hooded jacket emerged, just as the fog started to close, and as Xavier stepped through he shuddered, spinning slightly.

Xavier's body fell to the ground, hands outstretched in supplication as he fell. Bright red bloom stained his white shirt, she tugged on the belt, screaming in fear. "Xavier!"

She wrenched on the webbed belt and pulled hard, but it wouldn't give. The car rocked as Javed pulled himself from the vehicle and sped toward the vampire lying on the ground. Fear enveloped her, as she watched Javed lift Xavier into a standing position, and, supporting him, they moved toward the car.

He leaned heavily on Javed. She wanted to help, but the stupid belt wouldn't release, and she sobbed her frustration. The door opened and Javed helped him in. Xavier's shoulder smoked curiously, and he seemed to struggle saying something.

"It's all right, Xavier. We're here…" Her words were frantic. She touched him, needing to feel the warmth of his skin for reassurance that he still lived.

He said just one word, before slumping back into the corner of the seat in a faint. "Talisman."

She thrust a shaking hand to his chest, but the rise and fall assured her he still breathed. "Javed, find the talisman, then head up to the house. We need to get a look at that shoulder and his chest wound."

A quick nod from Javed, a shouted instruction, and the car moved onward, speeding up the long drive as she kept a worried vigil.

When the vehicle drew to a stop, she wrenched off the seatbelt, finally wrestling the clasp open. She shouted instructions to the staff to carry him to a secured room. She snatched up her crutches and followed as swiftly as she could.

A young maid helped her find the room, where the staff already attended him. His shirt lay discarded on the floor in a smoking and bloody mess.

She shook uncontrollably, fearing the worst, until someone stated, "It was a holy water hit. We need to treat this by cleansing the wound site with the blood of a vampire. That will neutralize the spread of the burns then wait until he regains consciousness and give him blood to help the regeneration process."

She watched, fascinated, as one of the maids stepped forward, eyes shining while she tore at her wrist with long teeth. Blood welled forward, and the vampire held the torn wrist over the injury to Xavier's chest and shoulder.

For an instant jealousy rose, with a nasty oily feel that churned inside her gut. *It should be me.* She pushed the thought away. Now wasn't the time for pettiness, but the thought had free rein. If she fed him, would he be able to stop in time? Another thought intruded, leaving her breathless for a moment. She really didn't want to embrace the virus…did she? All it would take is one bite to begin the process. Would he be able to stop before he reached the death drop? The thought was both enticing and horrific.

Hope moved forward, seeing the blood trickle over his skin, evaporating as it touched the injury at first, but then sliding down in a red river, over his exposed chest. The helpers turned him over, the action repeated on his shoulder, her stomach churning as she watched their unhurried movements.

Emotions overwhelmed her. She wanted to push the maid away from him. Didn't they realize he was hers? Right now, he needed something she couldn't give him, so she had to be thankful they could care for him. Didn't mean she had to like it.

The smell of copper rose in her nostrils, and she gulped watching the proceedings. Javed moved into the room, stepping close and hugging her. She took the comfort he offered with a whispered, "Thank you."

The vampire maid took a step back. Xavier moved. "Hope?" The words were quiet, but the most beautiful thing she'd ever heard. She moved to him, controlling the tears that wanted to escape, touching him.

"Don't you ever frighten me like that again." Then she leaned forward to chastely kiss his lips.

The whisper of his breath upon her mouth felt like a magical gift bestowed, and she let a short prayer of thankfulness loose in her mind. The knot that had been in her chest from the time he'd fallen forward let go and she relaxed against him.

He made to sit up and she pushed him back down. "You need to rest, Xavier."

"I'm fine. I need to drink and then I will heal."

She looked at him. Who would he feed from? The narrowness of his pupils told her it needed to be soon. She thrust her wrist forward, her stomach quivering slightly as she shook.

"Take it from me, Xavier." He looked at her, and shook his head.

"Not this time." His eyes were sad, but his voice was firm. "I may not be able to stop myself in time, Hope."

She pushed her wrist forward again. "You'll be fine. Take it from me." No way would she watch him feed from someone else. That would kill her, seeing the deeply erotic movements as he fed from another, knowing that many vampires found it incredibly arousing. If he was going to be aroused, then she was damned sure it would be by her...and her blood. The primitive attitude wiped every other thought from her mind.

"Hope. Please not this time. I don't know that I could stop in time." His tone was insistent, but when she glanced around, she noted the room was empty and the door shut.

"It's just you and me, Xavier. Please take it from me." Her lips trembled and he sighed.

"Come here then. Take off your top, I don't want to stain it." He closed his eyes and reclined into the bed he was lying on, as if the effort was too much. She pushed the crutches to one side, steadying herself on the edge of the bed and reached for the waist of her top, pulling it over her head and flinging it to the floor.

With eyes closed, he motioned for her wrist and pulled it to his mouth, shifting so that she slumped beside him. She raised the leg still encased in the ugly boot, so it lay on the bed, and she followed it down to the soft mattress.

Now she lay beside him on the bed, her arm stretched to his mouth, where he kissed and laved the sensitive flesh. She closed her eyes, and let the pleasure of his touch wash over her. The feel of his tongue and teeth, rasping over the skin of her arm, was both shocking and exciting at the same time and she moaned.

He moved from her arm, the skin tingling as he touched her. Flames ignited inside her body, and she squirmed beneath his lips as they roamed over her bare skin, hot and needy. Now he loomed over her, pushing the straps of her tiny white bra away with trembling fingers.

She panted with need, aroused at the eroticism of the moment. Her breasts peaked and dampness pooled between her legs. He moved to her throat, and she moaned again, on fire with hunger. Finally his teeth grazed her skin, followed by the sharp instant of penetration, the sting replaced with draws, as he took his sustenance from her. Elation roared. She gifted him with the one thing that would heal him.

Her heart rate increased at the feel of him reaching down her body to pull up her skirt, and his hands quested under the little white panties. He combed his fingers through the damp hairs, seeking her cleft, and the part of her that ached with need.

She arched upwards, welcoming the twin pleasures at her neck and between her legs. He enticed her with his fingers, entering her core, where he found her hot, slick and ready. He groaned his pleasure against her skin.

Hope moaned again. He raised his head. It wasn't bloodlust, but passion that darkened his eyes, and he moved his lips to hers. For an instant the coppery tang of her blood shocked then aroused her further. She licked the drops from his tongue and fire streaked through her system.

"More," she demanded against his lips. She needed more of that lightning taste, her body urging her on, and once more she swept her tongue over his lips, still wet with her blood, uncaring now of anything keeping them apart.

Hope reached for his zipper while he unhooked her bra lost in the passion of the moment. Undulating against his hand as she freed him from the constriction of pants and boxers, she palmed his cock, warm in her hand. She gloried, knowing that it was hard and engorged with want for her. The thick ridges beneath her fingers told her of his readiness, as did the bead of liquid at its tip.

He grabbed her skirt and pulled. The sharp noise as it ripped rent the air. She arched beneath him, wild with passion, and she felt the air on her nearly naked body.

"Oh, God!" she cried. He tugged on her panties. "Don't rip them. I love them." Her head thrown back, her nipples exquisite points of sharp, hard pleasure, she realized he'd pulled them down over her boot. She splayed her legs wide. Wanting and needing the pleasure of his body, his hands, even his mouth on her. She keened in her throat, once more in appeal.

He fastened his lips to the skin at her throat, positioning himself between her thighs. "More, Xavier! Please!" Her words were hoarse with arousal and she shook.

His touch roamed over her sweaty flesh.

She felt his blunt shaft at her entry, felt his push, as his teeth once more entered her skin, his movements mirroring his carnal feeding. She pushed his mouth away, and instead demanded his kiss.

He thrust within her body and she met it, pulling him deeper, both of them gripping the other, demanding the ecstasy just beyond their grasp.

She pulled his face to hers, seeking the coppery taste once more of his wet mouth. Swiping a hungry tongue over his blood-tainted lips while she exploded around him. Aware of the coppery tang filling her head, so heady and rich, her body splintered beneath his.

The long pulls of her body's muscles welcomed his orgasm, milking him, and the wish of one last thrust, one last pull, filled her to bursting point, as she felt him come apart in her arms.

The sensation of him jetting into her body completed her as never before.

They stilled, panting in each other's arms, the aftermath of their cataclysmic loving a revelation. She smiled sleepily, as she lay quietly until a sharp pain racked her, tearing through her head, intense and sharp.

She gripped both sides of her head, but the pain grew exponentially. "Ahhh…"

All other senses dulled with the pain of the initial explosion that continued to grow. Her stomach roiled in defense while she curled against the tremors that were now racking her body. "Dear God, what's happening to me?"

She was even more shocked to realize she'd asked the words out loud, but the pain in her head increased. She moaned loudly, bile rising in her throat.

She slumped back in his arms, her breath coming in wild pumping gasps. Her mouth stung viciously. Hot tears leaked from between tightly closed lids.

Xavier swung his arms around her, as she experienced vertigo and her limbs going almost soft and boneless. "Oh, I really don't feel so great," Hope moaned, holding onto her head, the seesaw sensation increasing.

"My eyes hurt," she whimpered. He swung her up into his arms. The grip of darkness filled in at the edges of her vision, creeping closer before finally overtaking her.

CHAPTER TWENTY

ope woke. The buzzing nearby was annoying so she flicked at the mosquito, finally realizing that there wasn't one. The noise continued, but she couldn't pinpoint exactly what it was. Hope opened her eyes, and the light, shining brightly above, hurt them. She moaned. At least she thought it was her. Loud and guttural.

Her mouth hurt, it was dry and irritated. In fact, her whole head hurt, but especially her jaw, and she tried to think if there had been an accident.

Thinking back hurt, but all that came to mind was the amazing sex she'd enjoyed with Xavier, after he'd fed from her.

The intensity of it had caught her unaware. Hope attempted a smile, groaning as the move made her face throb. She raised her fingers to touch the side of her mouth. Something protruded from her aching gums. Something sharp. Long. The touch stung her flesh a little, and she gasped at the unfamiliar sensation.

What is going on? The thought reverberated through her aching brain.

A movement close by caught her attention. A hand. Male. Short hairs dotted along the pale skin. She looked up. Xavier.

"Where am I?" The words slipped from her lips. Awkward, muffled and almost lisped, and it certainly didn't sound like her.

"You're awake. How do you feel?" Xavier leaned over her, and she thought about how anxious he sounded, the soft touch of his hand upon her skin. She took a quick inventory of how she felt. Her leg no longer ached and she felt full of energy.

"I... Fine. Actually, better than I did before the attack on the cars. Why?" Her head still had that filled-with-cotton-wool sensation, but even now that was dissipating. "Where am I and what happened?"

He looked uncomfortable, opened his mouth, closed it as he seemed to think better of his original answer, then opened it again. "We're at Cressida's." He swung away, stepping to the end of the bed and coming back, his hair standing up in crazy spikes that made her smile. She grimaced again. "There has been a slip-up, though." He seemed so upset, leaving her puzzled and wondering what could have happened.

"What's wrong, Xavier? Why does my head feel odd and my mouth hurt?"

"Oh, God!" Xavier's lids closed over his pained green eyes for a second, before opening again. A seed of doubt filled her... "Hope, I don't know how to tell you. There was an accident...when we made love." Did he drink too much? Leave her with too little blood that needed some attention? Had he been a little rough?

"Xavier, I told you to drink. Did you take too much? I'm still here, so all is fine." She relaxed, but his face was still white and drawn. "It's okay. Really." Somehow he didn't look like that was sufficient to absolve his guilt, and a seed of dread sprouted in her mind. "Xavier?"

"It isn't that, Hope. When I fed from you, we got a little carried away. It seems the antibodies and virus within your body do not make you immune to the virus. You must have ingested some of your own blood. We already knew I wasn't susceptible unless I..."

She watched him closely as she swallowed. "What? What happened?"

When he opened them, there was devastation on his face. A deep pain evident in his eyes. "Hope? I turned you. You're now a vampire."

Hope scooted back on the bed, away from his words. *Turned?* "No.

No. No." The words dripped like icicles, and even as she said them, sharp pains crashed through her head. "No way. You have to exchange blood for that, and I sure haven't ingested any of yours." She shook her head from side to side.

He moved forward, and with each step he took closer to her, she scooted a little farther away from his touch, as if it was going to brand her.

The pained expression on Xavier's face caught her attention. Pained! What about her life? She didn't want to become a vampire. It had never featured in her daydreams.

She hadn't been one of those kids who wrote 'Dear diary, when I grow up, I want to be a blood-sucking, eternal, light-denied vampire!'

Hysteria grew. "No. I don't want to be a vampire."

He winced. "I'm so sorry, Hope. Sometime during our lovemaking, you must have ingested some of my blood. Do you remember..." God, his faced turned red, as if he struggled with the words. "Ahh...being... with me?" His words seemed uncertain, and she nearly threw up, as she knew exactly what had happened.

She'd been hot and so very ready. Something had begun, when he'd taken her wrist and his mouth had wandered up her body. God help her, she'd been turned on by the time he'd finished. It had been rough and wild. She had a vague recollection of kissing him, tasting...

That was it! When he'd kissed her, she'd tasted it. The blood with its coppery tang and she'd wanted more. The thought crashed as another surge of pain rocketed through her. Her head felt like it was going to split on either side of her mouth.

"Ahhh!" The pain took voice, and she reached to grab either side of her head. She could see his face, horror filling his visage. "What. Is. Happening. To. Me?" Her stomach roiled and her mouth was dry.

"Your fangs are descending for the first time. The pain will pass soon, but we need you to feed." He thrust out his wrist, and she noticed the shirt sleeves rolled up.

"How long have I been...changing?"

"Three days. At first you were like a...corpse. There was no rousing you. That is when we removed your boot. The second day you moaned a lot, but I stayed here with you. I know you don't have any recollection, but Cressida has been in to check you a couple of times as well." He tried to keep her calm. She could see the agitation he was trying to cover with the quiet voice and slow movements. The clenched fist, the tight way he held his lips and the set of his shoulders. "You need to feed first, and then we can talk." The voice called to her, as a ripple sounded through the room, the pulsing sound mesmerizing her. What was it?

She sniffed. Her mouth watered, and her vision narrowed to a pinprick. She saw him, the red glowing pulse of his veins as they throbbed with the liquid she wanted. Needed. She licked her lips. Her head ached viciously, and she knew she needed to feed to stop it. Hope closed her eyes.

The sound grew louder, the rhythmic whooshing, as footsteps came closer. She felt the touch of a warm hand on hers, gently extending his wrist to her. She felt it being guided toward her mouth. She snapped her eyes open.

His wrist rested mere inches from her lips, the veins tracing under the pale skin, and the thirst raged inside her. She snatched it up to her mouth, as her stomach churned painfully. She tasted the saltiness of his skin, and slid her tongue along his arm. He pressed up with a quick jerk, piercing the flesh with her teeth, like a rich ripe peach, and the first spurt hit her taste buds. The taste! So full and delicious!

The first draw exploded on her tongue, just as a fine full-bodied wine would, and she drew again, more this time and faster. Each suck seemed to do something to her. The first opened her to the taste, the second eased her thirst, but the third, dear God, her body tightened with the third.

The erotic pull of the act filled her and left her empty at the same time. Made her loins ache, an ache that only he could assuage. It pulled at her, from her mouth to her heart and all the way to her cleft, and she felt a heat pool once more, deep down inside. This was stronger, deeper and far more primitive.

Hope pulled away from his wrist, as he leaned forward, toward her lips. His deep green eyes were darker and more mesmerizing than she'd ever noticed before. Deeper and greener than the pools she'd originally likened them to. Like the bottomless ponds she'd seen on some of the estates she'd visited. His were so warm and inviting, surrounded by thick lashes that reminded her of the fine fern fronds that fringed tropical pools, inviting wells of forever.

She whimpered at the loss of the dark liquid, but the exhalation of pleasure that quickly overtook her was filled with a longing she couldn't contain. She watched as he reached for her. Hope closed her eyes once more, against the tight and lustful look upon his face, but other senses took over. She could smell him—his aroused musky scent filled the air.

She reached out, letting her touch skate over the tight planes of his chest, covered in fine cotton. She wrenched it out of the way, hearing the tear of material. The heaving chest below, then she heard the hiss of his breath.

She opened her eyes and gazed at him, taking in the golden tinge around his irises, as his passion for her rose.

This time the pleasure was rough and quick. Tearing at each other's clothing with sharp questing fingers. The need was a pain that had to be stilled. She arched. Her sensitive nipples met his hard chest, rubbing and abrading against his skin.

Only him. Only he could fill her need. "Xavier?" Buttons flew, as his pants tore under her quick hands. The sheet that had covered her was flung to the floor, forgotten, as it lay with his discarded and ruined shirt, joined by his leather belt, pants and boxers. The shredding, loud in her ears, and tongues quested in wet-seeking mouths, even as their clothes fluttered to the floor, forgotten heaps of torn cloth.

"I'm right here. With you." And he was there. Oh, God! On the bed with her, above her, so fast there was no time for any foreplay as he shoved himself into her body, but she was as wet and ready as he was hard. His fully engorged shaft entered with a swift thrust, and she cried out, glorying in the sensation of him moving within her tight, hot sheath, pushing her toward completion. He filled her totally, and the sound of their movements rang loud in her ears.

Slapping flesh thudded loudly while they moved and undulated on the rumpled sheets. The smell of sex filled the room, enhancing the senses that already cried out to her. "More! Oh, please, more!"

The explosion was cataclysmic. They orgasmed together, the long hot pulse of his jetted semen, salty in fragrance, mixing with her damp musky fluid. The dying sounds of their incoherent words of passion echoed in the room.

They lay still, one holding onto the other, hearts screaming as they beat against sweaty bodies, still heaving as they gulped down air.

She held onto him while their skin cooled. Their smells still filled the air, enticing, and she opened her eyes. She cleared her throat and he watched. Dear God, he was still inside her, watching her. "Will it always be like this?" Too late, she realized she'd said the words aloud.

"I have never experienced anything like that before." His words were uneven and strained, as he raised a shaky hand to her face, pushing back strands of black hair that tangled in his hand.

He chastely set his forehead against hers. She closed her eyes too, letting the silence slip around them like an old glove.

What would happen next? For a moment she didn't care. She had Xavier in her arms, and whatever came next she was sure they would face it together.

"Yes." His word came out of nowhere, ending her reverie.

"Yes? Yes, what?" She jerked upright against him.

"Yes, we will work this out together." She pulled back, confused. She'd just thought about them working it out—in her mind. Now, he was answering. A cold prickle at the nape of her neck rose as suspicion grew.

"I just thought that." She felt her brow furrow with confusion. "How did you know what I was thinking?" The words tumbled out. Hurried and harsh and needing an honest answer.

"Because you and I are linked now. By blood." He watched her. His face was devoid of emotion, and she felt a cold shiver pass through her system. No secrets? "What do you mean linked? Does that mean you can read my mind?" *No way!* That was so wrong if he could read her mind. She looked for something to cover herself with, but there was nothing. She made to disengage their bodies, but he stopped her.

"Wait, Hope. Not in so many words." Twin sensations of hurt and sadness, formed a hollow pit in her stomach at the loss she heard in his voice. "I can sense your emotions, and when you're unguarded, I can read your thoughts. Before you wanted to know whether we could or would work through this together, and I answered you. Verbally. If you drop your defenses, I can talk to you in other ways as well."

She slumped back. The enormity of the link overwhelmed her but she was prepared to try. For Xavier.

Now that you have dropped your natural shield, I can talk to you this way as well. Yes. I can hear you and you can hear me. It is a kind of defense mechanism. It allows me to keep you safe. To be in constant contact, and aware of your physical condition so that I can protect you. Xavier closed his eyes, as if trying to decide how best to explain. "It works both ways, stops me from putting you in danger, allowing me to communicate distress or defensive tactics, and it stops us from surprising the other with an attack."

His lips curled up with self-derision. "It only works if we are open to each other and both want it." He reached toward her, but Hope shied back, pulling her hand away, and his dropped back down.

"Do we have to be in the same room together, and how did this link thing form anyway?" Questions. So many questions to be asked and things she never knew to learn.

"No, we don't need to be in the same room, but within a reasonable vicinity, depending on age, experience and ability. As for the other, that is simple. We shared blood when I turned you. In turn, you fed from me. All those things come together, like a chemical reaction. My age also played a part. I am several hundred years old, so my blood is strong and you benefited from it. You took sustenance from me." He dropped his eyes for a moment, and she felt a frisson of alarm race through her system. Hers or his? She couldn't tell.

"If you want me to leave, though, just say the word and I will go. I'll leave you with Cressida. I know she would ensure your safety and placement in a suitable nest." He pulled back from her, and she felt a wrench, not just physical but emotional. Like he was tearing her into pieces with his emotional distance, and her whole body rebelled at the thought.

"No!" The words erupted from her lips. Anguished. She grabbed his shoulder. "Please don't go." She was confused, hurt, angry, frightened and when all was said and done, this had not been his fault, and to be brutally honest, she wanted him to stay with her. No matter what had happened, she wouldn't lie to herself.

And yes, though she wasn't ready to tell him, she loved him. She let the thought filter, as she imagined a thick brick wall between them, hiding the words from his view. God, she hoped it was enough. It had to be enough, at least for now, until they were ready to face their emotions together.

He didn't react, so she hugged the knowledge to herself, taking stock of her situation. They could talk telepathically. She was a vampire, now wholly reliant on a blood supply. Damn. How would her parents take that?

The times were a-changing, and she had to work out what she needed to do in order to survive her new reality. Needed to know what she had to do to emerge whole and intact, physically if not emotionally, at least. She closed her eyes, and breathed in and out heavily. "What do we do now?" She let the question hang in the air, as she searched his face.

'*What do we do now?*' The words were a gift. He wanted to whoop with exultation. Ever since the session on the night he was attacked, he'd been waiting for her to wake. Yell at him. Rail that she'd been changed against her will, even though they both knew it was an accident.

"Cressida needs to see you, but you may want to shower and dress before seeing her. Then, I guess we need to work out how the... change...affects the dynamics of our problems."

She watched him, her face luminous as he'd never seen before. The shadows below her eyes were finally gone, her lips redder than he'd seen before, while her eyes themselves sparkled with a new light and strength. The whole time she'd been unconscious, during the change, he'd stayed beside her. How could he not? It was his fault, even if accidentally.

"Well then, I guess you had better show me to the bathroom and help me find some clothes."

He helped her off the bed and she smiled at him. He slipped a robe over her naked skin, and found a matching one for himself, thankful that the day shades were pulled down. The sun would set very soon, but even dappled or darkening sun would fry her to little more than ash, and having come this far, he wasn't willing to take chances with her safety. Not when forever was a possibility yet to be explored.

"Through here." He padded to a large door and opened it onto a luxurious bathroom. Black marble on the floor and walls, and she gasped, taking in the deeply sunken bath. One large slab of etched marble was fitted with pressure jets, the shower opening to the bathroom, large and fitted with a power spray head. The silver metal used to make the taps had been polished until it shone brightly.

She stood, looking around, obviously fascinated and he had to remind himself her senses, now enhanced for the first time, would be seeing things in detail she'd never before encountered.

He closed the door behind them, and watched hungrily as she shrugged the robe from her shoulders. The dim lighting, enough for his sight, allowed him to see every curve and dip of her body and slowly she turned to look at him, and he could see the hunger banked in her eyes. She stepped toward him, loosening the knot in his sash, letting it spring open, so the air caressed his skin.

"Well, Xavier, now that we're both vampires and the night hasn't settled yet, we have time." She grinned, and her little twin fangs peeked at him from between the luscious cherry red lips.

She pushed the covering back off his shoulders, and the slide of the material made him shiver as nerves reacted to the erotic sensory delights.

"Hope, you are such a deliciously sexy woman." He watched her.

Giving this woman total completion was quickly becoming his drug of choice.

She moved closer and placed her hands on his shoulders, slowly running her soft fingertips down his arms, finding where the fine cotton had snagged on his elbows and pushing it down his arms where it fell in a heap upon the floor. His body pulsed in reaction, and he could smell her arousal. Soft and musky. He moved to touch her, but she pushed his hand away.

"No. This one is my turn." Her voice was husky and sultry in the silent room and he gulped while he closed his eyes.

She reached out, grasping his erection in her hand. His cock stood hard and proud springy hairs covered his sac. He groaned, and let his head fall back, accepting her wordless worship of his body. Widening his stance he gave her what she wanted, which he knew was everything. "I want you, lover. All of you."

Then she swooped, letting her wet, hot tongue traverse his chest. A damp trail lit by fiery electricity followed in the wake of the magic she made. She found one nipple, licking it lightly before suckling. Then she moved and he felt the stroke of her breasts, as they abraded him when she swayed gently.

She laved the other nub with mouth and tongue, and all he felt was her tender touches, while he fisted his hands against the wall. The gentle pump of her hand on his cock, the other holding his shoulder as she moved from side to side, had him short of breath and sweating.

He raised his hands, grasping her shoulders, but not touching her in any other way, though the scent of her musk grew heavier in the air around him. He drank it in, accepting her arousal. Feeling her beautiful distended buds growing harder and tighter with each pass of her skin on his.

Oh God, Hope. Let me touch you. He pushed the thought toward her and her breath hitched. Instead of stepping away and letting him help, she slowly sank to the floor as she tongued a hot wet track down his belly toward his pelvis.

Her hot breath washed over his erection, and he knew what was going to happen. He felt the welling of fluid and squeezed his eyes tighter, as the wet glove of her mouth surrounded his hot engorged flesh.

Her lips sucking on him made him rock slightly, and she moaned. *Oh yes, Xavier, just like that.*

His body ignited. He was on fire with burning need. The stimulation of her tongue, setting off tiny firework like explosions all over his skin, drove him to the edge. She touched his sac and he nearly exploded.

Enough. The thought was a growl, and he wrenched her away, pulling her up, so that they were finally lip to lip and chest to chest.

She swung her legs around, encased his hips, then he slid into her warm, tight sheath, groaning with pleasure at the heat and wetness surrounding him. She cried out, and he pumped her, their rhythms matching, while she rode with a wild abandon. Her lips had opened and his tongue found its way into her mouth.

He grabbed her ass, squeezing and kneading while they moved, hot and fast.

Oh God, Xavier. Give me more! He could hear her thoughts, and he gave her the same back.

So beautiful. I want to touch you all over, rub you, suck you until you come, screaming. He pushed the thought toward her, pumping her, his engorged penis thrusting in and out of her tight core until the final push.

Her body started to milk his length, tight movements while her womb worked its final magic on him. He felt the rush, and he emptied his seed within her. She screamed in time with the warm jetting of fluid, while he held tight to her.

Her scream of delight faded, as he held her against his thumping heart.

I will never let you go now. You are mine. Body and soul. He wordlessly vowed to her, one he'd never given before. He held the most precious bundle in his arms. This woman, so beautiful and giving, was now his.

Their skin started to cool and he released her enough to slide down his body to the floor. She smiled, and his heart thumped once more. He reached for the shower and ushered her in.

CHAPTER TWENTY-ONE

ear God. I have become the most wanton female ever. What was I thinking in the bathroom? Not that she was embarrassed—far from it. Perhaps now, knowing she was a vampire had removed the restrictions of her upbringing, allowing her to finally express who and what she was. She shook her head. No. She allowed herself the honesty she swore by. It was all Xavier.

Yes, she wanted him, but there was more. Her hunger for him was fueled by the wish he would never leave. She reminded herself he'd never promised her love. She pulled on the black pants she found in the bottom of her bag, and teamed it with a red bustier top. She usually wore it under a shirt with the top buttons undone, but his naked approval of her outfit made her rethink the shirt. It was still warm, though the nights were cooling. He threw her a leather jacket and nodded when she held up the long black boots. A weakness her mother had always detested, but, she reminded herself, what her mother wanted no longer mattered.

Hope fastened her hair in a loose knot at the top of her head, while watching Xavier choose his own clothing including an open-necked white shirt and black shoes. She raked her gaze over his rugged form and she had to close her eyes.

Keep up those lecherous thoughts and we will never get down to Cressida. Then we will have a problem when she comes up here to check on you. The thought was filled with mirth and she laughed out loud.

"All right, I'm ready now. Take me to your leader." She giggled again, and realized she didn't do that very often.

"No, you don't. I love the sound." He smiled, and she saw his eyes crinkle as he held a hand out to her. She took it and together they left the room, moved along the hallway and down the wide stairs. They descended together, and she could see Cressida, immaculate as always, in a pale cream suit watching them. A broad smile wreathed her face.

"My darling Hope and Xavier. I am so pleased both of you are well. Now, Hope, has Xavier explained about the change?" Her eyes sparkled and for an instant Hope was amazed. This strong woman was excited that she'd changed?

"Umm. Sort of." How else could she answer? She glanced over at Xavier.

"I have explained what happened, how she turned. I haven't explained the hierarchy, though. I thought you may wish to do that." He bowed slightly and Hope goggled. She imagined him as a courtier, and was shocked at the reminder of how little she knew of his past. That was something she would remedy. *Soon*, she promised herself, giving her full attention to Cressida.

"Yes, we should start with the hierarchy. Come and sit down while we work through this. It will take some time." Cressida indicated a love seat and she quietly took one side, arching an eyebrow as Xavier took the other. She looked back at Cressida, and saw the approval in her eyes. Cressida always had a kind word or smile for her, Hope realized. What else had she missed?

"There are layers in our world. You know a little of the Council. We have one Overlord on each continent, and the head of the Council acts as an adviser to the Overlord. Our Overlord is Gianna. You will likely meet her at some point, but not yet. Unless this goes badly, that is." She wondered at the distraction in Cressida's words, but kept her counsel. After all, she could ask Xavier later. "The Council is made up of fifteen vampires, each representing a group of nests. We are elected by our peers and hold the title until death, or in some circumstances we can step down."

"I formed an alliance with Philippe, as you know, and on his death, Cyrus assumed his position on the Council."

Hope sat up straight at that. "No. I never understood why you left or how Cyrus ended up Master. Only that in the last six months he ascended to the Council." Hope watched as Cressida harrumphed angrily.

"Fine, briefly, when you were taken, we had no formal alliance. There are some important facts you need to learn, but because we lost so many of the vampire members of the nest, there was no protection once I came for you. So we tied ourselves to many nests. We formed an alliance, which became the basis of all our current alliances with other nests, making us stronger."

Hope sat still, fingers twined with Xavier's as she listened.

"As you know, once we take the death drop or the final drop from a body, it can bring the feral and primitive aspect of our nature to the forefront. That is the reason I had to leave. I wasn't safe around humans, because I took so many that night. Cyrus joined the nest, bringing some of his nest mates with him to bring in and train new guards. Ensuring your safety at all times." Cressida paused.

"It was only a temporary option, as he was always meant to be the next Councilor. Once Councilor Philippe chose to die, Cyrus had to accept the call to ascend. Xavier was the next best trained for the role, which is how he became Master of your nest. It was a sad loss to our community, yet Philippe passed doing what he believed was the right and honorable thing. The nests had to make the necessary changes once again." Cressida placed a trembling hand to her lips and Hope waited, understanding that it was still hard for her to discuss her own losses, after having been friends for so long.

"Back to our hierarchy. Each nest has a Master or Mistress to whom all other vampires are either placed as guards or staff, dependent on their skills, abilities and training."

Cressida stopped, watching Hope and for a moment she felt like she was under a microscope. "Other than that, any other vampires are considered rogues and untrustworthy. Each and every vampire makes oaths at the time of changing, and then they assume positions. Hope, I must formally ask you to declare your oaths to Xavier as your Master, to me as Council member and to Gianna as Overlord." Each word now carried magic and she felt the words as physical bindings, wrapping around her, unseen but tangible.

Her chest tightened.

"Can you and will you uphold our hierarchy, our way of life and our commitment to the common goal of a peaceful existence? Will you give your future service to those who would guide and protect you? Will you give your life for your brother and sister vampires, and for the protection of the nest you are assigned to?" The air filled with electricity, streaking around them as lights sparked here and there.

A choice. She must make a choice. In the end, what choice was there? "What happens if I refuse?" The words filled the silence, and for a moment the crashing of lights blinded her.

"A good question, Hope. We either declare you rogue, turning you out and upon the mercy of others who will likely kill you or use you for their own ends, or we work to educate you. Quickly." Cressida's eyes were clouded and tired, and for the first time Hope appreciated the enormity of the task this vampire had accepted.

Xavier squeezed her hand. She turned to him, knowing what must be in his mind already. She could sense his concern and worry. She smiled and he carefully smiled back, but his eyes remained grave. "I accept the oath." She whispered the words and felt the tension rush from Xavier's body. The air around them skittered once more. She smelt a vanilla essence on the air and closed her eyes, inhaling.

"You have chosen to abide by our oaths. It has been accepted and I welcome you to our world." Cressida moved forward and quickly hugged Hope, whose hand was still in the grip of Xavier's. She got the impression of genuine delight, which filled her with warmth all the way through her body. "Now Xavier has requested you be entrusted to his nest, and I cannot see any reason to decide differently. I believe, Xavier, you have a further request?"

Hope swiveled to look at him, who was looking very uncomfortable.

He cleared his throat, and Hope was surprised to see a blush creeping up his face. "Cressida. She isn't ready yet." He glared at Cressida who seemed amused.

"I believe you may be surprised by her answer." She reached a hand over Xavier and Hope's joined hands. "I believe you will make an excellent life partner for Xavier. I could declare it by decree, but that wouldn't be fair. To either of you." She grinned, and, letting go, sat back upon her seat, her eyes on Xavier.

"Hope, I know it's early, but when this is over, I would be so proud if you would consider becoming my life mate." His chest heaved as he spoke the words rapidly.

Something inside her bloomed, like a flower.

Xavier wanted her? As a life mate? Did that mean he loved her? She was unsure—it had only been weeks. Sure, he'd been kind and caring, good-natured and the world's most fabulous lover, but that didn't necessarily mean love.

"Xavier, I will consider it, but…" She floundered for the words that would give her time to think. She blinked rapidly as she cleared the burning sensation that filled her eyes. Xavier wanted her! She needed time, to find out what he thought and how he felt. "We need time. So, I will think about it." She smiled weakly. He looked at her and the crimson tide remained, but some of the wariness that had flashed into his eyes during the short speech had disappeared.

Cressida stood up, obviously satisfied with the conversational direction. "Xavier, you and Hope have some serious work to do, and I have a Council meeting to convene. I have cleared you to use the salon. Xavier, dear, you know where it is. I must go."

Xavier and Hope stood. Cressida turned to leave, but as she reached just beyond the seating area, she turned. "I really am pleased you joined us, Hope." Then she left the area, unhurried, and Hope listened to the tapping of her heels and the opening and closing of the door. Then it was quiet again.

It had been a long session, talking over the last dream, which now seemed like a faraway nightmare. Each time she replayed it, she saw something new. The way Estersham talked, the stones beneath the feet of both Javed and Xavier, but, somehow, something seemed just out of reach. There was some facet that eluded her.

For hours they had to'ed and fro'ed over the details. And now exhaustion pulled ruthlessly at her.

"It's time to call it a day." His amused voice sounded behind her, and she sagged against the chair, head hurting once more. "Are you all right, Hope?"

She simply shrugged. She was tired, but surely this was normal? It was probably nothing to get concerned about.

"Yeah, just a bit sleepy." Her voice must have given away the depth of her exhaustion, though. He moved around the sofa to pick her up.

"Hey, what are you doing?" She moved in his arms, hoping he would let her down.

"It's almost sunrise and you are dead on your feet. Come on, time for bed, my princess." He hefted her, and she swung her arms around him, holding on for dear life. He moved toward the heavy door and beyond it, across the empty foyer and up the stairs. To the room she thought of as theirs.

Tiredness played at the edges of her mind, and she let herself rest against him, thinking over the dreams they had discussed. Something had definitely changed and she could almost see the answer, dancing just beyond sight. She sighed and snuggled closer, floating in a haze of well-being.

Xavier carefully placed her on the bed, his touch gentle as he brushed her hair from her face. The fog invaded her mind, though she could have sworn the last words she heard before dropping into the arms of Morpheus were, "I love you, Hope."

Then there was darkness.

CHAPTER TWENTY-TWO

After a goblet of blood-infused wine, well before dawn, Hope stretched. The first classes and self-defense had her muscles tightly bunched, and she knew that, no matter how hard she tried, Xavier knew of her discomfort. His eyes shone with concern for her.

"We can do this tomorrow night." In his hands was a sheaf of papers and she knew it was the addresses of the real estate holdings.

"No. We need to get it done tonight. I sense we're running out of time." She placed the goblet down and leaned both elbows on the table, placing her chin in her hands. "We need to try to work out the property, so we can take adequate measures to safeguard the people who are within." Her stomach knotted at the thought of what she saw each day. Bile burned in her throat as it did each time she considered the situation. The scenes from her dreams continued to revolve in her mind.

She was tired, just as she always seemed to be at this time of night. It had been the same since her turning, but she had to keep going. Too much time elapsed, and a sense of urgency gripped her. Seven nights had passed and, realistically, she didn't know how much time they had left. Each night the dream grew more vivid and detailed.

Xavier laid the first sheets in front of her, and opened up a laptop.

"These are the properties the Council owns and controls." She looked down the list. Blood banks, hospices, residential units and shops. The list was extensive, detailed and long.

Addresses were written next to each holding. She pulled the laptop closer, peering at the screen. Methodically, Hope started working through the list, checking each location and searching for a corresponding image on the Internet. It was time-consuming and mind-numbing, and before she knew it, she was reliving the dream from the night before.

Darkness gathered as the booming sound echoed across the street. She, Javed and Xavier were running as fast as they could toward the building, her heart thudding in her chest, threatening to choke her. The building, stark white before, was now lit up from within. There was a crash of thunder, or it could even have been an earthquake, and the ground around them shuddered from the force.

Lights or fire flashed from the windows and people screamed, filling the air with blood-curdling sounds of agony and despair. Black clouds billowed from windowless openings, and rolling creaks and metallic groans emanated from the building as it shuddered in its death throes. Some people made it out, and the smell of blood filled the air that threatened her with a hunger, fierce in intensity. She pushed it aside. People, their clothes and bodies blackened by smoke, spilled out of the building. Others screamed from within, rending the air.

A wicked blade slashed in front of them and an army of vampires appeared, smiling broadly amidst the chaos. Xavier pulled a UV gun from the holster he wore, but was too slow and took the first hit on his arm. Hope battled another, the whip in her hand slashing through the air, the crack lost in the cacophony around them. She slashed again, and hit one in the face. He went down screaming. She pulled a UV gun and shot him. It hit him in the center of his chest and his body stilled, turned gray and disintegrated in front of her.

She felt a slash across her back and a white-hot burst of pain seared her. She heard Xavier call and turned. One vampire stood behind him, his sword raised, and she yellled a warning. He turned and the blow from a sword connected with his chest. She screamed when he fell, saw him raise his gun as he went down and let loose another round. Yet another vampire was there and he rolled. A blond vampire came forward, and with one tremendous thrust found Xavier's throat. Hope screamed, over and over again, high-pitched sounds of anguish. Beyond Xavier, Javed lay still. His blood spilled on the dirty concrete.

This couldn't be. It wasn't right.

She'd woken screaming. Xavier's arms tight around her. He spoke words of comfort as she shook uncontrollably. The door had flung open and Cressida herself had rushed in.

Hope had been only dimly aware, though, while she shuddered and shivered. The screams that hurt her throat slowly died down to sobs that racked her body. She shivered not from the cold so much as from a reaction to the hideous sounds and sights, but she had instinctively curled into the warmth of Xavier.

He rocked her back and forth, holding her close until exhaustion brought with it a dubious calm. She lay in his arms, unable to move away for fear the dream would come back. She refused to shut her eyes.

"Hope, it's okay. I'm here. No one will hurt you." His words had finally penetrated the cloud of fear and despair gripping her and she vaguely remembered clutching at him with nerveless fingers. She'd heard murmurings, and the door had closed while she'd huddled pitifully in his arms, waiting for the shudders to stop.

She knew from the drag of sleep that it was daytime, but she fought off her exhaustion, knowing she had to tell him everything.

"I saw it all. The explosion, the fight. I saw how you died and Javed too." The words croaked into the room.

"It's a dream, Hope. We're getting closer. Each time you see more." In his voice there was a wealth of fury and exhaustion. She'd known then that the nightmares were telling on Xavier too. "We're getting closer each time. I hate what you go through, but we're so much closer. We'll crack this in the next few days. We just have to hold on." The words were brave, but she could discern the broken quality in them.

Hope pulled her mind back to her work, requesting a highlighter pen, and began circling the more likely properties as she went. Each that was circled felt wrong, but she kept working through the list. The chill of early morning was in the air, and the house started to settle around them, growing quiet. She knew sunrise wasn't far away, pulling at her, demanding that she rest her body.

"Come on, Hope, you've been at this now for hours. It will be sunrise in under an hour. Call it a day and we can start again tonight." His voice was seductive, and how she wanted to stop.

"Just let me finish this page." The words were dogged, but she didn't have a lot of energy left to use.

Hope kept pushing herself, as the screen grew blurry in front of her gaze. The hum of the computer and the tapping of keys made her sleepy, and she wasn't quite through when she felt her body sway forward.

"Go 'way. Not finished yet." She swiped ineffectual hands at him, as he slid his beneath her, lifting her close to his chest. The metallic rattle of shutters filled the air, deployed against the sunlight that would soon shine.

A sensation of weightlessness shimmered through her once more as he carried her up the ornate staircase to their room.

"You've got to stop carrying me everywhere." She allowed the words to mumble out of her mouth while he laid her down on the deep bed. Before she could hear his answer she was asleep.

Xavier woke with a jerk. Another nightmare. It shook him to the core. How much longer could she continue like this? He reached for and enfolded the shaking woman in his arms, holding her close to his body, willing her to accept the warmth and love of his embrace—needing to comfort her.

Each day had become her personal torment, and she held herself together, arms wrapped around her waist and chest. As if, by doing so, she could control her reactions, or stop the dream from invading her very mind.

Once the shaking stopped, Xavier passed her the goblet of blooded wine without a word. There didn't seem much to say when she woke screaming, the sounds shrill and chilling. He'd held her through her shudders, running a hand up and down her back, warding off the icy cold chill of her skin, while seeking to give her comfort as she'd sobbed brokenly.

Quiet had descended in the room once more, and he drew himself upright, knowing that sunset was near. If what she saw came to pass, they didn't have much time, and the need to protect and hold her roared at him to take her as his.

"Hope? In the eyes of the Council you are already as much my life partner as you would be with the ceremony, but formally, I… I want to ask you to be my consort, my lover. Please be my life partner." He held his breath as she sat still in his arms. His stomach churned.

Dear God, let her say yes. The silence grew and the greasy bubble that had coated his insides felt like it was congealing. She was going to refuse him.

"Why?" The simple word contained so many subtleties, yet he knew what she was looking for. What she needed.

"Because I love you." The words escaped. He'd never said that to another person, human or vampire. No woman had entranced him, aroused him or pushed him quite like she did. "Because for however many days and nights are left to me, I want and need you with me." His hands shook and so did his voice, but he felt no shame.

This was the most important question of his long-lived life. As a human, he'd not taken a wife, even when his father had urged him to for the sake of his household. In several hundred years as a vampire, he hadn't found the one person he would trust by his side forever, that is until now. Until Hope. Now it was so important, he had to do this right.

"Yes." He heard the word, and knew a moment of utter peace. He closed his eyes and kissed the top of her head, holding her close to him.

"Thank you." What more was there to say? He held her tightly and inhaled her scent. Just needing to be with her.

"You know, you could have waited until I was dressed or had at least washed my face." Her voice was truculent, and he smiled at both her comment and her tone.

"I could have, but this was right." She chuckled a watery sound, and his chest filled to overflowing with pride.

Now, he just needed to find a way to make forever something that they could achieve.

She was bone weary, but elation colored her actions as she clung to him, resting her body against his, accepted the warmth he exuded.

She'd just taken the biggest leap in her life, accepting Xavier as her life partner. It wasn't a step taken lightly.

Now she needed to tell him, match the declaration he'd made. She felt ready to tell him what lay in her heart. "Xavier? I love you too." She knew the minute the words found him, when he roughly turned her in his arms. His sophistication ripped away and he kissed her hungrily. The kiss was scorching but brief. Xavier pulled back and she lifted a shaking finger to her passion-stung lips.

"You have given me the most perfect gift, Hope." They sat together, quietly entwined for a while before rising in silence. There was little time for celebration now, yet she felt the glow of love and, glancing his way, saw his face shine.

With difficulty, Hope dragged her mind back to their problem, how to stop Estersham carrying out his evil plan. To do that, they still had to find where the attack would take place.

They dressed hurriedly, then moved down the staircase toward the room where the computers waited, and took up their spots in front of the flashing monitors.

Hope lifted the sheaf of papers, running through them, starting at the page she'd been working on the night before. Residence by residence and building by building she searched, in the hopes that the *one* would catch her eye quickly. Hope crossed off any that didn't meet the criteria she'd mentally prepared, understanding that it would continue in the same time-consuming and laborious way.

While they worked, Xavier told her of the information he'd received, reading from the emails which he'd found in his inbox. The message must have arrived while they slept, from the human and vampire investigators the nest used periodically.

"Estersham was seen in the Mandrake Bar last night again. There is some talk he has a group of rogue vampires affiliated with him. We believe they are members of the Brethren." He scrubbed a hand over his face. "It looks like one of them is possibly the guard from the execution. That would explain how he got away."

"So, he has associates. That makes sense, but how long ago did he make those connections? Are they the same people he was with straight after his…turn?" She lifted her eyes to look at him for an instant, before focusing on the screen once more. "And didn't anyone, you know, check to make sure he was dead?" Something about the whole thing felt wrong to her. The thought ate at her, like an itch irritating in the back of her mind. "I mean, don't you have like a ledger or paperwork? And what about whoever was the witness?" She let the words hang in the air.

"Excellent points—but at the time, we had no expectation that we would be crossed like this. We believed that the membership was stable. I'll make more enquiries, but not tonight. We need to have everything in place, in case it tips them off to a change in our plan." He stood gracefully, and once more she found herself watching his movements. "How are you doing?" His eyes narrowed as he moved around the desk to see what she was checking.

"I'm about halfway through the list. It's difficult, because what I see is smoky or foggy, and so damaged that it really bears little resemblance to the buildings in the pictures. I know it is in color when I see it in my dreams, but I can't make out distinct aspects of the building. The only thing I know for sure is there are multiple levels and a lot of glass. That lets me eliminate the individual houses, but not businesses, commercial buildings or apartments." She sighed heavily. "This is going to take forever."

"Want me to help?" His voice was quiet, but she shook her head.

"I'd love you to, but there really isn't much you can do. I need to go through each one and look for a landmark or something that pings…" She shrugged her shoulders, dismayed that it wasn't easier to find the right building. "I'll keep on with this." She gulped, looking back at the screen. There was one more question she had to ask, but she felt ill at the thought of the answer. "Have you got the results of the tests yet?"

They had taken a blood sample since arriving to check her blood values, to see if they continued to carry the same antibodies that made her a siren.

"No. They may not come in for a few more days. However, the main thing is, so far it seems none of the Brethren appear to have heard of your change, which means that they don't know potentially what they wanted you for is gone." A light hand settled on her arm. "Meanwhile they continue their aggressive campaign, while we prepare to fight them. And win." He smiled quickly, but she could see from the tight lines around his mouth and eyes that it was falsely bright, She read his concern through their shared mind link.

"It's okay. I understand. You need bait for the trap. I can accept that." Hope touched his shoulder. It was a concept she hoped he found reassuring.

"The dreams are changing. Each night there is a difference, subtle, but there. Soon we'll find the key." She watched as his face changed, waited a heartbeat before continuing. "I didn't think you had picked that up yet. Yes, there are changes each night. I've been keeping a document on the computer in the last couple of days, tracking what I'm seeing. Highlighted the changes I'm noticing." She brought up the file, showing him. He scanned it, smiling. She saw the muscles in his arms relaxing. "I'll send it through to you after. Right now, we need to get back to work, to find that piece of information that will give us the advantage."

He looked steadily into her eyes, and she felt something inside her shift slightly. "You are one hell of an amazing woman, Hope."

Warmth flooded through her. He rose, moving back to his side of the desk. For an instant, she fancied the air around her cooled, in the absence of his proximity, and she reminded herself inwardly those thoughts were fanciful.

Hope crossed off another building, turned the page and started typing once more.

Xavier watched the graceful, slim body, waiting in figure-hugging black yoga pants and a fitted sports top. Hope gripped the head of the whip in a firm hand and he could see the intense concentration on her face. She lifted her arm and the whip jerked, thwacked with her quick motion. She moved again, this time the supple leather coiling and dropping back to the ground with an audible slap.

"Let me do it again." The sheen of sweat on her skin glowed under the lights, but it was the glint of determination in her eyes that filled him with pride. After two hours, she'd managed several decent cracks and pretty much each time had hit the target, which was a step toward being able to command the whip, as both a defensive and offensive weapon.

She bared her teeth and gave a grunt as she wielded it again. This time the crack echoed through the room.

"That is sufficient for tonight." Xavier moved to take a step forward, but she turned.

"No. I need to…" He knew what she was about to say. Yes, she needed to master it, but for now, it was time to rest.

"No. You need to feed and we still have some work to do tracking that building." Her eyes narrowed as she looked at his face.

"You've heard something?" She dropped the arm she'd raised and stalked forward, the muscles of her body moving in a sensual wave.

Xavier grinned. He knew he smiled. He stepped back waiting for her to follow. A competitive streak had emerged with her change, one he appreciated fully. "I think you might like to take a quick shower first."

"What?" She sniffed the air before wrinkling her nose. "Yes, I probably should. Geez, that is a huge drawback to my increased sense of smell. However, that doesn't get you out of it. Walk up with me and tell me what you have found out." She turned, not waiting for him while he watched her graceful movements, curling the whip up in her hands as she walked toward the door of the gymnasium.

Her gliding gait was mesmerizing, her hips swaying slightly to and fro. She mounted the stairs and the muscles of her backside clenched and released, while she made her way along the landing, slipping through the door and heading toward the large built-in wardrobe. She stopped, snatching clean clothing before heading into the bathroom.

Hope left the door open. He reclined upon the bed, listening to the sounds of her movements. "So? Now that I know you have news, it would be unfair to make me wait." The water rushed from the head of the tap and he closed his eyes, imagining her stepping beneath the spray, the water beading over her luscious curves. The ever-present arousal raised its head and he opened them again, willing away the sexual awareness that had dogged him unceasingly since meeting her.

"Yes. Well, we have your test results back. They are all negative. Which means the siren factors in your blood are now absent." He waited for her to absorb the information.

"So?" She stopped talking for an instant, and he would swear he could almost hear her thinking, she was probably weighing up the information. She'd mastered the ability to erect a barrier between them when she needed to. The barrier was like a block wall. "Okay. He obviously doesn't know yet. Do you think that will work for long?" He heard the quick, efficient twist of her hand when she turned the shower off and the way she pulled the towel from the rack. He strained hoping to hear the rub of the fabric over her skin.

How he wanted to go to the bathroom and make love to her, sink within her body as his arousal demanded. He couldn't, not now. That was for later, when there was time to show her how much he cared. Right now they had to solve the problem. He refused to be sidetracked into forgetting—it was one that needed a swift resolution, as time bled away.

Sounds filtered through the open door, that of clothing slipping over her skin, and he curled his fingers, as the heat simmered below the surface once again. "Do you want to get straight back to work?" *Keep it light and innocuous,* he thought. As far away from the temptation that would wrap him back into the veil of sensual thoughts.

She came through the open doorway. "Yeah, I guess we should." In her eyes he could see the same awareness that wavered between them. Her cheeks were slightly flushed, and her beautiful violet eyes glittered with arousal. He stood quickly.

"Let's get out of here." His words sounded rough, but he was unashamed of the reaction to her. She was his life mate, the one he'd waited empty centuries for.

She moved forward, twining her slender fingers through his and drawing him close, her lips whispering over his. The kiss nothing more than a promise, but even so, the electric touch set him aflame.

Xavier pulled away, regretfully putting space between them. "Come on." He led the way out of the room.

CHAPTER TWENTY-THREE

Once more she concentrated on the vision glowing before her. She was sure she knew the building. The smoke haze choked her, and the sound of crying humans was so loud she wanted to clap her hands over her ears. The humans who'd escaped wore smeared white coats. Lost in the middle of the nightmare, she was sure this was important as she looked around, seeing the fear in their eyes, smelling it in the acrid, coppery tang of their body odor. Their hearts beat and blood pumped faster than ever before through their veins. Her mouth ached, and she fought to control the unfamiliar urges her body experienced.

The leather grip of the weapon in her hand moved as she flicked it to and fro, waiting for the moment they would appear. They would come, she knew it instinctively now. They always appeared in her dream.

Xavier waited beside her, as did Javed and the house guard. Each held their favored weapon—Javed, a long scimitar that looked both ugly and beautiful, and Xavier carried a long slender sword in his hand. At his hip, she could make out the ultraviolet gun.

They waited, standing still, searching back and forth, scanning the gray choking cloud. They would soon be here.

The crunching and crashing from the building finally ceased, and all she could hear were the humans as they moved and huddled in groups, crying out. A scream rent the air while the ghostly dust started to dissipate, and finally they saw the hunters.

They moved with an unnatural grace—a predatory army. A moment of hysteria descended, gripping her.

A thought occurred before she could beat it back. What if they didn't prevail? What if these creatures, these Brethren won the day? Then what?

Who would be the defense of the humans then? "No. I won't let that happen." She voiced the words, taking strength in them.

"It will be okay, Hope. Breathe. Watch. Look for a weakness." She could hear his voice as it filtered through the gray cloud. He was there. With her.

Then the Brethren moved. Circled. Looking for a gap they could exploit in their formation.

Javed feinted as one tried to launch a forward assault. He parried the attack while everyone watched in silence. The Brethren vampire lifted his sword and Javed parried again, holding his opponent off. The sound of grunts and clashing steel filled the air.

The others had engaged, but this was the main game, she knew. Javed got the upper hand and a quick silent thrust was followed by a jerky movement. It finished with a rolling head falling to the rubble strewn ground.

A roar filled the air, and finally the circle around them broke free from the mystical arrangement. The Brethren vampires surged forward, their animalistic grunts filled the air.

Clangs and cracks met with the sound of whips and chains and they each found an opponent. One tried to engage her. She flicked her whip, wielding it with accuracy. It snaked through the air and she hit the one who came at her.

He ducked and dived, slid and slipped, trying to move out of the way of the flying leather.

The scent of blood was pervasive. Her jaw ached. She fought against the urge to drop the weapon and tear at him, to rip his throat and drink him dry. The vampire tried to wrest control, pulling on the leather, but she restrained her instincts, instead flicking it free of his hold. She watched, moving forward, advancing on the opponent. He moved back. Swipe. Into the arcing blade of one of her guards and the sound of flesh hitting the ground filled her with a mixture of pride and disgust.

She turned, seeking another opponent. Now wasn't the time to be squeamish.

The humans watching were howling with fright now, but she blocked the sound and advanced on another Brethren. He swiped gore and sweat from his fine Italian suit, then raised his rapier. The feral look in his eyes met her gaze. Crack! Once more the whip flayed at the air. He ducked and the dance of death began again.

Again and again she replayed the scene. The fight was vicious, but the Brethren outnumbered them. Exhaustion started to pull, when she saw Javed fall. She cried out, but too late for him to move away. Saw the blade separate head from shoulders.

"Noooo!"

Xavier moved forward and she knew: This was the minute she would relive over and over again.

They moved forward, circling around him, swords and chains raised. Her stomach roiled, knowing what was to come, but still dreading it.

Estersham moved out of the gray dust cloud that swirled around them.

"Finally. My friend, you should have joined me. I would have preferred that. However, the girl, once she joins my army, will more than make up for the disappointment of your intractability." He grinned, the look in his eyes feral as they glowed a deep burnished gold. His teeth, long and ready to rip and shred, had descended. Drips of crimson running down his chin. Her stomach roiled.

"No. You will not kill him. I will not let you." She cracked the whip, anger lending her speed and agility. She ran at him. Some of the Brethren moved in front, like a living wall of protectors.

"Nooooo!" The whip slashed and cracked in the air. She hit one across the neck, watching as it curled around in her deft movements and she jerked, tearing the ligaments and flesh. She screamed as she moved forward and for the first time, the scent of fear rose from the Brethren. In her eyes they had seen something. She didn't dwell on their faces, though. Estersham sucked in a breath.

"You're no longer human?" He hissed the words, anger evident in the cold English tone of his voice.

"Just worked that out, did you?" She stalked forward. A cry broke her stride, and she twisted back, in time to see the knife sever Xavier's head.

"Xavier!" The primal howl rent the air.

She opened her eyes and panted, sucking air into her heaving body. "Xavier!" This time the sound was broken by the vicious sobs tearing from her being. "Xavier!"

Slowly she became conscious of the warm arms around her bitterly frozen frame.

"I'm here, Hope. I have you." The words soothed the hideous sense of loss and despair and she gulped for air, exhaustion pulling at her senses. She let the heat of his body seep into her. Drew comfort from the closeness and scent of him.

"It's okay. I'm here and alive. You are with me."

"It happened, but this time it was different. This time he found out. He knew. And I think I have a better idea of where." The words tumbled out, low and broken, but she now knew they just might have found the key. The one they had been searching for.

"Where, Hope? What did you see?" This time, it was Cressida speaking quietly. She turned her head and noted the woman standing beside the bed.

"Cressida? Why are you here?"

"Because the whole household heard you." No matter that her words were quiet, they may as well have been shouted and Hope winced. "It has been getting gradually louder with each night. You were close this time, though, weren't you?" Nonetheless, the soothing words demanded an answer.

"Yes. White coats. The humans are wearing white coats. We need to check factories, laboratories and places where they wear those sorts of coat."

"Well done, Hope. I know it has been an ordeal, but now we have a fighting chance. Tonight I need you to focus on those types of locations. Can you do that?" Her gaze was steady.

"Yeah." Hope raised her eyes one last time to the woman, the vampire Councilor. "I can do that." She would beat Estersham. There was no way she was going to lose Xavier and the sense of belonging that she'd finally found. The conviction in her voice must have reinforced her commitment to Cressida, as she left the room and once more, it was just her and Xavier.

He pulled her against his body. "What happened?"

She couldn't answer. The pain of the loss she'd experienced was unbearable to her now. She refused to give in to the tearing agony. Not now. If she did, it would swallow her and she'd be lost.

"I can't, Xavier."

She felt the nod, a jerk of muscles against her, and burrowed into his arms. "Just hold me. Please?"

They lay like that for a long time.

CHAPTER TWENTY-FOUR

*E*vening came and they rose, with limbs that ached tiredly. The ongoing pressure of the constant stress wearing them down. Xavier could see the dark circles and gray pallor on Hope's face. Lack of sleep and the demands of her dreams were draining her. If it wasn't so important, he wouldn't keep pushing, but as it stood, time was running out. They had to find the answer, because otherwise it would be too late for all of them. They had to solve the problem, and the knowledge weighed more heavily as each day passed.

"Sit down, Hope. I'll grab your sustenance and then we can start. Are you okay with that?" He waited, watching her until she responded.

She nodded—the movement jerky and graceless. Since waking in the night, he'd felt a distance growing between them, as if she was retreating behind a shell, and he wanted to knock down the wall she was building, but didn't know how. It angered him, but he acknowledged the sense of helplessness. Xavier had already attempted to use the link, but somehow she'd managed to lock him out.

Xavier didn't know what else to do, so he waited and watched. Impatience ate at him as effectively as acid. How long could she continue like this? Her behavior was both robotic and jarring. Yet in her eyes he could see determination, so instead, he moved to the side, retrieved a goblet of the heavily blooded wine and moved back to where he'd left her. She'd already booted the machine and was working through the list of properties, clicking and flicking paper.

He waited by the doorway, knowing she hadn't yet noticed him.

"I won't lose him. I need to find out where. When." She muttered the words.

Xavier watched her shoulders slump again, and a general air of loss and sorrow fell upon her. So much had happened in a short time. Even while he stood in the shadows she straightened again, her spine once more aligned. "This isn't going to help anyone." His heart constricted while he closed his eyes against the burning sensation that built behind their lids.

Knowing she wouldn't wish him to see her like this, he made a thudding noise, alerting her while he stumbled his way back into the room.

Hope turned slowly, her eyes shone with the tears she fought to contain. "I'm ready to start again." The unnecessary words were teamed with a hand movement. It was to keep his gaze from her face, no doubt, he told himself.

"Excellent. Show me what you're looking at now." Xavier kept his words gentle, but she shook her head.

"No. Not right now. You keep going with your things. I have a few ideas I want to try." She kept her face averted, and he detected the huskiness in her words, but let it be. There was nothing to be gained by making her feel worse.

Xavier settled in, checking messages and emails. The government had finally contacted him about the attack. He read the incident report. The constant tap of the keyboard as she worked kept him company.

"Ohhh…" The sound had him lifting his head.

"What?" He looked closely at her face, seeing the surprise and dismay.

"I think I found it."

Xavier rose, moving quickly around the desk to crouch down beside her. "Show me."

Hope pulled up the image of the old blood hospital across town. Of course, what else could possibly be the target? Yet, he was sure the nest had sold that property.

"See this? That building, the lines. It all seems so clear now. It's one of the old clinics set up not long after I was abducted. Later we sold it. It's in an industrial zone, which explains why there weren't lots of cars and other people in my dreams." Hope looked up at Xavier and his chest tightened. "That's the location. I'm sure of it."

He moved quickly, the adrenaline rushing through his system. Time to move. They had to hurry and make arrangements. Xavier lifted the phone to his ear, while she slumped into the chair. He closed his eyes, turning away from the sight of her. The pinched white look on her face haunted him as he began to speak.

Hope sensed the daylight pressing down on her. She had to know. "Does he know, do you think?" She gripped the goblet tightly.

"I don't believe so. I have mobilized people to begin the preparations, though. If he is aware, it's too late for him to do anything tonight. When we wake, I will contact the rogues. Have them pass along the message to meet."

The knowledge sat like a lump in her stomach, but she fought off the sensation of fear that choked her, the one she'd experienced endlessly since her change.

Hope sipped at the blood, but she couldn't finish. It settled at the base of her stomach, which wanted to churn, a sensation she'd felt more than enough. She walked to the small dresser and placed the goblet down, watching, as the liquid moved within the fine-cut crystal.

"What about…?" Hope couldn't continue the thought, but knew he understood as Xavier pulled her against him.

"No. We don't believe he knows about you. Otherwise, I'm sure you would know now. That is one of the strongest positives on our side. Add in the fact he doesn't know your change has removed the siren strain from your blood, and we are streets ahead."

The words were as she expected, but it didn't lift the heavy weight she felt pressing her down. With the coming dawn, exhaustion pulled at her body and mind.

Hope climbed into the bed, pulling the light coverlet over her lace-clad body. Xavier settled in behind her. His warm breath brushed over her neck in an intimate lover's touch. She wanted to turn in his arms and seek the reassurance of his most urgent caresses. That was the coward's way, she reminded herself. Tonight, she was ready. Prepared for whatever her dreams threw at her.

He encircled her body softly and she wanted to cry at the tender emotions that rose in response to his touch. His actions affirmed the emotions settling inside her heart. Her eyes burned and she waited, listening for the sound of his breath to settle into the steady cadence of sleep. Hope controlled her own breathing, keeping a steady in and out rhythm while she settled her emotions.

"I know you're awake." His voice rumbled at her ear. Hope closed her eyes. She'd forgotten about the bond between them.

I can still hear your thoughts, his voice intruded in her mind. *I'm happy to make you feel better, but only if you want to.* How in heaven's name was she supposed to keep herself apart, when his thoughts called to her, like the most enticing promises ever known?

"Not tonight. It would be as if I was using you. I'll never do that, Xavier." She sniffled loudly.

"Hope, I…"

"Not tonight, Xavier. We need to sleep, to be ready." Sleep was the one thing Hope feared, almost as much as the battle to come. The dreams, the smells and sounds kept filling her with dread. His death. She was sure it would come again in her dreams.

"Okay, we'll do it your way, tonight." She could hear the dissatisfaction in his voice at her comments and she smiled, just a little, before snuggling against him. Hope closed her eyes and willed herself to sleep.

It took a long time.

CHAPTER TWENTY-FIVE

The layers of sleep lifted from her consciousness as Hope woke. The sensation of Xavier wrapped around her, filling her with pleasure and warmth, while she stayed as still as possible, not wanting to wake him and lose the feeling of well-being that bloomed inside her.

"Good morning." His voice flowed over her like silk, making her shiver with sensual anticipation followed by the rippling sensation of laughter. "Much as I'd like to make love with you, we need to move."

His words stripped away the happy contentment she'd cloaked herself in. It was the day she feared. Hope nodded unsteadily then rose, reaching for the clothes she'd laid out the night before. The black pants and close-fitting corset top. The thigh-high boots with carefully reinforced toes and heels. The black leather belt with the whip hook teamed with a matching leather jacket, all in a glossy leather shine. She smiled at the thought of just how much her clothing tastes had changed. Or had they? Had she just lost some of her inhibitions?

Hope stopped abruptly as another thought occurred to her. Maybe it was more than that… Perhaps it was a physical manifestation of just how much she'd found her own way. The concept fascinated her, but there was no time to consider it.

He laid a hand softly on her shoulder. "It's time. Before we go… Carry this with you. I don't know if it will help, but it would ease my mind knowing you have it."

He held a small silver stiletto, elegantly engraved. He pressed it into her hands, folding her fingers around the handle. He looked at Hope and she could see concern shining. Intrigued she looked, seeing a small clip, which she pressed, watching as a copper spike shot out. She grinned, knowing what this was. He took it without a sound and showed her with a deft twist how to retract the spike.

She nodded, and slipped it into the pocket of her coat, zipping it up. She knew there was a story to this knife, one she was determined to ask him later, once the threat had passed and they were able to breathe easily. She clung to the notion and took a last, long look around.

"I'm ready." They left the bedroom, and Hope refused to look back at the room that had been a haven during a time of upheaval. She knew, whatever happened now, there was only one way to deal with the aftermath of whatever took place. Looking to the future and accepting what happened, no matter how personally devastating it might be.

Once downstairs, Hope noticed the men and women milling around, many dressed as she was, in uniform black, and the majority were decked out in leather. So many more than she could ever remember seeing. New faces filled the crowded foyer, but she looked harder for those she knew. There was Catriona and her partner Emily, holding hands. Near the door stood Javed, a grim half-smile covering his handsome face as Cressida waited by the stairs.

There also had to be at least a hundred vampires watching and waiting in the silence, as she and Xavier stepped off the last tread.

"Ready?" Cressida's voice was husky and Hope nodded uncertainly, while her stomach pitched and roiled. Cressida clapped once, and several members of the household appeared in the doorways, carrying trays with goblets of the blood wine that most of them had come to prefer. Cressida had chosen to wear leather as well, but with her usual style, it was red. Actually crimson, and stark against her pale skin and blonde hair. Hope smiled. That was Cressida all over, making a statement.

The human staff moved silently among the warriors who waited, the quiet only filled with the sound of steps and crystal moving on trays, and the barely discernible throb of a heartbeat here and there.

Cressida stepped forward, taking the first step up the staircase before stopping. Hope felt the ripple of tension that wove through the room as Cressida slowly turned.

The Mistress' eyes glinted in the reflected light of the chandeliers. "For hundreds of years, we have lived and died, keeping to the single basic understanding that humans are more than just food. For hundreds of years, we have acted as their guardians. Now, it is time for us to be their avengers."

The company assembled within the room stood still, mesmerized by Cressida's words. "Tonight, we take the first step in ensuring the safety of the innocents, and reclaim our place within humanity. Some will fall. We will mourn them together, but it is in our victory that we shall celebrate their life!"

A hand crept around Hope's waist. Warm and welcome, she felt Xavier move closer and she leaned into him. Drawing strength, even as she watched the others grinning with growing excitement.

"We will work together to vanquish those who would destroy our way of life. The Brethren would use humans as a food source, to be rounded up like cattle to the slaughter with no thoughts to their place and ours in this brave new world." Hope watched as Cressida paused, waited a beat and scanned the room. The energy flowed around, buffeting her.

"We will protect the innocent and rid the world of this unworthy scourge. To the battle for the innocent. To victory!" Her voice rose, urgent, while the room erupted in cheers. The atmosphere was now electric, as the chamber rang with 'hurrahs', before the assembly drank deeply of the blooded wine.

Cressida looked at Hope and winked conspiratorially, shocking Hope for just an instant. *She wants you to know that she is pleased to have you among us. That she sees you as an asset.* The words from Xavier's mind had her goggling.

"I can't see how she could possibly think I'm an asset. It's not like I can fight hand to hand in any useful fashion or fly through the air." Hope muttered the words, yet she felt his movements, the shaking of his head behind her.

"No, you're not ready for that yet. You will do what you must to protect all of the innocent. That is what counts tonight."

Perhaps it was, but then she still might lose Xavier. For the first time, she knew she would move heaven and earth to make sure that wouldn't happen. Hope squared her shoulders.

"Everyone here has strengths. Emily was a police officer, so she already knows how to fight. Catriona can't fight worth a damn, but she has the most amazing ability to disseminate information, so she'll be doing that tonight. Everyone has a role to fulfil."

He would protect her. The instinctual knowledge was there, in the glint of his eye and the way he held her tight against his body. She too, would protect her mate from a possible death, and the agony of a never-ending grief she suspected would engulf her if he was lost.

Without a word the warriors turned to the door, placing empty glasses on sideboards and any available surface, before making their way outside to the vehicles.

"Where did the others come from?" she asked, as they crunched along the gravel to the car that waited for them.

"Other nests affiliated to Cressida. The word went out this morning. There are more to join us at the rendezvous point. We might just manage to outweigh the Brethren yet." He indicated the door of the vehicle.

It's time for us to leave. Hope nodded, understanding the time for pondering and planning ended now. He took her hand, grazing his lips over her knuckles. *Stay by me. You are the one he wants.*

Together they stood quietly while she took one last deep breath, inhaling the scents of jasmine and rose, before climbing into the beast they had arrived in. The glass between them and the driver was carefully tinted and the body of the car was empty. "I wanted us to be alone and quiet before it began." She smiled at his words. Even in the depths of planning for battle he'd taken a moment to arrange time for them.

Xavier watched her face, pale in the dim light of the vehicle, yet her eyes were clear. The car accelerated up the long drive and he sat, taking in her subtle fragrance, the one that drugged his mind. Something felt different. It gnawed at the edges of his consciousness, chipping away at the concern that had settled in his chest over the long weeks. The constant pressure he'd felt since they had arrived here dissipated slightly, but that puzzled him more than reassured.

"Do you have a sense of…?" Xavier stopped. He wasn't given to seeking reassurance, and the such sensations were alien, leaving him off balance.

"A sense of what? That something has changed? Perhaps… Last night…" She stopped. Her cherry red mouth opened wide as she realized the change had occurred without them even noticing. "I didn't dream. I didn't dream at all." She breathed the words and smiled.

Xavier reached for the phone, pressed a button then waited. She hadn't dreamed. The dream had been plaguing her for weeks and it was suddenly gone?

"Yes?" He could hear Cressida's tension over the line.

"Hope didn't dream last night." What else was there to say? He waited, tension filling him once more, as he reached out to Hope, grasping her cold and shaking fingers.

"Put her on speaker."

Cressida's command spurred him into action. He depressed a button, and dropped the handset back to its cradle as a crackle sounded through the cabin.

"You're on, Cressida." He waited, tense and wondering what she had to say.

"Excellent. Hope? You didn't dream last night? Nothing at all?"

"No, Cressida. I went to bed, expecting a bad night, but I slept through and woke refreshed." Hope's hand shook in his grasp and he wrapped an arm around her.

"Nothing? There was no dreaming at all?" Cressida sounded as puzzled as he felt. "Has it ever happened like this before?"

"No… Well, one time, when this girl was threatening me at school. It was a stupid childhood incident. I dreamed about it for weeks. I finally told Mother…" Her voice tapered off. Something had obviously come to mind.

"What? What happened, Hope?" Cressida demanded the answer. The one he was sure he already knew on an instinctive level.

Hope scrunched up her face as if remembering as much as she could. "She talked to the girl's mother. Kat. The girl. She left the school not long after. Do you think…? Could it really be that simple?" Hope's eyes looked into his, demanding an answer to the unspoken question. Was it possible that by sharing the information, planning for the worst, they had changed the outcome? Did the fact that Hope didn't dream mean that they had changed what was meant to be?

"It could be. We can't take it at face value. Cressida? I think we go ahead with the plan."

"I agree, Xavier. Everything is in place." The phone disconnected, leaving the jarring signal pumping through the air. Xavier reached over, stopping the sound by punching the button, and letting the thoughts of a possible future swirl through his mind.

Since Hope had told him that he would die because that is what she'd seen, he'd been consumed with ensuring she would be left protected and cared for, knowing there was little chance he would survive.

He'd worked tirelessly, ensuring that in the event of his death in battle, she would receive everything owing to him. Not that he'd told her. Instinct warned him she would have refused to accept what should rightfully be hers, something he'd had no intention of letting her do, of course.

The vibrations of the car slowed and he tensed. They'd arrived.

. . .

Hope waited while Xavier got out of the car. Some of the vampires were already milling around, though she noticed they weren't all there, preparing for the battle ahead. The lump in her throat got bigger. *Xavier? Where are the rest?*

Not now, Hope. Just in case. He smiled, softening his words, as he strode to the corner they had chosen for its view of the building. He stepped before a burly man, who bowed deeply to him. "Everyone is out now? You have set the cameras to play old footage as we agreed?" Xavier's voice cut through the air, sharp and cold. Controlled.

"Yes, Xavier. We haven't seen anything that would indicate that he or his rogues are nearby currently." They drew into the shadows of the building across the way, watching in silence as Xavier fitted an earpiece, listening intently.

A truck pulled up. A delivery. Xavier cursed, moving forward, but Javed flung out a hand. "I have this under control." He nodded to another who pulled out a remote and began working it. They could see the driver clambering out of his truck, adjusting his clothing and hat. Something seemed familiar about the human, and she watched as they loped inside, out of view. Hope guessed that the package carried something to cause the explosion she knew would soon take place.

Hope's mind searched and hunted through the people she knew. The hooded jumper jangled her mind. Who would wear a jumper in summer, anyway? The driver came back out, tucking the clipboard they carried under one arm. As soon as they were clear of the doors, ostensibly out of sight, they pulled off the cap. The long golden tresses falling from where they had been confined left Hope shell-shocked.

"Oh, my God!" Hope whispered the words, unable to contain them as the identity came to her. The person making the delivery was her sister-in-law.

"Javed? Get people working on the how and then report it back to me. Heads will roll." Hope felt Xavier's arms surrounding and supporting her, but right now, she stood in her own private hell. She'd never been close to Alexa, but the knowledge of the betrayal left her reeling. Her brother David... Was he also involved? Were her own parents? Hope closed her eyes, willing the pain away as the ground below her feet rumbled.

"Hope?" Xavier bent over her. "Hope? We can't do this now. We'll find a way to fix it, but not now. We don't have time." His urgent words snapped her out of the fog. The building rumbled and she watched as it rocked and swayed. A ripple surged through the walls then slowly, very slowly, the building collapsed to the ground, sending up plumes of gray smoke, filling the air.

Swiping away tears, she let the anger flood her system, looking into his forever green eyes. "No. Not now, but the time will come." Hope straightened. "Now, let's go deal with Estersham."

Together the small group moved forward, and just as in her dreams, the gray smoke hung in the air, choking living things in its wake. Hope was now a vampire and consumed with anger at the depths of the betrayal experienced.

Her whip balanced on the hook at her hip, but she caressed the end, ready to use it with a second's notice. She knew, when the time came, it would be speed, agility and her ability to hit the target dead on that would make the difference. Her vision narrowed to a pinpoint, as she waited for figures to emerge from the billowing clouds.

This time there was no sound from the innocents caught up in the battle. The silence overwhelmed her for an instant, catching her off guard, until she balanced herself. They had managed to save the innocents by clearing the building. Running a fake vision reel at each window had taken some planning, but no matter. They had done whatever it took, clearing the office during the lunchtime, and carefully staggering it so it remained believably busy.

She let her hands move back and forth over the grip of her weapon. Much as Hope wanted to employ it when they moved out of the choking smoke, she waited, letting the leather bite into the soft flesh of her palm.

Xavier stood beside her, so did Javed. Both men held their favored weapons—she noted the ultraviolet gun clipped into the holster at Xavier's waist, his muscles locked and ready for action. They looked carefully from side to side. She felt a frisson of alarm before she controlled it. They would be here any second now.

The ghostly gray dust started to dissipate and she could see the Brethren, moving with an unnatural grace, making their way toward them. Cocky as they advanced, smiles on their faces. Not knowing that steps had been taken to ensure they never achieved their victory.

"It will be okay, Hope. Breathe. Watch. Look for a weakness." Xavier's words, unknowingly the exact phrase he'd used in her dreams, soothed her skittish nerves in the tense atmosphere, as much as his physical presence and the one in her mind too.

The Brethren vampires moved forward. Circled around them as the three of them turned, eyeing off the threat. Hissing viciously at her. She let the sounds die away, watching them and looking for an opportunity.

Javed feinted, as one tried to launch a forward assault. She held her breath. One quick movement after another from Javed was effective at holding him off, until, with a final jerk and thrust, Javed got the upper hand, finishing with a rolling head falling to the rubble-strewn ground.

One down, but many more to go, she thought. Hope watched, as the disembodied head rocked back and forth until it finally came to a stop. The body had slumped to the ground and his brothers watched in silence.

A roar filled the air, and the boiling sea of combatants moved toward the three. A sharp whistle rent the air and one of the flanks of vampires from Cressida's personal guard appeared. Clangs and cracks met with the sound of whips and chains. Each warrior found an opponent.

One of the Brethren attempted to engage Hope. She flicked the whip, saw the opponent fall to the floor. She had little time to watch him writhing on the ground in pain. Another advanced. She flicked her whip again—leather snaked through the air, making contact with another vampire close by, but he ducked and dived, slid and slipped trying to move out of the way. She cursed loudly, trying again and again, fending off the attack she knew would keep coming. A final flick of the whip finished her opponent. A loud crack and crunch sounded as the bones and sinews of the neck tore apart. The body slumped to the ground slowly.

Hope turned seeking another opponent. The fight was ferocious, but the Brethren were weakening, although, she noted angrily, so were they. There had been numerous casualties on both sides, neither sparing the other. Exhaustion started to pull when she saw Javed fall, just as they had planned.

She cried out. "Noooo!" Her scream cut through the air, even as she continued to battle those around her. *One more step*, she reminded herself. *One more scene and one more act. That is all it will take.*

Xavier moved forward to engage another and the final scene of the battle began. This was the minute when she truly felt the danger was acute. So much could go wrong now. The Brethren stepped back, forming a circle and watching the battle of the two warriors.

The vampire moved forward, circling around Xavier while others watched, their swords and chains raised, ready to attack once more. Her stomach roiled knowing what was to come. She flicked her whip, threatening any who moved to advance on either of the men. Particularly Xavier. There was no way she would allow him to be ambushed by the on looking crowd. Once more she flayed the air.

Estersham moved out of the miasmic cloud that swirled around them. Immaculate, except for a fine layer of gray dust that coated his hair and clothing, and she watched as he flicked it from his shoulders. His blond hair was fashionably short, but it was the look in his eyes that chilled her to the bone. Red eyes. The eyes of a predator. She quaked, but refused to back down, even as the queasiness in her stomach grew to a heaving churn.

"Finally, Xavier, you have come. My friend, you should have joined me. I would have preferred that, to this outcome. However, the girl... Once she joins my army, she will more than make up for the disappointment of your intractability." He grinned, a cold smile that didn't reach his eyes. His teeth, long and ready to rip and shred, had descended and drips of crimson ran down his chin, so obviously he'd recently fed. Her stomach rebelled at the fetid smell that filled the air.

"No. You will not kill him. I will not let you." Hope moved quickly, knowing that this was the minute when she needed to be strong. "Nooooo!" The whip slashed and cracked in the air aiming for the man who entered the battle at the end. She hit the one who stepped in front of her across the neck, watching as the tail of the whip curled around. With her quick movements she jerked, tearing the ligaments and flesh. It howled, until the sound suddenly stopped.

She screamed her fury, advancing in a lope. For the first time, she noted the fear rising from the Brethren as some moved back. Estersham sucked in a breath, hissing as he exhaled.

"You are no longer human?" His anger was evident in the cold English tone of his voice.

"Just worked that out, did you?" She stalked forward, baring her own fangs at him.

The sudden motion around them broke through the silence. "Estersham. You should have stayed dead. Now, you and yours will pay the price." Cressida. Hope remained tense, waiting to see what would happen next as Estersham shot out a hand. "Not before I destroy your prize."

Xavier roared his anger. "You will not harm her!" Hope twisted and turned in his cruel grasp, the bite of fingers steely on her leather-covered flesh. She looked over toward Xavier and saw the fury on his face, but he was held back by three of Estersham's own.

His movements were wild and uncontrolled as he fought to break free, but Hope had prepared for this moment.

Hope dipped one hand into the pocket of her jacket, finding the small stiletto knife Xavier had given her. Cold and solid in her grasp. She moved again, hiding her intentions and whipped the hand free of the pocket and whirled back toward the one who held her, while depressing the lever, letting the copper spike shoot forward.

She only had one chance to free herself. The arc was quick and true. The spike found Estersham's chest. He shuddered wildly while he shrieked in pain, then she pulled back quickly, taking the small stiletto knife with her.

Hope moved quickly away, hearing a whine then thud, looking

back to spy the remains of Estersham on the ground. The smell of burning flesh filled the air, and she turned back to see Xavier waiting, gun in hand, watching her. Estersham's guards stood still. Obviously stunned to see the end of their leader, they dropped their weapons.

For Hope, the battle was now over. Xavier stepped forward to grasp her in his arms, winding them closely around her trembling body. "Tell me it's all over now." Her gentle demand was made against his leather-clad shoulder.

"Not yet. We need to round up the Brethren here, but Catriona has done an excellent job of keeping our men apprised of their location."

Hope shuddered as he led her back to the car. Cries of anger filled the air, but the sounds of battle had now quieted. They watched the others rounding up the Brethren vampires.

CHAPTER TWENTY-SIX

The journey back to Cressida's house was silent. Cressida opting to join them in the vehicle, sitting primly across from them, looking out of the window at the passing buildings. Hope waited quietly, twining her fingers firmly in Xavier's as they made the trip in silence. The vehicle sped through the night, before finally turning into the sweeping drive. The glow of dawn was a distant hint of color on the horizon as they entered the house.

In the hours that had passed since the battle, the human government had become involved, overseeing the transportation of the prisoners to carefully reinforced cells. Each of the vampires they had captured was now fitted with a collar, copper on the inside and silver on the outside. Each now wore a tracking system, which would keep tabs on them until they were to be brought before the Council.

"What will happen to them?" Hope's question was met with a sad smile.

"How about we discuss this inside?" The car stopped, the door opened. They carefully climbed out of the car and swiftly made their way up the shallow stairs. Other cars stopped at the steps to disgorge their passengers. All were weary, and many limping, carrying their injuries. Each face bore testament to the long and hard-fought battle.

Those who required extra help were given support toward the doors and beyond into the cool interior.

Within the safety of the house, they watched the doors sealing and the shutters slowly dropping, as Cressida led them to a room Hope hadn't entered before.

The room was comfortably furnished with deep lounges and chairs in blue. Hope dropped down next to Xavier. Those who could do so dropped ruined coats and shirts at the door, others disappearing briefly only to return moments later wearing clean attire. Hope felt dirty in her battle-stained clothing, but took the lead from Cressida taking a comfortable position. She sighed as she relaxed in the deep cushions.

Even as she watched, the humans of the household once more entered bearing goblets, and she grinned to see Javed limping into the room, his arms around a blonde woman, her mouth going and him nodding furiously. Something in his eyes told Hope this was more than a passing acquaintance.

Emily, bearing scratches and scrapes, and Catriona also entered, hand in hand. Once everyone had settled in, Cressida held her goblet up, taking a sip before declaring, "We have won this battle, but it's not the end of the war. It will continue through the ages, just as it always has. Tonight, we have lost good men and women. To those who gave their lives in the sacrificial defense of the innocent we salute them." Her quiet words met with weary nods.

"Yet, we have prevailed once more. Tomorrow we shall mourn them, but for now, we may celebrate our victory." Her tone was somber, and Hope felt the rippling emotions on the air.

"Cressida, what will happen to Estersham now?" Her voice was uncertain, but it was closure she sought on this front.

"His remains have been transported to a location where they will be left for the sun to finish the job started so many years ago." Hope nodded, understanding exactly what that meant. There would be no memorial for them to mourn his passing. He'd cast away that right once he'd turned against his own kind.

A quiet sob erupted from the back of the room, a rustle of movement, and she turned to watch another vampire kneel before a woman, and others hurried to attend to her also. Hope's eyes burned at the sounds of sorrow but when she looked back, Cressida was watching them intently.

"Xavier, you and Hope will wish to return to your house, tonight. There is some nest cleaning to do, I fear."

"Cressida... Before we retire, I just have one question." Hope's voice caught her attention, or at least the puzzled quality.

"Yes, my dear?"

"When Xavier was injured, you let him feed from me, knowing that I had that thing in my blood? Why?"

Hope watched in fascination as a crimson tide appeared on Xavier's cheeks. Cressida chuckled quietly. "Yes, that's a good question. Xavier knew about the anomaly in your blood. He also had it tested against his. Since you were already intimate, he was concerned about the ramifications. There is one thing about blood sirens."

Cressida leaned forward conspiratorially and unconsciously Hope mirrored the move. "They only have one perfectly matched partner. There is only one who is unaffected by their blood. That is how they know their perfect mate, it is said."

Hope's mouth formed an 'O' as she looked at him. He swallowed. Now she knew, and she felt her face forming a smile.

"Indeed." He cleared his voice, changing the subject. "Together, Hope and I will look to the future and rebuild our nest." He held her fingers tight, even as a yawn tried to break through. "For now, Hope is tired and I must admit to being wishful of retiring too."

Cressida chuckled. "Yes, Hope is just a baby and it is past her bedtime. Go." Cressida waved her hands at them in dismissal. They left the room hand in hand as they walked, albeit unsteadily, toward the stairs.

CHAPTER TWENTY-SEVEN

*X*avier watched Hope's face as they entered the hall. Lisi moved quickly toward them and dipped a small curtsey to Hope, who grinned and caught her in a hug. "It's so good to be back."

He looked around, spying David and his wife Alexa waiting with the guard behind them. Their expressions sour, but he knew not half as sour as they soon would be.

The report he'd received, the links forged in hate, fueled his anger.

Javed followed behind giving directions for the baggage to be dealt with, looking at the bright flares of light. He strode forward to the waiting couple.

"David? Alexa? Please join us in the office." He turned to watch Hope pull away from her friend and step forward, taking his side. He caught a flash of panic in Alexa's eyes, realizing Hope was no longer human. *Finally, the worm turns.* He smiled at the whimsy, even as he indicated for them to go before him.

"Master? I just have to…" Alexa's words died away. He stopped her.

"No. Now." There was no way he would put this off, giving her time to regroup or get away. *She must be made to pay for her decisions and actions,* he reminded himself. He nodded to the guards, knowing they would follow at a discreet distance in case she chose to run.

She'll run if we leave the option open. Hope's angry thought made him smile. She was ready also.

There was still more she didn't yet know, and he chained that knowledge away. Soon enough she'd be ripped apart again by revelations of the evil doings of people who should have protected her.

They entered the room. Two matching chairs now sat side by side. One for him and one for Hope. He watched David's eyes widen at the tangible evidence of their union and waited. Hope took the position he indicated to her, not saying a word, just quirking a fine eyebrow and smiling.

He waited until they were settled. "Alexa. We have a problem. Why were you making a delivery to the medical center last evening?"

Her eyes widened, and if he hadn't been a vampire he may have been fooled, but the scent of fear filled the air. "I wasn't… Who said that?" Instead Alexa feigned a startled expression, laying a hand on her flat stomach.

"We know. We saw you, Alexa. We also know about your parents, your background. Not the carefully crafted one that everyone seems to have swallowed." He let the words settle, watching her in silence. She continued the ruse, though.

"It's lies. Whoever has told you anything else is lying." Her blue eyes hardened once more.

"Alexa Yvonne Dunlap. That's not really who you are, is it, Alexandra Maree Monson?" She made to stand, but Xavier was around the table, hovering above her. He read David's confusion.

Hope, your brother may need your support very soon. He let the message float through the shared link, knowing she would understand soon.

"You were a child of the head of the rogue clan. Your father and mother were killed in their service. Estersham took you, educated you. Showed you how evil we were. Told you he was your benefactor and father. Didn't he?"

Xavier reached for her. Alexa—no, Alexandra—rose, pushing him away with hard fingers, her nails long and sharp. He let her go. She wouldn't leave the room, though, not with the guards outside the door. He'd already given instructions to Javed for his men to be in position. She had nowhere to go now.

"You and your nests. They are an abomination." Her tone now turned frigid. "They took the free will from those who would make their own decisions. He promised to turn me, once this was over. Make me one of them. One of his own. It was my birthright. All I had to do was pretend to love this helpless bastard. Marry him and become one of the nest." She laughed, and it was a cold and angry sound. "I had a plan, the one we formulated together. Once I knew about Hope and passed my mis-information on, it was all too easy. Then her father..." She stopped her eyes shining with contempt. "You didn't know that though, did you? He knew. He'd already been helping himself to the accounts. Wanted nothing more to do with you and your people's leadership. We joined forces. Agreed that we'd alienate the family. When the time was right, his people would once more attempt to hand her over to Estersham. Her own father orchestrated the latest plan." Her chest rose and fell. Her gaze on Hope.

Hope's gaze flicked to him. *You knew this?*

Xavier's fingers clenched, the only outward reaction while struggled to keep his visage impassive. *I received a report tonight from one of my people. He'd already determined your father was in league with Alexa. I'm sorry.*

In her mind, he read the final thrust of betrayal. *My father knew about it and was complicit.* It wasn't a query.

Yes. The urge to reach out and take her hand rose and he gave in, well aware that right now she needed an anchor against the pain slicing at her insides.

Alexa watched his hand twine around Hopes, realizing finally, he was sure, there was no way she could escape the charges that would be laid against her.

Her eyes took on the look she'd perfected for David and Hope's mother. Her face softened, but he wasn't fooled. "I can help you." Her voice now turned crafty. It sickened him.

He knew there was more. To clean out the wound, you had to release the poison first. So, he went to work. "You undermined Hope with her mother and brother, feeding them false stories of her wild college antics."

"My father told me to. He said it would make taking her easier if she was alienated. Her father was well aware of what I was doing. He assisted somewhat." Alexa shrugged. "Nothing big, just some pointers here and there."

"Why did you need Hope?" His anger built, but he held it back. He needed a full confession from this woman, so that David could see, and maybe salvage something from the shipwreck of the nest.

"My father would use her skills. Create others in his likeness. Set those free who had no wish to remain vampires. Then we would take the city. Start with that, and then the country. Removing the strictures that kept them bound for centuries to archaic ways." She smiled, it was cold and brittle. Alexandra's voice was totally devoid of warmth and he stopped the shiver that wanted to escape at the lack of penitence.

"And David?"

She shrugged nonchalantly, not even sparing him a glance. "He would be discarded when the time was right. Dealt with, as was appropriate at the time." She turned to her husband, smiling that cold, heartless smile she excelled in. "And I'm not pregnant, you fool. It just got me what I wanted in the short term. I wouldn't want a mewling brat by you anyway. Ruin my figure and future as a vampire? I don't think so." She tossed her hair in a cloud of gold that signaled her disdain.

"It's too late, Alexa, for that future now. The authorities will be here for you within the hour."

She laughed and Xavier knew the woman still thought no one would touch her because of her position in the nest. It was erroneous thinking, of course. "Only if they can find me." She turned lightly, racing to the door, opening it to find the guards. "You bastard!" Xavier heard the hiss of her words.

"Take her away."

Alexa screeched while they grabbed her arms and manhandled her from the door. Once she was gone, Xavier turned back to those waiting in the room. Hope sat in silence, watching David.

David's face was bone white and he breathed harshly as if he'd just run a marathon. For several moments he looked at them in silence. "She never loved me. They both lied and cheated." He muttered the words bitterly. "They were both using me all this time."

"I doubt she ever felt anything for you. She used you to further her own ends. As to your father? Well, he too will face retribution." What else could he say, except to tell the truth? "She needed a way into the nest, and they both believed you were the easiest option."

"David. I didn't know everything either. Xavier only found this out last night and told me some of it." Hope rose and moved to David, laying a hand on his arm. "Do you want…?" Xavier watched David pull away from her soft touch. He felt Hope's devastation at the movement.

He'll come round in time. He needs to work through the truth and she messed with his head so much. He's confused and doesn't know what to believe. He sent the message, hoping she would understand. The glint of a tear sat on her lash, but she turned away from her brother.

I just want to help him. Her despair cut him.

I know.

And my father? Hope glanced in his direction.

Cressida and the council will deliberate on that. It's out of my hands.

He moved toward her, laying a soft hand on her shoulder. "Come. David? Let us know what you wish to do. We will help any way we can."

Hope rose in silence. "Wait." Hope's voice cut through the air. "Mother?"

"They are both at the summer house." David's voice was quiet.

"Will Mother be all right?"

"Why wouldn't she be, Hope?" David's tired voice broke as he turned away.

"She's sick…"

"No. She's not. Father instructed her to say that, so you'd comply."

Xavier felt the impact of the words on her, moving soundlessly to her and grabbing her hand as David left the room.

"She lied to me." The words filled the air, and he wanted to take her pain away. She slumped miserably against him. "What about David?"

"All we can do now is be there for him. It will take time for him to heal. I hope in time, too, your mother will understand, and be willing to reconcile. It'll be tough."

"You don't believe…?"

"She's involved? No. However our people will continue with their enquiries and apprise us of what they find in due course."

She breathed raggedly, and while the knowledge of her pain hurt him too, he felt a determination to begin their life together on a happy note. "Come. Let us go share the celebrations with our guards. I have given orders that the entire household join us in the ballroom."

She smiled, watery and distressed though it was. She lifted her chin, and his chest filled once more with pride at this strong and generous woman who would be his life partner through the ages. "Yes, they are our household, aren't they?"

He stopped her at the door, stole a quick kiss. "They are indeed. Just as you are mine. Forever."

As they stepped through the door into the room, he knew it wouldn't be easy. As Cressida had said, they had been victorious in this battle. The war remained to be won, but he was thankful, right now, it wasn't his war to fight.

EPILOGUE

In a far corner of the room, watching the celebrations, the old woman smiled. The young girl whom she'd watched over from childhood had grown. True, she'd become a vampire, but she'd also found her life mate.

Jemima's job here was now complete, and the sense of satisfaction made her grin. This part of the renewal of life was complete. Xavier and Hope, together, would fulfil their part in future vampire lore.

Meanwhile her next role was waiting. She grabbed a sherry from the tray moving past her, and took a gulp. Not bad, and she certainly hoped the household of her next charge had good taste in wine and food too.

It was time for her to move on, she reminded herself sternly, placing the glass on the table quietly, before looking around to ensure no one was paying her any attention.

Oblivious to all, she crept away, and no one noticed as the older woman walked down the long gravel driveway, and, with a shimmer of magic, became young once again.

When Cupid—otherwise known as Diocail— is banished from his home on a remote Scottish Island, he's set a series of tasks by the great god Lugh, who also happens to be his father.

In **Blame The Wine**, he must bring two lovers together... BBW Cara and James, the man she's lusted over from afar who happens to be a super geek and head Veha Industries.

In **A Stranger's Embrace**, Diocail is driven to help an emotionally fragile Jane and Davis, a famous author. The task is more complicated, with the existence of Carstairs her could-be ex-husband and teenage daughter, Frannie.

In **Revenge on Cupid**, Diocail must take the ultimate chance and find his own happily ever after with Simone. Sometimes the past gets in the way and HEA's don't come cheap though.

The dusty, dingy little diner was full, even with its current state of cleanliness—or lack thereof. People from the surrounding offices didn't care about anything except the incredible, well-prepared food at a reasonable cost. They flooded in, like waves to the shore. As one tide left, another swept in.

"Honestly, Simone. I'm going to try getting his attention one more time. If that doesn't work, I'm out of there. I mean, how long can I keep trying?" Cara picked at the caramel tart she hadn't been able to resist with the cheap metal fork and flicked the blob of fresh cream that sat on top to the side of the plate.

"You've said that tons of times before. Besides, what are you going to do to get his attention? Hmm? Walk naked through the typing pool?" Simone bobbed the straw in her smoothie as she eyed her friend with a frown. "It's been what? Eighteen months since you saw him, and you've mooned over him from a distance ever since you met him. You need to move on, Cara. That is, unless there's something you haven't shared?"

The query was arch. Cara shivered even as she shook her head. "No."

Simone quirked an eyebrow, obviously unconvinced with the answer. Cara let out a deep sigh of frustration. "There's a position...it's only temporary, for a PA reporting directly to him." She speared a forkful of tart, chewed quickly and swallowed, before continuing. "In his office, full-time for the period of the engagement. I saw the memo yesterday. I mean, I have the skills, right? I can type, answer phones, make coffee, file, greet people. What's more, I can probably do it better than all those size eights in the typing pool that Ms. Jackman seems to prefer." She nodded thoughtfully. "All I have to do is get past the ogre in Human Resources."

Simone stared at her, disbelief clear on her face. "Girl, I so remember that woman. If you think you can get past her, you're doing better than I ever did. That's why I left Veha Industries, remember? Maybe it's time to haul out your resumé and consider some other options. Look for something better." Simone shook her head and billows of her crimson hair swirled through the still air.

Cara understood Simone only had her best interests at heart. But this time she knew the outcome would be different. Hell, she could feel it in the air. The tingle of expectation.

"Cara, the HR ogre will hang you out for breakfast before she offers you anything like a position in that office. Remember her mantra? Good looks and good work make for a positive workplace!"

Simone didn't sugar-coat anything. It was another great reason for their long- term friendship. Honesty. But Cara didn't want to hear the truth in the statement. Even if it was exactly as her friend said.

Cara nodded quickly. "Yeah, I know, but if I don't try, then I won't know how close I can get to him, right? And the only way to catch his attention is to get past *her* and see him in person." Cara quaked a little at the information she needed to share. The favor she needed to ask. "Anyway, I tidied up my resumé and dropped the application into a memo envelope yesterday, so it's too late to back out now. I mean, fortune favors the brave. Doesn't it? If I don't snag an interview, I'm going to visit the career advisor across the street and register with them." She shrugged. "I'll look for temp work until something more long-term shows up. I can see what they have on offer and well...who knows? Maybe a job with the right boss is just waiting for me. But I'd rather this worked out, to be honest." Her voice trailed off into a whisper. "I really wish he would notice me."

Simone took a long slurp of her banana drink, and Cara noticed her questioning gaze even as she squirmed. Finally, Simone nodded. "It's your funeral. So anyway, you'd better show me this memo if you want me to be a referee for you. I'm guessing that's what you need, right? I'll have to know what I'm supposed to say about you before they ring."

Cara smiled. "Thanks, Simone. I knew I could count on you." She slipped a piece of paper out of her handbag and handed it over. "Sorry it's a bit creased. It was in the bottom of my bag, I stashed it so none of the others from the pool would see. You know how it is."

Available from Love Books Publishing
books2read.com/CelticCupid

Direct Autographed Copy
http://bit.ly/2vs7wtS

Can a cyber-enhanced warrior and a ship's captain find love together?

Levia Endrado never wanted to be a warrior, but at seventeen she was deemed suitable for battle. After intense training and multiple enhancements, which gave her superior strength and healing ability, she was sent off to defeat the enemy—a killing machine with a mission.

When the war was over, she had to find a new life. At twenty-seven she's a washed-up veteran without a future. Or she was, until she met Sandon Daria.

Serving as a pilot aboard Sandon's spaceship the *Golden Echo* makes Levia long for a different and gentler life. But old hurts and even older enemies aren't so easily forgotten. Particularly when they come back for her.

Sandon is determined to show Levia that she's more than just a BioCybe…she's the woman who completes him. Getting close is just the first step, keeping her alive is an even bigger challenge, but one he's willing to take because the prize is their combined future.

Levia scanned the long line of other hopefuls entering the chamber. The large building in the center of town was cold, and she dragged her wrap around her body, even as she craned her head, looking to the high ceiling. She'd never before had an occasion to enter the testing complex, yet she'd seen the lines of teenagers every time they passed the building.

Once she'd asked her parents why the teens were lined up and her mother's face had shuttered. Her stepfather had just shaken his head and growled. They'd stopped her questions with a carefully uttered, "You'll know soon enough, Levia." The pain in her mother's eyes had been enough to shush her questions. For endless months afterward, her parents had traveled different routes to the educational facility she attended and Levia lost interest in the puzzle of that building.

Now, as she looked around, remembering that long ago spring day, it was her opportunity to find out. But she felt a surge of concern at what lay ahead. She likely wasn't the only one, given that there were probably two to three hundred seventeen-year-olds gathered in the one place. Ahead of her, she caught sight of a couple of girls, their arms linked together and wide smiles on their faces. Scanning the crowd, she became aware that, by far, a majority of those gathered displayed both fear and trepidation.

"All female subjects will enter through doors three, six, and seven. All male subjects will enter through gates four, eight, and ten." The speaker above her was loud, and she jumped before checking the numbers etched on the black metal sign over her head.

The massive doors beside her swung open, and now an uncertain silence reigned. Many of the youngsters hung back, clearly discomforted by whatever testing regime lay ahead. This was where they'd been told their futures would be determined.

"Oh gosh, I hope they only have an aptitude and psych eval. I don't think..." Levia turned to see the white face of the girl behind her. The girl had uttered what many must silently be thinking.

Levia dragged an unsteady breath in, her hand resting flat against the plane of her belly as she looked around. No one had entered yet. It was clear many were on the verge of taking the step, but still they hung back.

She straightened her shoulders. "I'm not afraid." It was always wiser to approach things head-on, she believed. When her biological father had died, she'd been one of the few to view his capsule before it was sent into the massive gray structure built to accommodate those who'd moved onto the next life realm.

Her legs shook as she wobbled toward the entrance. Beyond the doorway, she spied sealed cubicles and her heart stuttered. Why cubicles? Usually testing—med and psych—were in eval-units, hidden only by billowing white curtains. She glanced back, noting that others had taken the first step.

"Move along, subjects." Once again, the androgynous voice of the address system blared.

Of course, given it was her seventeenth anniversary of birth, she was technically considered an adult now.

She thought longingly of baby Rald and her half-sister, Elda, waiting at home for her to return, and the celebrations to be held that night. That made her smile. She would need to make them proud of her.

She entered a row and the tall Educational Specialist, the edu-specs as her peers laughingly called them, stopped her. "Present your credentials to the scanner."

She'd done this many times since the tiny implant had been slipped below the dermal layer of her skin at birth. The small unit in her wrist heated as her details were checked.

"Enter the first cubicle, Levia Endrado, and follow the instructions to complete your assessment."

Thus dismissed, Levia moved to the first unit, laid her palm against the scanner, and the door slid open soundlessly.

"Welcome, Levia Endrado. Take your place in the eval-unit." The soft contralto of the voice echoed after the door closed silently behind her.

"What are you evaluating?" Her voice was breathy, and she peered around.

"Your skills—physical and psychological. Your emotional and medical status. Your educational attainment levels."

It was an answer that shed little insight into the many things she was hungry to know. "Why do all seventeen year olds—"

"Take a seat, Levia. Then we may begin your testing."

If she'd expected an answer, she was sadly mistaken, she considered sourly. She dropped into the seat, the soft leather-like surface molding to her body.

"Levia Endrado, you are required to remove all non-specified apparel."

She jolted in the chair. "It's cold."

"The temperature will be amended. Remove the non-specified apparel."

Her misgivings grew as she dragged off the light wrap she'd brought with her, and then threw it to the floor at the side of the unit.

"We will begin, Levia Endrado. At any time, should you experience any malfunctions of the unit, simply depress the red button." It glowed and she grimaced.

Levia reclined against the chair and waited for the testing to begin.

The first examination was based on her understanding of the

political system, where she saw herself, and her knowledge of the rights and responsibilities accorded through citizenship of both her planet and the commonwealth.

The second test was mathematical and scientific proficiency. It felt like hours had passed by the time she'd finished, and she lay limp on the seat, exhausted.

"Levia Endrado, you may rise. The sanitary unit will emerge once you trigger the yellow button at the door. Should you require refreshment, press the blue button and a restorative will be made available."

"Can I leave?"

"Negative, Levia Endrado. Your needs will be catered for in this capsule."

"Why?" Her voice hitched and true fear rose for the first time. Why did they keep her in the alcove?

"All will be revealed at the end of the testing cycle."

Levia looked at the now empty screen before hurling a curse word. It was met with silence.

The urgent throb of her bladder reminded her that she needed to use the facilities, so, with

a sigh, she rose and clambered from the seat. After attending to the needs of her body, she walked around the unit, peering at the door, but it was obviously programmed remotely. She poked and prodded, but it made no difference. With a huff, she headed back to the chair.

The moment she'd settled in, the viewing screen shone bright. "Welcome back, Levia. The next sequence will evaluate your psychological reflexes, then that will be followed up with the general knowledge portion of the evaluation."

"When can I leave?" It seemed better to ask bluntly, she told herself.

"Once the examination is completed. After the next set of evaluations, you will be subjected to the physical aspect."

"Then I can go home?"

"Levia Endrado, you will now complete the psychological test. This will be undertaken by one of the center's personal evaluators."

She frowned. Personal evaluators? She bit her lip, and the sting reminded her that this wasn't something to joke about. In her seventeen years, she'd only heard of personal evaluators being brought in once before, and that was when one of the girls at her academy had been in a serious accident. Both legs were amputated and her body's ability to keep her alive had been gravely compromised. Her peers had been informed that the girl had requested the assessment before she could request her support systems be disconnected.

"Levia Endrado, are you ready to recommence processing?" The emotionless voice echoed once more and she gulped.

"Yes."

Available from Beachwalk Press
http://www.beachwalkpress.com

Direct Autographed Books
http://bit.ly/BioCybe

I DREAM OF ZOMBIES

What if the zombie plague careening through Australia was the result of a government conspiracy? One that goes all the way to the highest levels.

Seasoned Mission Specialist Julia Carter lost her mother and sister to the virus, and she's sure her stepfather is involved. The only question is *how*. When she's given a team to lead into Canberra to retrieve him and a passel of scientists, she's not happy.

Complications arise in the form of Damien Leroy, who arrives at Camp Queanbeyan running from the loss of his fiancée. He has secrets that could split apart the fragile networks between the existing camps.

But when the chips are down and there's a possible cure on the horizon, things will only get worse.

Content Warning: contains some graphic fight scenes, a couple who come together against great odds, and sexual content

---

Leroy

0700

The clock ticked over the hour, and I blinked once, twice. Just checking in case my tired

eyes read it wrong. Since I'd seen the notice on the board, I'd been waiting for the time to click by. Slowly. Right now, my backside felt numb as I swilled the last of the coffee in the mug in my hands. It was rough and black. I doubted I'd ever get used to that.

I'd only been at this base for a handful of days. Hanging around one base or another meant making acquaintances, and often that led to friendship. More than once, it had also led to connecting with other humans who died, and I wasn't going to make that mistake again.

These days my best and only friends were the gun in my holster and the rifle I carried. I placed the rifle beside me with an audible sound. Clunk.

I pushed the mug back and rose, the leather of my fingerless gloves rubbing at the webbing between my fingers as I stretched them out and back again.

"Finished?" the shrewd woman who'd been making the coffee— Casey I think she called herself—asked.

"Yeah." I attempted to avoid her gaze while I scanned the room filled with the misfits and detritus of humanity. "Where's the Control Office?"

She sniffed and indicated the hallway to the left.

"Thanks," I flung over my shoulder as I marched in that direction.

Team patrols might be the norm, though my experience was that this was an unusual request. Extraction. That hinted of enemy engagement, which was about the high point of my life. Not that I expected my life would be long.

It was all there was now to look forward to, wasn't it, though?

I smiled thinly.

Before the door sat several chairs. All of them full. Against the wall lounged a group of

people. It seemed that the notice had brought out a range of interested people—among them, me. I sauntered over and rested my hip on the concrete wall, acting nonchalantly, and let the rifle settle on my shoulder as I summed up those waiting.

Three men, weary looking with a droop to their mouth. Likely veterans dismayed at the turn their lives had taken.

Two women huddled together, not talking but obviously comfortable with each other.

One had tightly bound, red-gold hair, maybe late twenties, and high cheekbones. The other one was older and appeared to be well-seasoned. Both of them looked at me briefly before turning back to face the wall. The others were a motley assortment of younger men and women of various ages and physiques, but these ones captured my interest.

Most of the younger men were brawny with close-shaven hair. They all wore similar clothing: the ubiquitous camouflage which had become the norm after the spread of the virus, or plague as many called it.

Before I could engage any in conversation, the door opened and an older man, clearly with a military background, if his bearing and air were anything to go by, invited us inside.

He grunted as the last of us entered the room, then he shut the door forcefully and turned to us.

"Interesting crew. Matthews, Jones, and Forster, you're not going to be completing this mission."

The three elder men, the ones I'd tagged as vets, opened their mouths, but the man in charge raised a hand.

"I need you here, training the youngsters who are almost ready to hunt."

They muttered but took seats at the back of the room, the skin around their mouths tightening. Clearly they felt their usefulness in the field would be a better use of their skills

"Madderns, you're needed here too. I need you to work with the younger girls. They need immediate training in self-defense. The older boys are getting restless, and there's too much interest in the girls right now for me to dismiss the growing problems there."

The older woman gave a curt nod and moved to the seats at the back of the room.

"Now, I know most of you, except..." The look he shot in my direction should have sent my spine tingling with alarm, but instead I raised my chin and eyed him off.

"I'm Leroy."

"And you're new here, aren't you, son?"

Hmm. A hard-ass wannabe military type. "Yes, sir. I've been moving between bases from

Townsville through to here. I arrived in Queanbeyan five days ago, and I'm looking for a place on your team."

His eyes narrowed on me, as if trying to read my reasoning.

"You need to earn your place. I need six to eight well-seasoned people. Anyone at your previous posts able to vouch for you?"

"Sure. I can give you some names." I named the previous five base commanders I'd stayed with. Any would tell him that I'd earned the right to call myself a slayer. It was a term I carried with pride and had inked into a bicep.

"Fine. If what you tell me is backed up by them, then you're on the team."

He turned away and made a notation on his electronic pad before turning back to us. He picked out those that obviously met his needs, and the others slouched, accepting their dismissal with ill grace.

"I want you to meet back here at 0700 tomorrow. You'll need to prepare to be on the road for a minimum of seven to ten days to complete this mission. I'll update you in the morning on the details. You're dismissed."

The six of us who'd been successful looked at each other. This wasn't like any team prep

I'd ever attended, and judging by the surprised looks on their faces, they were unused to this type of organization too.

I scratched my chin, the stubble catching on my fingers. "Sir, can you tell us—"

"Not now, Leroy. Tomorrow. 0700."

Dismissed, we filed out of the office.

I waited until the door was closed then turned and addressed the others. "I've never—" The single woman of the group shook her head. "Not here. Not now. Meet in the mess

hall at 1500 hours, and we'll discuss it then."

The others grunted assent, and I wondered at this woman who exuded leadership so

easily for a young person.

Then she turned and left us there.

I was also intrigued, perplexed that no one voiced any dissent. Strong women. I smiled.

They either made the team work or were quickly replaced.

With that I turned and headed to the bunkroom I'd been assigned.

Available from Love Books Publishing

http://books2read.com/DreamOfZombies

Direct Autographed Copy
http://bit.ly/2SAw5zS

ALSO BY IMOGENE NIX

Warriors of the Elector

- Star of Ishtar
- Starline
- Starfire
- Star of the Fleet
- Starburst
- The Star of Eternity

The Star of Ishtar & Starline - Print

Starfire & Star of the Fleet - Print

Starburst & The Star of Eternity - Print

Blood Secrets (Re-releasing 2020)

- The Blood Bride
- The Illuminated Witch
- The Sorcerer's Touch

The Search Duology

- Miss Elspeth's Desire
- Miss Isabelle's Craving

Reunion Trilogy

- War's End
- The Assassin
- Executing Justice

The Reunion Trilogy in Paperback

<u>Sex Love & Aliens</u>

- Tangled Webs
- False Webs (Sex Love & Aliens Vol 1)
- Covert Webs (Sex Love & Aliens Vol 2)

<u>21st Testing Protocol</u>

- Cyborg: Redux
- Children Of A Greater Evil
- When Evil Came To Stay (Not Yet Released)
- Finis: The War To End All Wars (Not Yet Released)

<u>Celtic Cupid Trilogy</u>

- Blame The Wine
- A Stranger's Embrace
- Revenge On Cupid

The Celtic Cupid Trilogy in Paperback

<u>Zombieology</u>

- The Reset (2018 - Love At The End of The World)
- I Dream of Zombies (2019)
- The Six Million Dollar Zombie (Coming 2020)

<u>Knights of Pleasure</u>

- Silken Knights (Not Yet Released)

<u>Single Titles</u>

The Chocolate Affair (also in Print)

Falling In Love Again (Previously A Sapphire For Karina)

BioCybe (also in Print)

Hesparia's Tears (also in Print)

Tomorrow's Promise

A Bar In Paris (also in Print)

Inheritance Of The Blood (also in Print)

The Plan

Loving Memories (also in Print)

Hero of Heartbreak Hill (also in Print)

My One & Only (coming 2020)

Raspberry Dreams (Not Yet Released)

Non Fiction

Self Publishing: Absolute Beginners Guide (With Suzi Love)

Written as Ciara Cave

25 Curated Ways To Get Rid Of Telemarketers

Book Signings for Absolute Beginners

ABOUT THE AUTHOR

Imogene is published in a range of romance genres including Paranormal, Science Fiction and Contemporary. She is mainly published in the UK and USA.

In 2010, Imogene Nix (the pen name not Imogene herself) was born. Imogene sat down and worked tirelessly for 3 months culminating in the book Starline, which became the first in a trilogy titled, "Warriors of the Elector." Since then she's had over 30 titles published and is now focusing on hybridising herself - with a mixture of traditionally published and self-published works.

In fact, she's taking control of many of her back catalogue books, which are slowly re-releasing as self-published titles.

Imogene is a member of a range of professional organisations world wide, and believes in the mantra of mentoring and paying it forward and is actively involved in mentorship (through NaNoWrimo and her vlog: In The Chair With Imogene Nix) and tutoring of new and upcoming authors.

In her spare time she loves to drink coffee, wine & eat chocolate and is parenting her spoiled dog and a ferocious cat along with her husband and 2 human daughters and looks forward to weekends away with her husband in their caravan "The Seven Year Hitch!" Do look forward to her caravan romance at some point!

To Contact Imogene

www.imogenenix.net
imogene@imogenenix.net

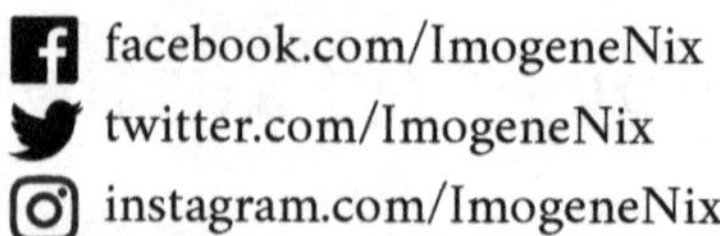

facebook.com/ImogeneNix
twitter.com/ImogeneNix
instagram.com/ImogeneNix

www.ingramcontent.com/pod-product-compliance
Lightning Source LLC
Chambersburg PA
CBHW060925190726
48286CB00002B/640